COPYRIGHT

D1595686

REVIEWS

He Completes Me by Cardeno C.: I was immediately drawn into the interesting lives of the two heroes, Zach and Aaron. Not only did they breathe life off of the pages they wormed their way into my heart and I loved every minute I spent reading about them. The intensity of their feelings toward one another was beautiful to experience. I thoroughly enjoyed watching both characters evolve into stronger, self-confident men because of the loyal, loving and supportive feelings they had for each other.

— *Night Owl Reviews (Top Pick)*

Home Again by Cardeno C.: The love between them was beautiful and inspiring.

— *Fallen Angel Reviews*

Just What the Truth Is by Cardeno C.: I am head over heels for the Home series and have been since I first read it nearly two years ago. I've also stated in the past that is near impossible to pick a favorite of the series, but there is one that I love marginally better than all the rest. Well, ladies and gentlemen, I would like to introduce you to Just What the Truth Is, my very favorite book in Cardeno C's Home series. ...Cardeno C is a master of characterization, and this story proves that. ... And the plot is engrossing. Ben's journey from momma's boy to his own man is something to behold. It is a bumpy, hard, and ugly road, but the outcome is beautiful. ... So, yes, I absolutely, hands down love Ben and Micah's story. It's emotional and lovely. In such a character-driven series, these characters are perfect.

DEDICATION

To Shirley Frances: Thank you for all that you do.

PROLOGUE

2008

"HARDER, OH God, Drew...harder!" Caleb Lakes flattened his palms against his headboard, locked his elbows, and braced himself against his roommate's animalistic thrusts. There was no way this was going to last long. Not with those familiar I'm-about-to-blow-my-load grunts flowing from Andrew's mouth in a steady stream while his thick dick shoved into Caleb with uncoordinated abandon.

Long fingers curled around Caleb's waist, muscular thighs wedged between his spread legs, and firm hips undulated behind him. Caleb knew what would come next. Andrew Thompson's body during sex was as familiar to Caleb as his own. That smooth long neck would tilt back, green eyes would clench shut, plump lips would drop open, and a pink tongue would dart out. Then Andrew would shout out Caleb's name and his body would stiffen as his cock pulsed, releasing his seed.

Just the thought of Andrew in the throes of passion was enough to make Caleb lose it.

"I'm there, I'm there, I'm there," Caleb stuttered as he looked down at his shooting cock, stunned at the sudden and powerful orgasm that rocketed through him.

Then Andrew's hold on Caleb's hips tightened, and he somehow managed to push in even deeper before stilling as his orgasm washed over him. "Oh, God! Yes, yes! Cae!" Andrew collapsed onto Caleb's back. He sucked in air while waiting for his heart to slow down.

The room was silent except for heavy breathing, which eventually quieted. Andrew's lips softly touched the back of Caleb's neck. Caleb turned his head and kissed the side of Andrew's arm. "I missed this so damn much," Andrew said huskily as his hand caressed Caleb's flank with what felt like reverence.

"I missed this too," Caleb responded. He paused before adding, "I missed you, Drew."

Andrew was quiet for a few heartbeats, and then he pressed his mouth next to Caleb's ear and whispered, "Yeah, me too." He rested his lips on the back of Caleb's sweat-slick neck and inhaled his scent before trailing openmouthed kisses from the top of his vertebrae to his hair line and back over to his ear. "What do we do now?"

CHAPTER ONE

1988

"CALEB, ARE you ready to go? Caleb?"

Caleb set his magazine down and sighed as he climbed off his bed. Well, his bed for the next week anyway. As far as family vacation destinations went, he decided he had no room to complain. When his mother had said they were going to spend a week in the woods by a lake, he'd thought she was kidding. His father was an investment banker in the city, and his mother spent her time planning various charitable events (she preferred that description to "socialite"). Anyway, the point was, they weren't exactly a back-to-nature type of family.

When he realized his parents were serious about this vacation, Caleb spent two weeks going through his considerable wardrobe and decided he didn't have anything he could possibly wear for such a trip. Thankfully, before panic over his clothing crisis could fully set in, his father handed him a brochure from the gorgeous Victorian Inn where they'd be staying. Dinner dress was formal, denim wasn't allowed in any of the main portions of the house, and the décor looked like it was done in full period style with beautifully refurbished antiques. Maybe the trip wouldn't be so bad.

"Are we going to have time to go antiquing tomorrow, Mom?" Caleb straightened his gray sweater-vest over his pale-yellow shirt and blue-striped tie as he walked out of his bedroom into the living area of their three-room suite and looked for his navy blazer.

"Honestly, Caleb, you're the only teenage boy I know who *wants* to go furniture shopping with his mother." Caleb's father wasn't really paying attention to what he was saying. He was busy going through the files he'd spread out on the mahogany secretary tucked away in the corner of the room, so Caleb didn't let the comment bother him too much. Besides, his father had expressed similar sentiments previously.

"Hal, stop it! Our boy has impeccable taste, and I enjoy his company," his mother said, and then she straightened Caleb's hair and kissed his forehead. "You should be thanking him because if Caleb didn't want to come with me, that'd mean you'd have to join me on these little expeditions."

That thought stopped Caleb's father short, and he snapped his head up. "Join you...I have work I need to get out tomorrow and..."

Barbara Lakes laughed and walked over to her husband, kissing him on the cheek. "And that is why you should be thanking your son. Okay, enough work for now.

Put those papers away and get your jacket. We're on vacation and we have a party to attend."

"BABS!" THE joy-filled voice carried across the entryway as a tall blonde wearing six-inch stilettos practically ran over, still managing to look graceful.

"Lizzy! It's been too long."

Caleb watched his mother embrace her friend warmly. It seemed to take the thin woman off guard at first, but then she relaxed and her expression softened as she returned the hug. After several long seconds, the woman pulled back, cleared her throat, and then approached Caleb's father.

"Hal, wonderful to see you again." She tilted her face toward his, kissing the air next to his cheek.

"You too, Elizabeth. You look lovely, as usual. Is Andy out back?"

Caleb saw his mother's eyes widen and heard her gasp quietly. Elizabeth's demeanor remained composed.

"Unfortunately, he got stuck in the city longer than expected, but he should be arriving any minute." She laughed brightly and waved her hand at nothing in particular. "The life of a doctor's wife... Anyway, come in, come in."

Once they were standing in the foyer with the door closed behind them, the blonde turned to Caleb and smiled. Her face seemed more relaxed, and her happiness reached her eyes when she looked at him. It was only then that Caleb realized she had been tense when discussing her husband's absence.

"And I guess this handsome young man is Caleb. I'm Elizabeth Thompson. You probably don't remember me, honey. It's been a few years since we've seen each other. I think you and Andrew were…" She turned to his mother as she continued speaking. "How old were the boys last time we all got together, Babs? Nine, ten?"

"No, I remember we had to make two connections when we flew here because we were living in Ridgecrest at the time. And we moved from there when Caleb was in second grade. I think the boys were eight."

"Six years! Time really does fly." Elizabeth shook her head and then turned back to Caleb. "Well, I'm sure you and Andrew will make fast friends again. We couldn't keep you apart the last time." She put her slender arm around Caleb's shoulder and led him into the house with his parents following. "Let's find Andrew. He'll be thrilled there's somebody his age here to keep him company."

Caleb and his parents walked with Elizabeth through a crowded living room and watched her smile politely at every guest and laugh at a few moderately amusing comments. When they ran into a man who Caleb assumed was an old college friend of his father's, his parents stopped to chat.

"I don't see Andrew out here, and I'm pretty sure I know where he's hiding. Come on, I'll show you the bat cave."

Elizabeth winked and walked toward a hallway at the end of the room with Caleb trailing behind. She knocked on a set of double doors before opening them and stepping into a nice-sized family room.

"Andrew, look who's here. You remember Caleb Lakes, don't you?"

The blond head facing the television turned and emerald eyes looked at Caleb over a bony shoulder. Thick eyebrows came together for a moment before a radiant smile took over Andrew's face.

"Sure, I do. Did you keep up with the swim lessons?" Caleb didn't understand the question, so he stayed quiet. Andrew waved him over. "I'm playing *Mario*, but you can choose a different game if you want."

"*Mario's* fine." Caleb shrugged. He walked around the back of the sectional sofa and sat down next to Andrew, who handed him a controller. Caleb settled into the couch and began playing the video game. He'd been at it for a few minutes when Andrew spoke again.

"So you don't remember me, huh?"

That distracted Caleb sufficiently to miss a jump and fall into a hole. He turned to Andrew and looked at him carefully for the first time. There was something familiar about those green eyes, but Caleb couldn't place it.

"Your family came out here for a long weekend one summer. You fell in the lake and started shouting that you couldn't swim, so I jumped in and rescued you. 'Course it was pretty shallow water, so the rescue consisted of helping you stand up," Andrew said. He elbowed Caleb gently in the ribs and smirked. "But hey, I was a kid, so I figure it still counts as heroics on my part."

Caleb's eyebrows scrunched together in thought, and a warm memory niggled at his consciousness. "Your hair's a little darker. It used to be, like, white blond, and now it's more golden. Plus, I think you wore it shorter back then."

Andrew cracked up and Caleb blushed.

"Can't say I remember much about my hair, dude, but I guess I'm glad it made an impression." He elbowed Caleb again and chuckled some more as he picked up his controller and faced the TV. "So I'm *Marioed* out. How do you feel about *NBA Jams*?"

THE NEXT morning, Caleb and his mother went to the Thompsons' summer house for brunch while Caleb's father stayed at the inn and worked. Caleb was finishing up his second plate of eggs Benedict and trying to decide whether it would be rude to ask for thirds when Andrew leaned over to him.

"Hey, are you all done? I was thinking we could go exploring." He smiled broadly, green eyes twinkling with excitement. "What do you say?"

Caleb gulped down the final bite of his breakfast.

"Exploring? Uh, sure. But what do you mean?"

"Cool!" Andrew jumped up and pushed away from the table. He stacked his plate on top of Caleb's and carried them into the house, returning seconds later. "Mom," he said to his mother. "Caleb and I are going for a walk."

"Okay, boys. Have fun," Elizabeth Thompson replied. Both of their mothers waved absently and then continued the conversation they'd been having with each other.

Andrew grabbed Caleb's elbow and tugged. "Come on, let's go."

They walked through the woods, with Caleb carefully making sure he didn't step anywhere unintended. He watched Andrew pick a branch up off the brush and turn it into a sword, swooshing it through the air as if attacking an invisible enemy. Deciding that looked like fun, he scoured the ground for a stick of his own, found one, and then dropped it seconds after lifting it. The thing was moist and a little muddy. He wanted to wipe the yuckiness off his hands, but he didn't want to dirty his pants.

"You got a problem there?" Andrew was looking at him with one eyebrow raised and a small smirk on his face.

Caleb glanced down at his locked elbows and outstretched arms, hands held up as if he were waiting for surgical gloves to get snapped on, and realized he probably looked ridiculous. Still, he didn't know what else to do with himself. He turned his head to look over his shoulder, trying to gauge how close they were to Andrew's house. They'd left for the walk about twenty minutes earlier while their mothers chatted. The house wasn't close by.

Caleb turned his head back and found Andrew right in front of him. Lanky arms reached for his wrists, held him firmly, and led his palms over to the red polo shirt hanging on Andrew's thin torso.

"What're you doing?" Caleb asked.

"Helping you get the dirt off. I can see it's bugging you." And with that explanation settled, Andrew dragged Caleb's hands down his shirt. "There, all better."

Well, that was…odd. At least it seemed odd. But Caleb's hands were clean, and that did feel better. Not knowing what to say and being decidedly uncomfortable, he continued walking through the woods as if nothing had happened.

"Umm, where do you go to school?" Not the most scintillating conversation starter, but it would be enough to get them past that little awkward hand-wiping moment and on to more comfortable topics. Well, it should have been enough anyway, but Andrew's mumbled reply made it difficult for Caleb to understand what he had said. "What was that? I couldn't hear you."

Andrew sighed and stopped walking. "Princeton."

"Oh, I haven't heard of it." Caleb thought he knew of all the good prep schools in the tri-state area, so he figured Andrew went to boarding school in a different part of New England. "I think my mother said your parents live in Somerset, so I guess you're away at boarding school?"

"No, I live in Somerset. Princeton University is close enough to drive every day."

Caleb's jaw dropped. "You go to *that* Princeton? But last night your mother said you were my age."

Andrew kicked at the ground and wouldn't raise his eyes. "Yeah, I'm fourteen too. But, uh, I'm good at school, or whatever, so I graduated early."

"That's incredible!" Caleb said excitedly. "My father would be thrilled if I got into Princeton. I mean, he's a Harvard alum, but any Ivy League school would make him so proud." Caleb was quiet for a moment and then nibbled on his bottom lip and started toeing leaves around. "Not that it's ever gonna happen. I mean, I study and everything, but…" He shrugged.

After a couple of minutes of silence, Andrew cleared his throat. "Hey, you wanna take a dip in the lake?"

"Oh, uh, I didn't bring my suit or a towel."

Andrew clasped Caleb's hand and pulled him along the path. "That's okay. This is all private property, so we can just go in our skivvies. It's not like anyone's gonna wander by. And it's warm enough that we can lay down on the deck to dry off when we're done. It'll be fun! Plus, I know CPR, so if you drown again, I've got you covered."

Andrew winked and Caleb wondered whether a little drowning would be such a bad thing. Shaking off the unwelcome thought, he followed along behind Andrew until they reached an old wooden dock next to a quiet lake surrounded by giant trees.

"Last one in is a rotten egg!" Andrew shouted, pulling Caleb's attention away from the pretty view. The red polo was already on the ground, as were Andrew's sneakers, shorts, and one sock. He bounced on one foot, peeling off his final sock, and then he ran across the deck and jumped off with his knees tucked against his chest and his hands wrapped around them. "Cannonball!"

Caleb slowly toed off his deck shoes and his stomach clenched in anxiety. It was one thing for Andrew Thompson to go swimming in his underwear. The boy didn't have an ounce of fat on him. Caleb was sure he could have counted ribs if Andrew had been standing still. Unfortunately, he wasn't built the same way. He was shorter and, let's face it, rounder than Andrew. Much rounder. Needless to say, taking his clothes off in front of other people was daunting.

"Come on in, Cae!" Andrew shouted as he splashed around. "The water isn't too cold."

Caleb had never had a nickname, and he instantly loved hearing the other boy use one. He didn't want to let Andrew down by refusing to join him in the water. Besides, he didn't have a believable excuse to get out of it. Deciding that jumping into the lake wearing chinos and a linen shirt would be weird, Caleb comforted himself with the thought that the water would probably hide most of his body anyway. He swallowed down his nerves, took off his clothes, and quickly jumped into the lake.

"Woo hoo!" Andrew yelled and swam over to him,

immediately instigating a splashing war.

The other boy's joy was infectious, and Caleb found himself laughing and splashing along. One well-aimed strike from Andrew had Caleb blinking lake water out of his eyes and spitting it out of his mouth.

"You're dead meat, Drew!" he threatened menacingly.

"Big words, Cae. But you'll have to catch me first!" Andrew swam away and Caleb found himself chasing the other boy across the lake.

It seemed as if Caleb was making a habit of following Andrew Thompson—away from brunch, through the woods, and now in the lake. Caleb decided that as habits went, it wasn't a bad one. He whooped and dove under the cool water, enjoying this week away from the city exponentially more than he'd anticipated.

CHAPTER TWO

1989

"ARE YOU sure you don't mind having us stay with you, Lizzy? We can get a room at the Inn again."

Elizabeth Thompson shook her head and lifted a suitcase out of the Lakes' trunk. Caleb blinked in surprise. The sight of a woman in high heels, a tight dress, updo hairstyle, and heavy makeup was incongruous with any sort of physical labor, especially at eleven in the morning.

"You're doing me a favor with this visit, Babs, and we both know it. Andy managed to come up with yet another..." She paused, looked at Caleb, and then smiled brightly as she walked to the front door. "Andy has to work again this week, so I appreciate the company. And there's plenty of room here for the four of us."

Once they got inside, Elizabeth pointed toward the stairs leading up to a large loft that had been converted into a bedroom at some point over the years. "Caleb, you remember where Andrew's room is, right?"

"Yes, ma'am." Caleb nodded.

He was halfway up the stairs when he heard his mother. "Tell me how you really are, Lizzie." Curiosity had him standing still and listening.

There was a sigh and possibly a sniffle.

"Tired. I'm really tired. Thanks for coming out here. I hope I didn't cause you any problems with Hal. It's just, I feel like I don't have anything left and—"

"You don't need to thank me. Hal's grateful for the uninterrupted work time, and I'm always happy to visit my friend. Plus, Caleb's been smiling nonstop since I told him he'd get to stay with Andrew for a week. Do you know how unusual it is to see a fifteen-year-old boy smile for longer than five seconds in a row? If I didn't know how well the kids got along last summer, I would have been checking his room for drugs."

The reminder that Andrew was just a few steps away overrode any interest Caleb had in his mother's conversation, so he finished walking up the stairs, dragging his suitcase behind him, and knocked on the white six-panel door.

"Come in!" Andrew's voice rang out over the sound of "It's the End of the World as We Know It."

Caleb turned the knob and opened the door. Deep, green eyes met his over the top of an *International Male* clothing catalog, and he desperately tried to ignore the flutter in his chest.

"Hey! You're here." Andrew tossed the catalog aside and swung his long legs over the side of the bed. He turned down the volume on the tape deck and then hustled over to Caleb, stopping when he was within arm's distance. He reached one hand out and clasped Caleb's shoulder, giving it a squeeze. "I planned to be downstairs waiting when you got here, but I guess I lost track of time. Sorry about that."

"That's okay." Caleb set his bag down and shifted from foot to foot. "So, ah, what're you doing?"

"Nothing," Andrew rushed out as he glanced in the direction where he'd thrown the catalogue. Then he cleared his throat and finished his sentence more slowly. "Just making a mix tape."

Caleb nodded. "R.E.M. Cool."

After a few moments of awkward silence, the side of Andrew's mouth tilted up in a small grin. Caleb couldn't hold back his own responding smile. And then both boys were laughing, little chuckles at first, followed by breath-stealing belly laughs that had them collapsing on Andrew's bed and holding their stomachs.

"I don't know how Michael Stipe would feel about hysterical laughter as a reaction to his music," Andrew gasped out as he tried to catch his breath.

"Wasn't la... laughing at the music," Caleb responded.

Then the song ended and Andrew's eyes widened. "Shit!" He hopped off the bed. "Hold on, I have to switch out to the next one."

Caleb sat up and watched Andrew fiddle with the tape deck until the music started again. "The Smiths, right? Is that"—he furrowed his brow—"'Asleep'?"

Andrew nodded. "Yeah. You know your stuff. Into music?"

"I guess." Caleb scooted down onto the floor and sat cross-legged next to Andrew. They stayed on the ground, shoulder to shoulder, and listened to the song. When it ended, Andrew paused the recording as he queued up the next tape. "Okay, let's see how many notes it takes you to guess this one."

The music had barely started when Caleb answered. "'Blasphemous Rumours'."

One blond eyebrow rose. "Impressive."

"I like Depeche Mode. So let me guess what else you've got lined up." Caleb pursed his lips and tapped his pointer finger against them. "Uh, a little Tears for Fears. Maybe 'Mad World'?"

Andrew's jaw dropped. "How'd you know that?"

"It goes with the whole I-wanna-slash-my-wrists anthem you've got going here. I'd ask how you've been, but I think the theme music pretty much sums it up. What's going on?"

It didn't even dawn on Caleb that his prodding might not be welcome. He hadn't seen Andrew in a year, but there was some sort of...connection between them. He'd felt it the previous summer, and being with Andrew again brought it all rushing back—not that he'd forgotten. He'd spent an embarrassing amount of time thinking about last year's summer vacation. Thinking about Andrew.

The blond boy collapsed onto his back on the floor and stared at the ceiling. "My father's a complete asshole." Caleb lay down next to him. "What'd he do?" he whispered.

"I think he's cheating on my mom."

Not knowing how to respond to that, Caleb stayed quiet. He moved his fingers slightly until they barely grazed Andrew's. When the other boy didn't pull away, he moved his hand farther until his palm rested completely over the back of Andrew's hand.

"I'm pretty sure it's a nurse or someone else from the hospital. I picked up the extension when he was on the phone a couple of weeks ago, and I heard him talking to some woman. My mom was at a charity thing, and my father probably didn't even realize I was home." Andrew snorted. "It was disgusting. She told him that she got off humping a pillow while she was thinking of him." Andrew's head tilted and he looked at Caleb, wetness evident in his eyes. "Can you believe that?"

Not sure how to respond, Caleb said exactly what he was thinking. "I'm sorry." He turned onto his side and met Andrew's eyes. They were close enough that he could feel Andrew's breath on his face. It was coming out in short huffs, like he was trying to hold back tears.

"Yeah." Andrew sighed. "A doctor sleeping with his nurse—he's a cheater and an embarrassing cliché all rolled into one." The song ended, and Andrew stretched a sock-clad foot up to the tape deck and pressed the pause button. Then he dragged his foot back and forth over the shelf. "Do you think I should tell my mom?" He bit his lip. "Not the details, I mean. But just, like, that he's cheating on her?"

Nothing in Caleb's short life had prepared him to be able to answer that question. He thought about the conversation he'd just overheard their mothers having. "Are you sure she doesn't already know?" he asked quietly.

"No way," Andrew said fervently and shot up off the ground. He began pacing back and forth across the small room. "My mom's all about my father. Always making excuses for why he's never around, talking about how hard he works. She even gives me presents she claims are from him, but I know she's buying them and putting his name on the cards to make him look good. If she had any idea he was off cheating on her with some tramp, she wouldn't do any of that. She'd leave him." He collapsed onto the ground and leaned against the bed, finishing in a whisper. "I mean, come on. Who would stay with someone who treated them like that?"

The rationale was sound, not entirely convincing in light of the way Andrew's mom behaved and the things Caleb had heard her say, but still sound.

"Do you, ehm, do you want me to tell my mom?" Caleb asked. "I know they're close, and my mom can probably talk to her or figure out how to handle this."

At first, Andrew looked hopeful, like he liked the idea. But then he slumped and shook his head. "No. She's my mom and I'll take care of her." He cleared his throat and then squared his shoulders. "I won't let him get away with what he's doing."

Caleb wanted to tell Andrew everything would be okay. But maybe it wouldn't; what did he know? He fisted his hands together to keep himself from reaching out and trying to comfort his friend, not sure if the touch would be welcomed. With the music off and neither of them talking, the sounds of birds chirping outside the window drifted into the room.

"I got a camera." Changing the topic was the only thing Caleb could think of to take Andrew's mind off his family problems. "My mom and I were antiquing, and I found this great Pentax SLR. It's not an antique, probably only twenty or twenty-five years old, but it's pretty cool. Metal body, a few different lenses. I've been taking pictures all around the city, and I thought it'd be fun to take some nature shots out here, change things up a little."

The blond head in front of him bobbed. "Cool. Let me get some shoes on and we can go outside, take a walk and see if there's anything worth photographing." Andrew sat up and looked back over his shoulder, his eyes meeting Caleb's. "Thanks for listening, Cae. Feels good to have a friend here right now."

"HOW'S SCHOOL?" Andrew asked as they walked through the woods and caught up on each other's lives.

"It's school." Caleb shrugged.

"Yeah, that much I already knew." Andrew laughed. "For real, though, how is it?"

"It's fine. It's school. There really isn't anything more to say about it. I, uh, like hanging out with my friends. Photo and music are okay. Aaaand, that's about it. How about you? Are you excited to be starting medical school, boy genius?"

"Um-hum." Andrew nodded and ducked his head, his long, slender fingers picking on an invisible thread in his shorts.

"What? I can't hear you when you mumble."

"Oh, uh," Andrew stammered. "Yes, I'm looking forward to it. I know that's not cool to like school or whatever, but—"

"Are you kidding me? I think it's great!"

"You do?" Andrew's tone made his surprise evident. Then he started talking excitedly, his words coming out fast. "I've been trying to decide what I'll want to specialize in. I'm leaning toward surgery. Not cardiothoracic, like my father, but another subspecialty."

"I bet you'd be great at that," Caleb said. "You have really big hands."

As soon as the words were out, Caleb flinched and squeezed his eyes shut. No, that wasn't weird at all. Everybody noticed the size of his friend's hands and commented on it.

He was sure he could feel the tension in the air caused by his inappropriate comment. When he opened his eyes, Caleb saw Andrew staring at his own raised hands.

"Well, you know what they say about big hands," Andrew drawled, causing Caleb's heart to stutter in his chest.

He had *not* been thinking about that. Nope. Not ever. And certainly not alone at night in bed. He gulped a couple of times before responding.

"What do they say?"

"Big hands"—Andrew waggled his eyebrows and smirked—"big surgical gloves."

Just like that, the tension broke, and both boys started laughing and shoving each other along the path.

"Are you getting hungry, Cae?" Andrew asked a few hours later.

"Uh-huh," Caleb answered. "Just let me get this last shot." He had the camera so close to one of the giant ash trees, they were almost touching.

"What're you doing?"

"I think the texture of this bark would look really cool up close." Caleb said.

He snapped the camera a few times before stepping back and putting it away.

"Did you get the picture?"

"Yup!" Caleb replied excitedly, and then his stomach growled. "Wow, I guess I really am hungry."

"Well, it's almost two. You were so into those pictures,

you forgot about lunch. Good thing I'm here or you'd starve for your art," Andrew joked.

"Yeah, right," Caleb scoffed. "This physique just screams starving artist. Not!"

"Goofball," Andrew laughed and bumped his shoulder against Caleb's. "Come on; let's head back to the house. What do you want for lunch? I think my mother has the fridge really well stocked for your visit."

"I'll eat pretty much anything, as you can tell." Caleb moved his hand up and down his body. "Well, anything except hot dogs. Do you know they have ground bones and stuff in them?" He shuddered. "It's disgusting.

"Seriously?" Andrew's eyes widened, and he looked slightly green.

"Uh-huh. Swear." Caleb nodded. "Look it up at the library when you get home."

"All right, note to self: never put a wiener in my mouth," Andrew said completely straight-faced.

Caleb almost choked on his own saliva.

CHAPTER THREE

1990

ANDREW THOMPSON III stood on the porch of his family's summer home and frantically waved at the car rolling down the curved drive. He and his mother had been there for two days, and he was more than ready to see his friend. If Caleb hadn't been joining them, Andrew was pretty sure he'd lose his mind. Not that he didn't love his mother, but lately he felt frustrated with her, confused. Thankfully, he had his driver's license, so he'd been taking the car out, going into town, scoping out places he thought Caleb would want to see, capture on film.

The passenger door was open before the car came to a stop and Caleb bounced out, a big smile lighting up his pale face, brown eyes sparkling. The guy all but skipped over to him, the wind blowing through his chestnut hair. He wore linen pants with suspenders over a pale-green button-down shirt. Andrew had to force himself to hold back a chuckle.

Adorable. Caleb Lakes was absolutely adorable. 'Course there was no way to say that to a sixteen-year-old guy without pissing him off and making yourself look like some sort of a fruit, so, yeah, Andrew held back his laugh. But he couldn't restrain his smile.

"Hey, Cae!"

"Drew!" Caleb gave him a hug, a real one, and Andrew shivered. "How are you?"

The voice was deeper than he remembered, but he still recognized the concern. Caleb was the only person who knew about what his father had done. What he was still doing. Andrew swallowed back the pain. That bitter taste was altogether too familiar.

"Better now that you're here," he answered quietly as he held on to Caleb, his fingers clutching the starched oxford and feeling the warmth of Caleb's skin radiating from beneath.

He heard a whispered "me too" before Caleb pulled away from the hug and walked back to the now-parked car. "Help us bring the bags in. That way we can do it in one trip, and then the two of us can hang out."

This time Andrew did laugh. "You're here for one week. How many bags do you have?" Andrew opened the trunk and counted four large suitcases along with Caleb's camera bag and his mother's purse.

Mrs. Lakes answered him. "You can never be too sure of what you'll need, so it's better to be prepared."

Yeah, his own mother chanted the same mantra, for which the staff at Barney's and Neiman's were endlessly grateful. They were on vacation in the woods, so a couple of pairs of shorts and some henleys seemed sufficient to Andrew, but he knew he was outnumbered, so he kept his mouth shut. Besides, he sort of enjoyed seeing Caleb fuss when he got dressed every day. He'd caught himself watching that show with fascination the previous summer, and he was looking forward to the sequel.

"Hi, Mrs. Lakes. How was the drive?"

Caleb's mother smiled happily. She was a nice woman. He was glad his mother had her for a friend. Even more glad for her son's friendship.

"You're taller than me now, Andrew. That means you can call me Barbara. And the drive was just fine, thanks for asking."

"Righteous." Andrew heaved a couple of suitcases out of the trunk and dragged them inside. "Mother!" he yelled. "The Lakes are here! Mother!"

Barbara laughed. "You boys head on upstairs and get Caleb settled. I'll find your mother without all the shouting."

That was all the invitation Andrew needed. "Radical! Which bags are yours, dude?"

"The one I'm holding and that one." Caleb nudged his chin toward the suitcase in Andrew's left hand. "Pretty tubular, like totally, right, dude?"

Andrew's eyes narrowed. "What's your damage?" he asked. "It seems like you're making fun of me."

"No duh." Caleb elbowed Andrew's side and smiled to

take the sting out. "You're not a California surfer, Drew. Quit talking like one. I missed my genius best friend. Bring him back."

With Caleb's camera bag slung over his shoulder, Andrew pulled a suitcase behind him and listened to it thump as he dragged it up the stairs to his loft bedroom. "I'm not a genius," he mumbled, disgruntled. Caleb grabbed the back of his shirt, unexpectedly halting his forward movement and almost making him lose his balance. "Hey! What're you doing?" He looked over his shoulder and met Caleb's blazing eyes.

"Don't ever pretend you're not smart, Drew. You're amazing and you need to be proud of it."

"I wasn't, I am, I..." Andrew didn't know what to say. It wasn't easy being so many years younger than his classmates. Nobody in school wanted to be friends with a kid, and he didn't really know people his own age, wasn't always welcome around them either. Well, except for Caleb. It seemed like the other boy enjoyed being with him during the weeklong visits they'd had the past couple of summers. For the first time in his life, Andrew felt like he had a real friend.

With a palm flat on Andrew's back, Caleb pushed him forward. "Good. 'Cause you're brilliant, you know. I brag about you to all my friends."

Andrew's heart rate increased in response to those words. Caleb talked about him? "Yeah? What do you say?" He kept walking and hoped his question didn't sound too needy.

"I tell them all about my incredibly smart friend with great taste in music and fabulous hair."

Andrew chuckled. "I do have great hair."

"That's what I'm sayin'! *Dude.*"

CALEB SHOOK out his pink Izod shirt and then slipped it onto a hanger. He turned his head to see Andrew lying on one of the twin beds, watching him. Feeling his cheeks heat, Caleb dipped his head and pulled a thin cashmere sweater out of his suitcase.

"Sorry, I know this is taking forever."

Andrew smiled. "I don't mind, Cae. I think it's cu...cool that you're into clothes, or whatever."

Blinking in surprise, Caleb looked up at Andrew's face, trying to measure his sincerity. It didn't seem as if Andrew was making fun of him.

"My dad thinks it's girly." He put the sweater into the dresser drawer and reached for his last pair of chinos. "I mean, he doesn't say it to me anymore, 'cause my mom told him not to, but I can tell from the looks he gives me that he still thinks it."

"Liking clothes isn't girly. It's...you." Andrew grinned broadly and something loosened in Caleb's chest. "Hey, if you want, we can make your dad an honorary member of the asshole fathers club. You already know that my father is the founding member."

Caleb flinched. He shouldn't have complained about his own father knowing what Andy Thompson had been up to. Yeah, his dad made some mean comments now and again—gave him a few looks—but he knew he was loved deep down. Plus, there was no way his father would ever cheat on his mother. Not ever.

"How are things with your father? Anything new?"

"Nah, I don't think so. I told you I confronted him about that phone call I overheard last summer, right?" Andrew asked.

Caleb nodded. "Yeah."

"Well, he tried to make all sorts of excuses, said he had *needs*, that it wasn't natural for men to be monogamous and I'd understand when I'm older. It was all a bunch of crap, and I told him if he didn't come clean with my mom, then I'd tell."

"What'd he say?" Caleb asked.

"He told her. I guess he promised never to do it again. She talked to me about it, told me how sorry he was, said I shouldn't let it impact my relationship with him." Andrew sat up, folding his long legs underneath him. "She didn't even seem pissed, you know? She just fell for his whole spiel, hook, line, and sinker. And then it was like she was protecting him, which is totally typical, going on about how smart he is, what a great doctor, how I'm so much like him." He sighed deeply and then continued. "I wanted to think like her, you know?

To believe he'd just made a mistake and he'd stop. The thing is—I know he didn't stop. I *know* it."

Caleb sat on the bed, his side pressed to Andrew's, both of them leaning against the whitewashed pine headboard. "How do you know?"

Andrew shrugged. "I can just tell. He's never around, claims to be working at weird hours. I know she wants me to forgive him, but I can't. I don't understand how she can." Tears streaked down Andrew's face. "And I *hate* that she thinks I'm like him. I don't want to be like him, Cae. It's bad enough that I'm stuck with the same name as that...that..."

"You're not like him." Caleb got onto his knees and faced Andrew so their eyes met. "You're not."

"But I could be, you know." Andrew blinked cheerless eyes rapidly. "I'm even in medical school, so I'll end up being a doctor like him. Lately, I've been thinking maybe I should drop out and do something else, which totally sucks 'cause I love my classes and—"

"Hey," Caleb interrupted. "Going to medical school doesn't mean you'll turn into your father, and you can't let him take away something you enjoy. If you want to be a doctor, be a doctor. That has nothing to do with being a cheating, lying asshole." Caleb cupped Andrew's cheeks and wiped his friend's tears away with his thumbs. His heart ached for Andrew. "You'll never be him."

"How can you be so sure?" Andrew whispered brokenly.

Caleb smirked. "Because I'll kick your ass if you even start to head in that direction."

The responding chuckle was a welcome sound. "Promise?" Andrew asked the question with a smile, but Caleb knew it wasn't a joke.

"Yup. It's my duty as your friend to keep you completely de-assholized."

"Thanks, Cae. You really are the best friend I've ever had."

"OH, I forgot to show you this position paper from the American Dietetic Association. I made a copy for you because I thought you'd want to read it," Andrew said to Caleb while they walked home from the lake.

"A position paper I'd want to read?" Caleb asked skeptically. "Drew, I don't even know what a position paper is. For that matter, I don't know what the American Dietetic Association is." He furrowed his brow. "Wait, is this an article about dieting? I know I need to lose weight," he said quietly, suddenly feeling self-conscious about the two hours he'd just spent in his swimsuit next to his wiry friend.

"No!" Andrew shouted. "I'm not saying you need to lose weight, Cae. Honest. I like the way you look." Andrew gasped after that admission and his eyes widened. It seemed as if he was surprised by his own words. "I mean, uh…" he stammered. "The, uh, American Dietetic Association is a nutrition group, but the paper is about vegetarianism. When I read it, I thought of your wiener. Hot dog!" Andrew was now bright red. "I thought of your thing with hot dogs. You know last summer? What you said about boners?" He groaned. "Bones. What you said about ground-up bones being in hot dogs. Never mind." He shook his head, seeming somehow defeated. "I'm going to stop talking now. The article's in the room in my bag. You can read it for yourself."

"Wow," Caleb smirked. "That may have been the least articulate and most unintentionally hilarious thing I've heard in my life. Thanks for that."

Andrew didn't respond verbally, opting instead to raise his hand and flip Caleb off. Caleb was still laughing when they walked into the house.

"Andrew? Is that you?" Elizabeth Thompson's voice rang out.

"Not sure who else it'd be," Andrew mumbled quietly before clearing his throat and answering. "Yeah, Mother. It's us. We're going upstairs to get undressed. I mean, uh, we just went swimming, so we're going upstairs to shower." Andrew stopped and a blush crept up his neck. "Each of us, I mean. We're each going to shower. Not together."

Caleb roared, tears streaming down his face, as he bent over and clutched his stomach. Andrew tilted his face up toward the ceiling and took a deep breath.

"I'm going to see what my mother needs. Then I'm

going to superglue my mouth shut."

Andrew stormed away, and Caleb chuckled the entire way up the stairs. When Andrew made it back to the room, he found Caleb next to his bag, flipping through one of his *International Male* catalogues. Caleb looked up when Andrew walked in.

"Do you think people actually wear things like this in real life?" Caleb asked, turning the catalogue around, showing Andrew a picture of a man wearing a satiny black thong.

"Oh, uh, I like the clothes in that catalogue. That's why I have it. For the clothes," Andrew said hurriedly, like he needed a justification for having the magazine.

One thin brown eyebrow arched. "Oookay, not what I asked. Plus, I've seen you wear that same pair of shorts for three days in a row, so I didn't realize you were into fashion, but, whatever, I guess."

"Did you, umm, were you looking for that position paper or something?" Andrew's voice was oddly high-pitched. He cleared his throat and talked more slowly. "I thought it was right on top in my bag."

"Oh, it was. But when I picked it up, I saw this catalogue underneath it, and I was distracted by the, ehm, clothes."

CHAPTER FOUR

1991

"SO WHERE are we going?" Caleb asked Andrew as they pulled out of the driveway.

Andrew had been so excited to head out that he hadn't even given Caleb time to unpack. He'd just left Caleb's suitcases by the bed, grabbed his friend's camera bag and gear, and led him outside, all within five minutes of Caleb's arrival at the Thompsons' summer house for his annual visit. The weeks he'd spent up here with Caleb during the previous three years had been the highlights of his life, and he'd been looking forward to this year's trip since the day Caleb left last summer.

"I was scoping out places I thought you'd like to photograph, and I found this great view, but we need to get there before the sun starts setting."

Caleb reached out and squeezed Andrew's shoulder. "That's really nice. Thanks, Drew."

"What are friends for?" Andrew tried to sound nonchalant, but he had a hard time holding back his pleased smile.

The drive winding up the nearby mountain took a while, which Andrew appreciated. It gave him time to catch up with Caleb, hear funny stories, listen to his voice. When they pulled up to the overlook Andrew had found, Caleb bounded out of the car.

"This is an incredible view!"

"Thanks. I thought you'd like it." Andrew's face heated and he smiled at the praise. "You can get some great pictures of the sunset here, right?"

Caleb reached out and cupped his hand around the back of Andrew's neck, giving it a light squeeze and then hanging on. "I sure can. I'll just get my tripod set up."

Andrew nodded but neither boy moved for several long minutes. Eventually, Caleb lowered his hand and walked over to the trunk to get his photography gear.

"What's your favorite subject?" Andrew asked once Caleb had everything ready and started snapping pictures of the orange sky.

"Umm, I don't know if it's a particular subject so much as the composition of a picture. I like capturing things that seem contradictory but actually complement each other. Like unusual color combinations or a mix in periods or styles. I got a great shot the other day of this, like, totally grunge, dreadlocked guy sitting on a bench and bopping to a Walkman next to a guy in a three-piece suit taking notes on a legal pad. Alone, they were, like, whatever, you know? But together they sparkled."

Andrew loved seeing Caleb glow when he talked about photography, so he didn't explain that he had been asking about Caleb's favorite subject in school. He knew his friend was a little insecure about his academic abilities, and truth be told, Andrew didn't really care about the answer to his question. He just wanted to hear Caleb talk, to learn what his friend had been doing over the past year, to reconnect.

"That sounds really cool, Cae."

Caleb stopped snapping pictures and turned to look at Andrew.

"Thanks. I, uh, brought my portfolio just in case you wanted to see some of my stuff, or whatever."

Andrew's smile was so broad his cheeks hurt from the stretch. "I'd love to."

They chatted some, stood in comfortable silence while Caleb took more pictures, and generally enjoyed finally being together again. Andrew was so happy to be in Caleb's presence that it took him by surprise when he looked around and realized dark had settled around them. "Are you still able to get anything with such low light?"

Caleb shook his head. "Not like this, but I'm gonna try something where I leave the aperture open for a long time and keep the camera on the tripod so it's perfectly still. I think there may be enough moonlight for me to capture the clouds moving."

The picture sounded nice, but the street they were on

was very remote, so there weren't any lights nearby. Being out in pitch dark gave Andrew the heebie-jeebies, not that he'd admit that out loud.

"Oh, yeah, cool. I'll just turn on the headlights so you can, uh, see your camera better."

He scrambled into the car and put the key in the ignition without turning on the engine. The car's high beams lit up the surrounding area and curbed Andrew's fear. He wiped his clammy hands on his shorts and then climbed out of the car and joined Caleb, who was standing next to his camera and looking up at the sky.

They stood quietly together for a few minutes, and Andrew's mind remained on high alert as his eyes darted around trying to identify the shadows beyond the trees.

"Boo!" Caleb yelled unexpectedly, causing Andrew to shriek in a very unflattering way as he jumped into the air and held his hand against his chest.

"What the hell, Cae?" Andrew gasped.

Caleb laughed so hard he couldn't get any words out. He just cackled and wiped tears from the sides of his eyes. Andrew squinted, his green eyes narrowing in what he hoped looked like a dangerous expression. It must have worked because Caleb stopped laughing. Andrew darted for him, but the boy moved away just in time, preventing Andrew from gaining purchase on Caleb's shirt. He was on the opposite side of the car faster than Andrew would have thought possible.

"I was only fooling around, Drew," Caleb apologized

as he rested his hands on the trunk and watched Andrew track him.

"Uh-huh. Sure. No problem." Andrew's expression and tone belied his words, which must have been obvious because Caleb refused to stand still as Andrew made his way toward Caleb's side of the car.

"Seriously, Drew. I didn't mean to scare you."

"I heard you, Cae." Andrew grinned evilly and Caleb's eyes widened farther.

The two continued to make their way around the car with Andrew stalking Caleb, and Caleb keeping the vehicle between them. When Andrew was coming around the trunk and Caleb was next to the car door, Caleb grasped the door handle and scrambled inside, closing each lock before Andrew could follow him in. Once he was safely inside, Caleb looked out the window to catch Andrew's eyes and then stuck his tongue out at his friend. Andrew jiggled the door handle and scowled.

"What are you? Eight years old? Open the door, Caleb."

Caleb put a thumb next to each ear and wiggled his fingers as he chanted, "You can't make me; you can't make me."

Andrew couldn't help himself; he started laughing. The situation was so ridiculous, and his friend was so adorable. He felt all the stress from medical school, his family, his loneliness—all of it melted away. He flattened one palm against the window and Caleb lifted his hand, meeting

Andrew's through the glass. They wore matching goofy grins.

Eventually, Caleb reached for the door lock and pulled it up. Andrew stepped back and Caleb got out of the car, promptly receiving a light punch to the shoulder. He pretended to wince.

"Was that revenge?"

"You'll never know." That evil grin came back and Andrew rubbed his hands together dramatically. "Bwa ha ha ha!"

Caleb rolled his eyes and made his way back to his tripod. "Whatever. I'm gonna get a couple more shots in. That okay?"

"Sure thing." Andrew reached into the car and removed the keys, causing darkness to settle around them.

"Not scared anymore?" Caleb asked, confirming for Andrew that his friend had incredibly good insight into what made him tick.

"Nah," Andrew replied as he walked up to Caleb and stood shoulder to shoulder. He draped his arm across Caleb's shoulder in a move that he hoped could pass for "casual buddy." "Besides," he bumped Caleb's hip with his own as he spoke, "it's more romantic this way."

Caleb didn't respond, just smiled and looked through the camera lens. And Andrew wondered how deep Caleb's perceptiveness ran.

"REMIND ME again why you wanted to do this," Andrew said as he read through the instructions on putting up the tent they'd purchased in town.

Caleb had all the parts laid out on the ground, and he was examining a metal pole. "Uh, *wanted* might be overstating it. More like I agreed when you said you wanted to go camping." He picked up another metal pole and connected it to the first one.

"When *I* said I wanted to go camping?" Andrew asked in disbelief. "I said no such thing! *You're* the one who said we should go camping."

"Riiiight. I said I wanted to sleep surrounded by bugs with no access to indoor plumbing. That sounds just like me."

Andrew furrowed his brow. Hearing Caleb phrase things that way made him question his own memory of their conversation the previous day. He could have sworn Caleb had asked to go camping, but then again, he'd have never pegged his well-dressed friend for a roughing-it type.

"Well, however we got here, we're here, and we need to figure out how to put together this…" Andrew's sentence trailed off when he looked up from the instructions to see Caleb draping army green fabric over a dome-shaped structure he'd fashioned from the metal rods. "What're you doing? Did you just build the whole tent?"

"Uh-uh, not quite." Caleb chewed on his bottom lip and examined what looked like a huge nail. "Do those instructions say what this is?" Caleb asked. Andrew had barely started

THE ONE WHO SAVES ME

reviewing the instructions again when Caleb seemingly figured out the answer to his own question. "Oh, I know! This is a stake."

"Uh, Caleb, not to burst your bubble or anything," Andrew said with a smirk, "but A, I don't think the tent manufacturer is an Ann Rice fanatic worried about a vampire infestation every time somebody goes camping, and two, vampires can only be killed by wooden stakes. Metal ones wouldn't do the trick."

Caleb's eyebrows reached for his hairline. "Ehm, no, I'm pretty sure the tent manufacturers aren't the ones obsessed with the vampire Lestat," he said meaningfully. "But what I meant was a stake to keep the sides of the tent secured to the ground. Find me a rock, would you?"

"Oh, right! Yeah, that makes sense." Andrew started walking around, looking at the ground while he mumbled to himself. "No, actually, none of this makes sense. In fact, this entire experience is officially bordering on surreal. The sun's going down and we're standing in the middle of nowhere getting ready to essentially sleep on brush and dirt. And here you are, like a camping savant or something, figuring out how to put a tent together in like thirty seconds without reading the instructions."

"Andrew!" Caleb interrupted the diatribe. "We're almost out of light. Just grab that one over there." He pointed to a large flat rock next to a tree.

"And now you're asking me to bring you a dirty rock,

which I can only assume you're planning to fashion into some kind of tool, MacGyver style." Andrew picked up the rock and brought it to Caleb, who crouched down and used it to hammer the stakes into the ground. "Yup, I'm pretty sure this is a weird bad-food-induced dream. I need to remember what I ate for dinner and never repeat it."

"Speaking of dinner," Caleb said as he stood up and clapped his hands together in an attempt to remove the dirt. "I packed us PB and J sandwiches and chips, and I brought marshmallows, graham crackers, and Hershey bars so we can make s'mores."

"Oh, that sounds perfect! Tell me the chips are salt and vinegar and I'll love you for life."

Caleb picked up the backpack he'd packed and unzipped it. He dug out a bag of salt and vinegar chips and tossed them over to Andrew with a smile, and then he got what looked like baby wipes and cleaned his hands. Andrew felt relieved to see Caleb's familiar desire to stay clean was still intact. Maybe things hadn't gone quite as topsy-turvy as he'd feared.

"Okay, I'm going to collect some sticks and stuff so we can get a fire going," Caleb said.

"You're going to start a fire with sticks?" Andrew asked in surprise.

"Uh, yeah. How else do you propose we start a fire?"

"With matches."

"Yeah, there'll be matches too." Caleb pulled a

matchbook out of his pocket. "But we need to actually light something, you know. The matches themselves would burn out too quickly, and they don't radiate any sort of heat." Sarcasm dripped from Caleb's voice.

"Okay, smartass. That's not what I meant," Andrew said. He set down the chips and started walking around picking up twigs to use as kindling. "After your impressive tent building display, I thought you were going to do the thing where you rub two pieces of wood together and they make a spark."

When Caleb didn't say a word in response, Andrew turned to look at him. His arms were crossed over his chest, and he was smirking at Andrew with one eyebrow raised.

"What?" Andrew asked. "Why're you looking at me like that?"

"You really don't do it on purpose, do you?"

"Do what?"

"Never mind," Caleb chuckled. "I think I have enough branches and twigs to get the fire started."

An hour later, the fire was out, the marshmallows and chocolate were eaten, and the sleeping bags were laid out in the tent. Andrew ducked inside with Caleb on his tail.

"How is this a two-person tent?" Andrew asked when his elbow bumped Caleb's. They were both trying to wiggle into their sleeping bags in a very confined space.

"Yeah, it is pretty small, huh? Well, at least we won't be cold."

Andrew's sleeping bag had twisted around from his fidgeting, so he straightened it out and then lay down. He was about to complain about the size of the tent again, but he became distracted by the feeling of Caleb's body pressed against his. Sure, there were two sleeping bags between them, but he could still feel Caleb's chest move as he took in air, could hear him breathing.

Figuring he had the small size of the tent as a viable excuse for getting closer to Caleb than would normally be acceptable, Andrew slowly scooted in tiny increments until they were pressed tightly together from toes to shoulders. He froze, waiting to see if Caleb would ask him to move back.

Instead, Caleb sighed contentedly. "You know, this isn't as uncomfortable as I expected. The ground isn't too hard and it's actually pretty cozy in here."

Understatement of the year, in Andrew's opinion.

"Um-hum. I agree," Andrew said. "It's really nice."

CHAPTER FIVE

1992

"I WAS sure your mom wouldn't let you stay up here with me anymore," Andrew admitted as soon as he and Caleb closed the door to his bedroom and started unpacking Caleb's bag.

Caleb furrowed his brow. "What do you mean? I've stayed up here with you the past four summers."

Andrew shrugged. "I know. But our moms talk, and now that I, ehm, you know, came out, I figured your mom might have something to say about that."

"Oh, she has something to say all right," Caleb scoffed. "Lots of somethings. She goes on and on about how there's absolutely nothing wrong with being gay and how important it is for families to support their gay kids. And then she tells me you're a great resource." Caleb rolled his eyes and shook his head. "Oh, the joys of having limousine-liberal parents who grew up in New York."

"Resource?" Andrew asked in confusion.

"Yeah, you know," Caleb responded as he made air quotes with his fingers. "About gay things."

"Why would you need a resource for that?" Andrew asked, sounding completely perplexed by Caleb's conversation with his mother.

"Seriously?" Caleb was slack-jawed. "Andrew, you do realize I'm gay too, right?"

"You are?" Andrew squeaked.

"Oh, come on. No way could you think a straight guy has my sense of style." Caleb highlighted his comment with a pose, one hand on his hitched hip and the other in the air, palm up. Then he started laughing. "Most of my friends know. And even though I haven't officially told my parents, I'm pretty sure my dad's figured it out, and my mom's definitely figured it out."

Collapsing onto the bed, Andrew remained quiet for a few moments and then said, "So have you done it yet?"

"Have I done it yet?" Caleb asked incredulously. "There are probably a slew of highly important things we can discuss—social stigma, family conflicts, assholes at school, even political stuff, but what comes out of your highly educated mouth is have I done it yet? Just what kind of doctor are you?"

Although he blushed, Andrew wouldn't be dissuaded. "Not a doctor yet, still have another year of med school. So have you?"

This time it was Caleb's turn to blush. "No," he admitted quietly. "But it's not because I don't want to," he finished in a stammered defense. "I know we're technically the same age, but it's not like I've been in college like you. I only just graduated high school."

Andrew stood up and chewed on his bottom lip. "I haven't either," he confessed. "Done it, I mean," he clarified unnecessarily.

Caleb rolled his eyes. "I know what you meant, Andrew," he said and then rolled them again for good measure, wondering whether his eyes could be permanently damaged if he kept rolling them. His mother sure thought so. He considered asking Andrew, but there were more important things to discuss. "So, do you wanna?"

"Do I want to what?"

Another eye roll. "Have sex. Or as you medical types say, 'do it.'"

"With you?" Andrew stuttered out.

"Yes, with me. Do you see anybody else here?" Caleb pointed around the room.

"Quit rolling your eyes at me, Caleb. I'm trying to catch up here, okay?"

"Sorry," Caleb whispered, suddenly feeling shy and insecure. He looked down at the ground and rubbed the toe of his shoe across the hardwood floor. "It's no biggie. It's just, I start college in a couple of months, and I didn't want to still be a virgin, but I know I have some weight to lose so you might not be interested and—"

Andrew's arms were around Caleb before he could finish his sentence. "I think you're perfect," Andrew said in a husky whisper.

That familiar face leaned forward, and Caleb's breath hitched. He was about to get his first kiss. He closed his eyes, pursed his lips, and tilted his face.

"Ow!" Andrew suddenly exclaimed. He had turned left when Caleb went right, and their noses made contact instead of their mouths.

Caleb giggled. "Sorry."

"'S okay." Andrew rubbed his nose. "Just stay still. I'm trying to be suave here."

"'Kay," Caleb agreed and didn't move despite a serious desire to wiggle. Then soft lips landed on his and all the air left his lungs. His heart felt like it was going to beat right out of his chest, his knees were weak, and he just hoped Andrew couldn't hear the whimpers he couldn't seem to hold back.

The first kiss led to another and then another. Caleb's lips parted, Andrew's tongue pushed into his mouth for a taste, and both men went wild. Hands grappled with buttons and fabric, hips rubbed and thrust desperately. And within moments, Caleb buried his face in Andrew's neck and cried out, coating his briefs with his release. He would have been mortified about his lack of control if Andrew hadn't followed him over the precipice.

"Wow," Andrew said in awe.

"Yeah."

"I think I like sex." The equivocal words were belied by shaking hands, a breathless voice, and a still firm cock.

Caleb raised one eyebrow, but didn't call Andrew on his understatement. Any insecurities he had about his body, about his experience, about anything, dissipated. It was just him and his best friend, the person he trusted most in the world, the one guy he knew would never look down on him. That security was unbelievably freeing.

"I know I'm a virgin and everything," Caleb's eyes twinkled as he spoke. "But I'm pretty sure that wasn't technically sex. Or at least, that there's more to sex."

Blushing, Andrew rubbed his cheek against Caleb's. "Yeah, ehm, I mean yes. As an almost medical professional, I can confirm the accuracy of that statement."

"As an almost medical professional, huh?" Caleb asked, resting his wrists on Andrew's shoulders and looking at his friend fondly.

"Oh, ah, yeah."

"Hmmm. Well, I wonder if the information you've learned at Johns Hopkins is consistent with the information I've learned from *XXX Showcase* magazine."

Andrew gulped. "Triple X?"

Caleb found a speechless, flushed Andrew to be an enticing sight. Then again, Caleb found any type of Andrew to be an enticing sight. Hell, he just plain found Andrew Thompson III enticing. He scraped his lips across Andrew's jaw and spoke softly into his ear. "Uh-huh."

"We could, uh, compare notes if you want," Andrew offered.

"You mean you'll show me yours if I show you mine?" Caleb lowered his hand and reached for Andrew's groin as he spoke and gave his friend a squeeze.

Andrew groaned. "This is going to be the best vacation ever."

"I'M GLAD you were willing to take a break from your time with Andrew to go get ice cream with me after dinner tonight, Caleb. I keep thinking this is going to be our last summer vacation like this. Next year, you'll be off in college, meeting new people, starting your own life." Barbara Lakes blinked back tears. "Oh, ignore me," she said while she dug through her purse for a Kleenex and dabbed the corners of her eyes. "I'm just suffering from empty nest syndrome a little early."

Caleb wrapped his arms around his mother and gave her a tight hug. "I love you, Mom. This isn't our last year having a vacation or anything else together. I'm going to college a cab ride away, not on Mars."

"I know, honey. I know. But it won't be the same once we're not living under the same roof." She linked her arm with Caleb's and kept walking along the path to the Thompsons' summer house. "Enough of this sad talk. Tell me about Andrew."

"Uh, what about Andrew?" Caleb asked.

"It looks like you two are really enjoying your time

together this summer."

"We enjoy spending time together every summer, Mom," Caleb said with an eye roll. "Andrew's my best friend."

"Of course he is, honey. You know, I was very good friends with your father before we started dating. Friendship is the best basis for a marriage. And I don't need to tell you that Andrew Thompson is a terrific catch."

"Mom! Andrew isn't a fish. He's my friend. And we're eighteen. We're not getting married." He stopped for a moment, feeling flummoxed. "Plus, we're gay! It's not like we can even *get* married!"

"Oh, pshaw. You know what I meant. The two of you could still have a life together. Look at Susan Sarandon and Tim Robbins. They're not legally married, but they've been living together for several years and they just had their second son."

"That's it," Caleb announced. "I'm asking Dad to cancel your subscription to *People* magazine."

"I do not have a subscription to *People* magazine!" His mother sounded truly affronted. So much so that her denial was almost believable.

"Uh-huh. You don't have a subscription, and you don't tuck that subscription into the *New Yorker* in an attempt to hide what you're actually reading."

Barbara blushed. "Oh, fine! You've caught me, but don't tell your father. He'll think I'm silly."

"Ah, Mom, I'm pretty sure Dad's on to you too. There

are only so many times we can see you holding a magazine upside down before we suspect you're not actually reading it," he said and smiled fondly at his mother. "But I don't get the impression Dad thinks any less of you for it."

She seemed frazzled for a few seconds, and then she pulled herself together. "Well, that just goes to show you that I'm right, now doesn't it?"

They had finally gotten back to the Thompsons' house and Caleb started opening the door. "Right about what?"

"Right about the best basis for a relationship. Only a true friend can know all your faults and love you despite them, or maybe even because of them." Leave it to his mother to bring the conversation back to her uncomfortable attempt at matchmaking. Caleb didn't respond, just rolled his eyes and walked inside. "Trust me, Caleb. I'm your mother and mothers know these things."

"Hey! You're back," Andrew said breathlessly as he ran into the entryway. "Good. We need to go." He clasped Caleb's arm and started pulling him out the door. "Hi, Mrs. Lakes!" he said with a smile. "Bye, Mrs. Lakes!"

"Bye, boys. Have fun!" Caleb's mother winked at Caleb and closed the door behind them.

"Where are we going?" Caleb asked.

"Drive-in movies."

Andrew walked them to the car and both men climbed inside. Caleb forced himself to shake off his disappointment. He had been looking forward to spending some quality alone time with Andrew that evening.

"What's playing?"

"No clue."

The clipped answers were getting on Caleb's nerves. Of course, those nerves were already pretty agitated because of the change in expectations for the evening. Caleb decided the best course of action would be to take a few minutes to calm down and regroup. By the time they pulled up to the half-empty drive-in, he felt moderately better.

That didn't last long when Caleb realized the movie was already playing. He bit his tongue while Andrew paid.

"Uh, Drew," he said once they pulled inside. "I think we already missed part of the movie." Caleb looked meaningfully at the screen where a few actors were engaged in some sort of chase.

"Yeah, probably." Andrew sounded completely distracted. A condition that was confirmed when, instead of driving to a spot close to the front or even in the middle, Andrew pulled into a parking spot in the back of the lot and off to the side. From that location, a portion of the screen was obscured.

"Good," Andrew sighed in relief and slumped against his seat once the car was parked and the ignition turned off. "We made it." He paused for a heartbeat and then turned an excited smile toward Caleb. "Want to get in the back?"

"Uh." Caleb furrowed his brow and glanced over to the backseat of the car. "I think that vantage point is even worse.

Half the screen will be blocked."

"Who cares about the screen?" Andrew unbuckled his seat belt and started climbing into the back, which required him to fold his long legs pretzel style. "We won't be watching it."

"We won't?" Caleb asked in confusion. "Why did you bring us to the movies if we're not going to, uh, watch the movie?"

Andrew raised one eyebrow. "It's dark out here. There's lots of noise from all those little stereos playing the movie. This backseat is roomy enough. And our mothers aren't here. Do you need me to draw you an actual picture?"

Caleb frantically grappled with his seatbelt, finally managing to unbuckle it. Then he scrambled into the backset ungracefully. "You really are a genius, Drew!"

"So I've been told," Andrew smirked. "Though never for anything this fun."

CHAPTER SIX

1993

"HERE'S TO my son," Andy Thompson said, raising his wine glass. "Medicine is an honorable profession, and I'm pleased Andrew decided to follow in my footsteps."

Andrew wouldn't so much as look at his father, let alone raise his glass to join the toast. Not even a discreet kick to the shin from Caleb was enough to get him to engage. Caleb sighed and lifted his water glass in acknowledgment, joining Elizabeth Thompson in a softly spoken, "Hear, hear."

"I would have thought you'd have let me know when you were choosing your residency matches." Andy Thompson was still talking, seemingly oblivious to the ill will pouring off his son. "I have excellent connections, even though you chose neuro instead of cardio."

Andrew peeled his gaze off his salad plate and looked pointedly at his father. "Seeing as how I matched with my top choice," he said, his voice even, stare unwavering and eyes unblinking, "it looks like I didn't need your help. Like always."

Oh, God. Caleb wanted to crawl under the table. They

were at what was supposed to be a celebratory dinner, and instead it was like a battle, with passive-aggressive barbs taking the place of weapons. It was more awkward than the time one of Caleb's buddies asked him to join an intramural soccer league. Turns out that "What color are the uniforms?" as a first question followed closely by "Do they have any jerseys with a tailored cut?" is enough to get an offer revoked. Who knew?

"This salad is delicious." Elizabeth's voice was unusually high. "Isn't your salad delicious, Caleb?"

It was romaine with a caesar dressing. He was waiting for the waiter to come back and confirm whether there were anchovies in it, so he hadn't yet taken a bite. Still, not having tasted it didn't seem like a good enough reason to squelch Elizabeth's desperate attempt at a distraction.

"Yes, it's great," Caleb answered.

"Cae, I think there are anchovies in it," Andrew warned from across the table.

"No, it's just lettuce and dressing, Andrew," Andrew's father corrected.

Oh, God, now they were fighting over salad. Poor Elizabeth, she'd really done her best.

"Just because you can't see the anchovies, doesn't mean they're not there. They could be hiding in the dressing. But hiding something isn't the same thing as not doing it."

Yeah, there was no way to pretend they were still talking about salad at this point. Caleb's gaze shot to Elizabeth.

She was pale, looking back and forth between her husband and her son.

"And let's just say there are anchovies in the salad. You can't see them. They're not in the way of the lettuce. I don't see the problem," Andy said to Andrew before looking at Caleb. "Just eat your salad, Caleb," he growled.

Caleb had his fork in his hand, spearing a piece of lettuce onto it before Andy could say another word. If he ate the damn salad, would somebody mercifully change the topic?

"No, don't!" Andrew sounded panicked, as if Caleb were about to commit anchovy-cide right there on the table. Then he glared at his father. "Caleb and I are vegetarians. I told you that when I came home for Christmas and then again when you chose a seafood restaurant for this dinner. But, as usual, you did what you wanted without regard to how it impacts your family. Now quit pushing Caleb to make accommodations for your choices."

He had seen a fire alarm switch when he'd gone to wash his hands before dinner. Maybe if he excused himself, he could go back there, pull the alarm and...

"It's too bad you didn't choose to attend your father's alma mater, Caleb," Andy said, reengaging Caleb's attention on the conversation. When had they stopped talking about *salad* and started talking about school? "If you were at Harvard, you'd be living in the same city as Andrew during his residency."

Oh holy shit. Caleb's gaze jerked over to Andrew. He had his palms planted on the table and was starting to rise to his feet. Those green eyes were on fire, the red lips pulled into thin white lines. Andrew was all sorts of pissed off. Rightly so. Going after his son's friend probably violated the Geneva Convention rules on family warfare. Regardless, Caleb did not want to escalate matters. At least not before the entrees were served. He mouthed a firm "sit down" to Andrew and then turned to his friend's father.

"I didn't have the grades or test scores to get into Harvard," Caleb admitted, hoping to take the sting out of Andy's attack. "But that may have been a blessing in disguise, because I found my passion in design school."

Andy scoffed. "That isn't a profession, it's a hobby. Look at Andrew's mother," Andy waved toward his wife dismissively. "She enjoys decorating, but that's not paying for this meal, now is it?"

The unsolicited attack on his mother was apparently the last straw. Andrew was out of his chair and leaning over his father. "No, I believe what's paying for this meal is Mother's trust fund," he spat. "Grandfather left me the same amount, and I know my annual earnings are significantly higher than what a mediocre cardiothoracic surgeon makes."

Caleb looked at Elizabeth apologetically, wiped his mouth with his napkin by instinct, not that he'd eaten a thing, and then calmly stood.

"Let's go take a walk, Drew. See if we can't calm down

a little." When Andrew didn't move from his stare down with his father, Caleb took the couple of steps necessary to reach him and clasped his elbow. "Come on."

Andrew closed his eyes, took in a deep breath, and then let it out as he opened them. "Caleb and I are going to grab some takeout and then we'll head back to his hotel." He looked directly at his mother. "Mom, if you want to meet for breakfast tomorrow, call me." There was no question the invitation didn't include a plus one option.

"I CAN'T stand him." Andrew stomped toward Caleb's hotel.

"Um-hum." Caleb nodded as he chewed the falafel they'd picked up at a little Middle Eastern place they'd passed by.

"I mean, can you believe him back there?" Andrew seethed. When Caleb didn't respond after half a second, Andrew continued, "Can you *believe* him?"

Figuring the question was rhetorical, he swallowed the food in his mouth and took another bite.

" '*You should have told me when you were choosing your residency programs,* '" Andrew mimicked his father in a derogatory tone; the demeaning expression on his face added to the mocking effect. "Like I can't get into a good program without his help? I got a two hundred sixty on my boards, for God's sake!"

Caleb thought about asking what that score meant, but the answer was pretty obvious. Andrew was always the top in everything he did. That thought warmed his heart, and he stepped in front of Andrew, halting his friend's forward progress.

"What?" Andrew asked.

"What what?" Caleb responded.

"You're smiling at me." The anger seemed to drain from Andrew's expression.

"Yeah."

"Why are you smiling at me?" One corner of Andrew's mouth was starting to rise.

"Because I'm proud of you, Drew. Like, really, really proud."

"You... Yeah?"

Caleb wanted nothing more than to plant a messy kiss on Andrew's smiling lips, but they were standing in the middle of the street. Instead, he reached his left hand up to Andrew's face and cupped his cheek, hoping the simple touch would be enough to express his feelings.

"Uh-huh. You're incredible. My parents told me that residency program you're going to is, like, the top in the nation."

Andrew shrugged modestly. "It's not a big deal."

"Yeah, it really is. Finishing medical school, starting your career, doing all of that when you're just nineteen. All of those things are a big deal." Andrew was blushing, but Caleb didn't stop talking. "You, Mister Andrew Thompson, are a big deal and I'm proud to be your friend."

With his gaze glued to the sidewalk and his shoe tracing circles on the ground, Andrew shrugged again and almost whispered, "I don't...I don't know what to say."

How was the same man who had been taking his father's head off minutes earlier suddenly shy? And why was that dichotomy turning Caleb on?

"Hmm, how about you say you'll eat that dinner you're holding"—Caleb tilted his chin toward the takeout bag in Andrew's hand—"and then take me back to my hotel room and show me just how big you can get?"

Andrew snapped his gaze up. "Was that a double entendre?"

"See," Caleb said, grabbing Andrew's free hand and pulling him down the street. "I knew you were smart."

CALEB CLOSED the hotel room door and turned the dead bolt. Five minutes ago he'd been horny and hard. Now that he was alone in a room with a bed and Andrew, he was unaccountably nervous. But still hard.

"Hey," Andrew whispered into his ear, his chest pressed to Caleb's back.

"Hey, yourself."

Andrew snaked his arm around Caleb's waist and

pushed under his shirt, skimming his belly and chest. "Did I remember to tell you how glad I am that you came?"

It was hard to hold back a dirty joke or three in response to that statement, but Caleb managed. "It's your graduation, Drew. Of course I'm here. Wouldn't miss it."

The hand caressing him was warm, big, gentle. It relaxed Caleb, and he leaned back, letting Andrew support him.

"I have butterflies in my stomach," Andrew confessed.

Caleb thought he could feel the heat radiating off Andrew's cheeks.

"Have you fooled around with anyone since last summer?" Caleb asked.

There was no censure in his tone, just honest curiosity. Andrew was his friend and he wanted happiness for him. He figured happiness had to involve an assisted orgasm every so often.

"No." Andrew shook his head, and Caleb felt the blond locks tickle his cheek. Then Andrew rested his chin on Caleb's shoulder. "I was busy with school and—" He sighed deeply. "I guess I don't really know how to meet guys. Plus...don't laugh at me, okay?"

Caleb turned around in Andrew's arms and rested his forearms on his shoulders. "I'd never laugh at you. *With* you, yeah. But never at you." He grinned and winked.

"Goofball," Andrew said affectionately and tugged a wayward piece of Caleb's hair. "What I was going to say was that I want to find a boyfriend, you know? Not just a one-night stand. Maybe I'll have better luck in Boston."

Raking his eyes over Andrew's body, Caleb leered. "I have no doubt." He cupped Andrew's bulge, giving it a squeeze. "And until then, I can help take care of you."

"Oh God," Andrew gasped and pushed his hips forward, seeking more friction. "That feels so good. Why does it feel so much better when you do it than when I do it to myself?"

Caleb leaned back against the door and spread his legs, then he cupped Andrew's ass and pulled him forward. It didn't take long for Andrew to get the picture. He bent his knees and thrust his hips up, letting his hardness rub against Caleb's through the fabric of their pants.

"Ungh," Andrew moaned, rutting faster, harder.

"Uh-huh," Caleb answered as he leaned forward and trailed kisses from Andrew's jaw to his ear and down his neck, moving his hips along with Andrew's rhythm all the while. "Uh-huh. So good."

"Can I...?" Andrew pressed his mouth to Caleb's neck and sucked in the warm flesh. "I want skin, Cae. Want to feel you against me. I..."

"Yes, ungh!" Caleb moaned in pleasure when Andrew moved at just the right angle. "Want skin too."

Their shaking hands squeezed between their bodies and tugged on zippers and buttons. It wasn't long before two pairs of pants and underwear were shoved down, leaving hard, hot skin exposed. The first touch of their naked bodies against each other had both men crying out.

"Can't last." Andrew swallowed hard, seemingly trying to stop himself from spilling so quickly.

"Let it go," Caleb said into his mouth before pulling his head down for a deep, probing kiss. He sucked on Andrew's tongue and humped against him with mounting desperation, relishing in the feeling of the runaway train gaining steam in his belly.

"Cae!" Andrew's neck stretched, his back arched, but he didn't stop pushing his hard cock against Caleb. "Oh, oh, oh!"

Liquid heat poured over Caleb's skin while Andrew shook and screamed his name. That was all it took for Caleb to lose it, crying and shivering, squeezing Andrew's hips and gasping for air.

With his forehead resting on Caleb's shoulder, Andrew started chuckling.

"What?" Caleb asked, reaching up to pet Andrew's hair.

"We're in the entryway." His laughter deepened. "We couldn't get any farther than the damn door before we started mauling each other."

"Couldn't get our clothes off either." Caleb joined the laughter and pointedly looked down at Andrew's body, taking in the still-buttoned shirt and the pants and briefs trapped at his ankles over his shoes. He knew his outfit was in the same state.

"You know, we have a bed in a private room this time? No parents on the other side of these walls. Maybe we can try this naked and horizontal."

"You have the best ideas!" Caleb pushed away from the door and grabbed Andrew's hand. "Come on." He took one step into the room and tripped on his own pants. He didn't plummet to the floor only because Andrew caught hold of his shoulder and kept him upright.

"Umm, maybe we should pull our pants up first," Andrew suggested helpfully before erupting in a fit of giggles.

Still only half-dressed, Caleb turned around and hugged his friend tightly, joining in the laughter. "Like I said, the best ideas."

CHAPTER SEVEN

1994

"SO HOW was it?" Andrew asked as soon as Caleb answered his phone.

"Who is this?"

"Caleb," Andrew growled in warning. "Did you or did you not get busy last night?"

"Mom? Is that you?" Caleb asked in a singsong cadence.

"Caleb Lakes, quit screwing around and tell me about your date!"

Letting out a low chuckle, Caleb settled on his bed and tucked his feet under his ass. "There wasn't any screwing, Drew. It was our second date, and I'm just not that kind of girl." He knew Andrew couldn't see him batting his eyelashes, but the action seemed to go with his role, so he hammed it up.

"So help me, Cae. If you don't tell me whether you got to touch a guy's dick last night, I'm going to get on a plane and fly up there to shake it out of you."

"I already told you, Drew, there was no dick in me so there's nothing for you to shake out. Plus, I'm not really clear on how the logistics of that would work."

"You are the most annoying person on the planet. Tell me about your date," Andrew said. Caleb stayed completely silent. "Caleb?" Not a word, not even a breath. "Caleb?" Still nothing. "Caleb, God damn it! Say something!"

"But you promised to come visit me if stayed quiet. I miss you." Okay, so he enjoyed torturing his friend, but the sentiment was sincere.

"I miss you too. This residency is kicking my ass, but I promise I'll come see you the first long break I get."

"Okay," Caleb sighed resignedly. "So what do you want to know about my date?"

"Everything," Andrew answered immediately.

"Hmm. Well, I tried on all my pants and decided my ass looked huge in all of them, and not in that sexy way. I seriously need to lose some more weight. But since that wasn't going to happen in one day, I went to the mall to look for a new pair of jeans. Not the super-casual kind, more the dressy jea—"

"In my mind I've already slapped you two times. Get to the good stuff, Cae."

"But you said you wanted to hear *everything*," Caleb whined.

"Please, Cae? There's not even an indicia of another homosexual within ten miles of me. I'm living vicariously through you here."

"Oh, that's total bullshit. They say ten percent of the population is gay. I'm sure there are even guys at your work that play for our team."

"You think so?" Andrew asked hopefully. "How can I figure out who they are?"

Caleb smiled. His friend was so unbelievably earnest. "Well," he said. "Have you ever noticed anybody violating the one three five rule?"

"The what rule?"

"One three five. You know, when you walk up to the urinals and somebody's already there so you choose the farthest one from him and if the only one open is right next to the guy, you just wait until he's done."

Caleb paused, waiting for Andrew to say something.

"Uh, yeah, I get it. Just didn't recognize the name, so what does that have to do with finding a guy I can date?"

"Well, if you notice someone violating the one three five rule, he's one of us."

"Okay, first of all, you cannot tell whether someone is gay or straight by their choice in urinals. And B, I am not going to meet my Prince Charming in a bathroom."

"Prince Charming?" Caleb asked quizzically. "I'm just hoping to find someone whose hair isn't in a mullet and you're looking for Prince Charming?"

"Yeah, well…" Andrew said hesitantly and Caleb was sure he could *hear* the blush over the phone line.

"I wasn't teasing you, Drew. I think it's sweet. I really do. And you're probably spot-on about not finding Mister Right in a bathroom. But I'm still sure there are plenty of great men around. You just need to look for them."

"You think so?" Andrew asked, his voice full of yearning.

Caleb wasn't so sure actually. He was in his second year of college, and he hadn't even found a Mister Right Now. But he didn't want to deflate Andrew's hope, so instead of answering, he changed the topic.

"So, my date last night…"

"Right!" Andrew refocused, the previous topic of conversation seemingly forgotten. "Was he nice? Did you like him? Are you going to see him again?"

"Umm, he was nice, I guess. But he wasn't my type," Caleb said.

"Why not?" Andrew asked. "What's your type?"

"Oh, I don't know. Someone with balls."

"He doesn't have balls?" Andrew gasped in shock.

"Jesus H. Christ, sometimes I have to remind myself that you finished medical school. Do you honestly think I met a eunuch in 1994 New York? I meant the comment figuratively, Drew, not literally."

"Right, right. I'm sorry," Andrew stammered. "I've been working almost seventy hours a week and I'm exhausted."

"Oh, babe," Caleb softened his tone. "I'm sorry. That sucks."

"No, it's okay. I really like the program, love the work. I'm fine, just a little tired. Now quit stalling and finish your story. I want to hear why your date needs to grow a pair."

Caleb laughed. "Well, we went to dinner in the Village. He seemed really nervous the whole time and that kinda stressed me out, so when we were walking out of the restaurant, I took his hand. Just trying to help him feel comfortable, you know? Calm him down."

"That's nice," Andrew said.

"I know, right? That's what I was going for. But he jumped away so fast he knocked down a barstool we were passing by. Then he, like, stomped out, and when I caught up with him on the street, he gave it to me because I tried to touch him in public. I figure if a guy's so deep in the closet that he can't even find his way out in Greenwich Village, he's not ready to date." Caleb paused. "Actually, that's not fair. Maybe I'll set him up with this guy in my computer design class. He's, like, militantly butch, so there'll be no worries about accidental outings. So I guess what I'm saying is, I'm not interested in dating someone like that."

There was silence for a few long beats before Andrew answered. "Yeah, I get that." Caleb could feel Andrew thinking, so he stayed quiet and waited for the always-interesting results. "So then, you didn't get any?"

He couldn't stop the laughter. "I swear, Drew," he gasped out and then started laughing again. "Your attention span amazes me. Nothing will distract you when you're focused."

"What?" Andrew chuckled. "It's a legitimate question."

"It is not. You're just horny and hard up."

"God, yes," Andrew agreed.

"I'll book a flight and see if I can't help relieve some of that...frustration."

"Really?" It sounded like Andrew was bouncing. "You don't mind?"

"Nah, my luck with men hasn't been all that great either, as you know. So I could use the company. Plus, I'm looking forward to kicking your ass in HeroQuest."

"Please, like you could ever beat me," Andrew scoffed.

"All right, it's on. I'll see when I can get out there for a little gaming and a whole lotta making out."

"Thanks, Cae. That sounds like the perfect weekend."

"DAMN, YOU'VE gotten so good at that," Andrew panted.

"Thanks." Caleb crawled up the bed and crouched over him. "I like doing it." He blushed. "That's not weird, right? It's okay for me to like...you know."

"I have no frame of reference for whether it's normal to enjoy giving head, but either way, I consider it one of your best characteristics."

Caleb scowled and bit Andrew's shoulder.

"Ow!" Andrew yelped. "Quit biting me."

"Quit being a jerk."

"I was complimenting you! How is that being a jerk?"

With a grumble and another nip to Andrew's shoulder,

Caleb collapsed on top of him. "Whatever. So now that we've gotten our hellos out of the way, what do we have planned for the rest of the weekend?"

"Umm, not much. There's a pizza place close by that some people from work rave about, so I thought we could try that and maybe catch a movie."

"I tell you that I'm going on a diet and you suggest pizza?" Caleb mock shuddered. "You're truly evil."

"You don't need to lose weight, Cae."

"Right," he snorted and rolled his eyes.

With Caleb's shirt pushed up, Andrew could skim his hot, smooth skin. Just the feel of his friend's body had Andrew's cock waking back up.

"I'm serious. You look good." Understatement if there ever was one. He thought Caleb looked gorgeous. Always had.

"You have to say that, you're my friend. That's the rule, right? Moms and friends are supposed to think you're good-looking even if your belly looks like an eighteen wheeler's tire."

"Honestly, I don't know where you come up with this nonsense," Andrew responded with a shake of his head.

"Well, I'd say my pathetic dating record speaks for itself."

"Hey, at least you have a dating record. I haven't even been able to manage that."

He moved his hands down to Caleb's ass and trembled in response. God, but did he ever want in there. They'd shared all their other firsts with each other, so Andrew hoped Caleb was ready to try this too.

"That's only because you haven't put yourself out there, Drew. You're a total hottie, and the guys will be lining up as soon as they know you're interested."

"I hope you're right," Andrew sighed. "'Cause I get lonely sometimes. Really lonely."

Deciding it was time to add some action to their Mutual Admiration Society meeting, he gripped one side of Caleb's ass with his left hand and trailed the fingers of his right hand into Caleb's crease. That move had Caleb trembling above him. Then Caleb dipped his head and kissed Andrew's chin, the left side of his lip, and the tip of his nose before he let their lips meet.

The kiss was slow at first, gentle. Lips pressing together and releasing over and over again. Eventually Caleb turned up the heat, parting his lips and pulling at Andrew's lower lip, darting out his tongue for little licks, and grinding his hips.

"Mmm. You're a great kisser, Cae," he mumbled into Caleb's mouth and leaned up for more of those drugging kisses.

He'd have yanked Caleb's mouth down to his, but his hands were busy exploring a fine ass. He slid his fingers up and down Caleb's crease, putting just a touch of pressure on the enticing rosebud at every turn.

"We doing this?" Caleb asked in between kisses.

Andrew pushed just the tip of his index finger inside that tight heat and nodded. "I want to. Are you ready for it?" When Caleb tilted his ass and ground it back onto his invading finger, Andrew got his answer. He met Caleb's movement and pushed all the way inside. Oh, damn. So hot.

"Let's hope this goes better than when we first tried blow jobs," Caleb said breathlessly.

The memory of both of them gagging in turn and a few inopportune teeth snaggings had Andrew laughing. "Oh, man. We were shit at it, weren't we?"

Caleb whimpered and thrust his hard dick against Andrew's belly. "When you laugh, it makes your whole body move...including your finger."

"That's good?" Andrew chuckled tightly, hoping the answer was yes because he didn't want to stop.

"Yeah." Caleb circled his hips and panted. "Really good."

Andrew's cock was trapped between their bodies, and every one of Caleb's movements had him gliding against sweat-slicked skin. It was a lucky thing he'd just come because otherwise he'd have lost it from the grinding-kissing-fingering trifecta of goodness.

"You have any thoughts on how we should do this, Cae?" Andrew was moving his finger in and out now, wanting to replace that digit with a different body part.

"Uh..." Caleb braced his hands on either side of Andrew's head and pushed his torso up, rocking his ass onto

Andrew's hand. "Tab A, slot B. Damn, Drew, feels so good. Didn't expect it to feel so good."

With one hand working Caleb's tight heat, Andrew moved the other to Caleb's upper back and then flipped them over so he was on top. He leaned down and kissed Caleb fiercely, teeth and tongue tugging and licking Caleb's swollen lips. And all the while he kept up a steady rhythm with his finger.

"I brought some lube home from the hospital. I think that'll help," he said.

"'Kay. I think…ungh…I think I want more of you inside me."

Though he'd never imagined words would be enough to make him come, it now seemed like a close thing. Andrew stretched toward the nightstand, hoping he'd be able to reach what he needed without severing his connection with Caleb's body, but that didn't seem possible. With a mental note to plan better next time, he removed his finger, dove toward the nightstand, and fumbled for the bottle he'd tucked away a few days earlier. He was kneeling between Caleb's outstretched thighs seconds later.

Caleb's lust-filled eyes met his, and they gazed at one another for a few seconds, letting the emotion of the moment and their ever-growing connection wash over them. With a shaking hand, Andrew opened the bottle of lube and drizzled some on his cock. Caleb clasped the backs of his knees and pulled his legs up and out, leaving his opening completely exposed.

"Oh, damn," Andrew gasped. "So fine, Cae. Seriously, you're so damn fine."

Andrew moved his slick fingers over Caleb's rosebud, getting it ready for him. Then he placed his cockhead at Caleb's opening and thrust his hips slowly. At first, his cock simply pressed against Caleb's body but didn't slip inside.

"'S okay, Drew," Caleb said as he gripped Andrew wrist, dragging his attention away from where their bodies were touching to Caleb's face. "Just push it in. I want you to."

Andrew gave a sharp nod, then gripped the base of his cock with one hand and laid the other on Caleb's outstretched thigh, holding him still. A steady pressure of his lubed cock against Caleb's entrance finally did the trick, and suddenly Andrew popped inside his friend's body.

"Oh! Oh, wow. Oh, wow," he stammered, voice full of wonder as he pushed forward into that warm heat.

Andrew's eyes were locked on the place where his body was joining Caleb's. Never had he seen anything so erotic. Combine that with the feeling of Caleb's body gripping his, and he knew there'd be no way for him to make this last. When he finally bottomed out, he dragged his eyes up to Caleb's. The wide pupils, parted lips, and rosy cheeks had him crying out.

"Caleb!" He pulled out and slammed back in with a hard thrust until his balls were pressed against Caleb's upturned ass. "Can't stay still," he grunted. "Need to move. Oh,

God, Cae!"

He dragged his dick out and shoved back in again and again, quickening his pace and crying out Caleb's name over and over. Almost by instinct, his hand reached for Caleb's dick and started stroking furiously.

"So close, Cae. I'm so close. Come with me. Ungh, ungh, ungh, Caleb!"

Andrew shouted, his entire body shook, and he shot deep inside Caleb. When Caleb called his name and warm seed pulsed over his thumb and hand, his cock throbbed in sympathy and pushed out more release.

"Oh my God, oh my God, oh my God." Caleb panted out the words.

He cupped Caleb's cheek with his clean hand and rubbed his thumb over that sweet mouth.

"Good?" he asked.

"So good, Drew." Caleb kissed the tip of his finger. "I had no idea anything could feel so good."

Andrew smiled broadly, feeling oddly accomplished. "It was pretty wonderful from this end too. Maybe after dinner, we can try it the other way."

"I thought we were seeing a movie after dinner," Caleb said with a wink.

"Are you kidding?" Andrew scoffed. "Now that we know about this, I'm not sure we should ever leave the bed again. I'll give the pizza guy a key and a blindfold and we'll be set for life."

CHAPTER EIGHT

1995

"I GOT my ear pierced."

"You what?" Caleb shot up in bed and gripped the phone tightly against his ear, certain he had a bad connection.

"I got my ear pierced. The left one. I got a silver ring with a small ball on each end."

"Andrew! You're a doctor. You can't have a pierced ear."

"I assure you that a ring in my ear won't impact my ability to perform complex surgical procedures."

Caleb found Andrew's too-calm, too-even tone to be more troubling than the seemingly out of nowhere piercing. He took a few deep breaths to calm down and think.

"Drew?" he began hesitantly.

"Yeah?" That tone was still completely flat.

"How's work?"

"Good. Well, really good, actually. I came up with a new way to do this one procedure. The attendings seem pretty excited about it."

Okay, so no problem at work then. "How's Brendan?" Caleb tried again.

"He's fine." Andrew paused. "At least I assume he's fine. I wouldn't really know."

Well, shit. "What happened?"

"Nothing much. He broke up with me."

"Oh, Drew." Caleb sighed. "I'm sorry."

"It's no big deal. I mean, we were only together for, like, three weeks. It happens. Right?"

It had been only three weeks, true enough, but Brendan was Andrew's first boyfriend, and Caleb knew how excited his friend had been to have finally found someone.

"It's okay to be upset about it. Even if you weren't together all that long, it still sucks." When Andrew didn't respond, Caleb kept pressing. "Do you want to tell me what happened?"

He heard Andrew breathing and waited for an answer. "He said I wasn't perverted enough."

"I don't...I don't know what to do with that," Caleb said honestly. "Was he into weird shit? You never told me anything like that."

"I honestly don't know. I thought things were fine until he didn't show up when we were supposed to go out. I called to check on him, and he said he wasn't coming and that things couldn't work out between us because I wasn't perverted enough. Those were his exact words."

"That's bullshit!" Caleb was incensed. "You are plenty

perverted."

"Uh, thanks?" Andrew chuckled and the sound eased Caleb's tension. His friend would be fine.

"You know what I mean," he grumbled. "I'm sorry, Drew. Clearly, Brandon's an ass and you're lucky to be rid of him."

"Brendan. And, yeah, I know. It feels weird that he found someone else while we were still dating, but I guess it's all for the best, right? This way I can meet someone more compatible."

"What do you mean, he found someone else while you were still dating?" Caleb screeched. "Did he say that?"

"Yeah," Andrew admitted, shame evident in his tone.

Caleb wanted to rant and rave about how wrong that was, about how Andrew deserved so much better, but he could tell Andrew was trying to look on the bright side and to focus on moving on. It seemed pretty clear the man's boyfriend had been cheating, plus he got dumped unceremoniously over the phone, but there he was looking at the bright side. Andrew always managed to find new ways to impress Caleb, and this was no exception.

"Whoever you end up with is going to be one lucky guy, Drew."

"'LO?"

"Hey. Did I wake you up?" Andrew looked at the clock as he asked the question and winced. With his on-call schedule, nights and days sometimes mixed. He'd woken Caleb on more than one occasion by calling at an indecent hour, and now he was doing it again.

"No, no. 'S okay." Caleb's voice sounded like it had been dragged over gravel. No way had he been awake.

"You want me to call back, Cae? After you get a bit more sleep?"

"Nah, I'm up. 'Sides, I'd rather talk to you than sleep any day. 'S up?"

Relieved he could get his worries off his chest, Andrew flopped down on his sofa, kicked off his flip-flops, and propped his feet on the coffee table.

"I did something stupid last night." Something, someone—there didn't seem to be a difference in this instance.

"What'd you do? I'm sure it's not as bad as you're thinking."

Typical Caleb—always assuming the best about him. This time he was wrong.

"I met a guy at a bar and went back to his place," Andrew confessed. He took a breath and continued. "And I fucked him."

"You went home with a stranger?" Caleb sounded angry. "That's really dangerous, Drew. Tell me you wore a rubber."

"Of course I did. I'm not a complete idiot. But we didn't even exchange names, which I only realized when I was walking out and he said, '*So what's your name?*' I wanted to crawl under the nearest piece of furniture."

God, he felt like such a sleaze. What he'd done the previous night was stupid and dangerous and a whole bunch of other words someone could put in an after-school special. Well, if they made an after-school special about anonymous sex.

"Ouch," Caleb said. "That is really awkward. So was it any good?"

The question took Andrew completely off guard. He was prepared for a long lecture about morals and relationships and who knows what else, but not for a question about the quality of the sex.

"Uh," Andrew stammered. "The during part was fine, I guess, but the after was beyond uncomfortable." He paused for a moment, thought about the previous night, and reconsidered his answer. "Well, no, actually, the during part wasn't spectacular either." He sighed despondently. "Great. I risked life and limb and made myself into a complete slut for shitty sex."

"I hope you don't mean that literally," Caleb teased.

"Huh?" Andrew asked.

"The shitty sex part. I hope you don't mean it literally."

"Ew, Cae! That's crossing a line. Quit being disgusting."

"Hey, it got a laugh out of you," Caleb responded.

"I wasn't laughing."

"Yeah, you were."

"No, I wasn't."

"Were."

"Oh my God!" Andrew shouted. "I'd tell you to stop acting like an adolescent, but I knew you back then and you were nowhere near this childish. Cut it out and help me here."

"Ehm, okay," Caleb said, and continued in a serious tone. "I read about a religion where you can become a born-again virgin. I can look into that for you."

"Fuck. You."

"No, no. If you do that, it cancels out the whole re-virginhood. Clearly you're missing the point here. The problem must be bigger than I thought."

"I assure you, my dick was not the problem," Andrew responded.

Caleb burst into laughter. "Nice," he drawled. "Well played, my friend, well played."

"Hey, if you can't beat them..."

"Oh, you can definitely beat them. Preferably while you're fucking them with that big *problem* of yours."

"All right, this conversation has gone completely off the rails and digressed into double-entendre insanity. Are we going to talk seriously about my screw-up last night?" Andrew stopped talking for a moment and then continued. "And so help me, if you make some pun involving the word screw, I'm hanging up."

Caleb snickered a little and then composed himself. "What do you want me to say, Drew? You had a one-night stand. It happens. I'd rather you not do it with complete strangers you meet at bars 'cause that's just not safe. But otherwise? You glove up, get off, and move on. No harm, no foul."

Something about that just didn't sit right with Andrew, didn't feel like who he wanted to be.

"If that's true, then why don't I hear about you hitting the one-nighter circuit?" he asked.

"I don't know." Andrew could picture Caleb shrugging, even though he couldn't see him. "I guess that's not my thing. If it's not your thing either, then don't do it again. But quit being so hard on yourself." Suddenly, Caleb fell into a fit of giggles. "I said hard-on."

"CALEB!" ANDREW called out as soon as he had his front door open. "Cae!"

"In here," he heard Caleb answer from his office/guest bedroom.

Thankfully, Caleb had a key to his apartment because work had gone late, and Andrew hadn't been able to pick his friend up from the airport or even meet him at home when he got in. He rushed down the hallway, anxious to see Caleb, and walked into the room to find the man sitting at his desk and looking at his computer.

"What're you doing...holy shit!" Andrew exclaimed when he saw a close-up picture of an erect dick penetrating a pale ass.

"I was bored so I went online, and then I thought it'd be fun to check out your browsing history. You can try to give me the same excuse you did when we were kids and you said you were looking at that catalogue for the clothes, but I don't think you'll get away with it this time, seeing as how there's not a stitch of clothing in this picture."

"Oh, God," Andrew groaned, his face burning. "Is there anything I can say to make this less embarrassing? And if so, can we pretend I said that and go to bed now?"

"Oh, hell, yes." Caleb flew out of his chair and grabbed Andrew's hand, pulling him to the bedroom. "After what I've seen on your computer, I'd say the afternoon just took on new, almost limitless possibilities."

Andrew laughed. "Oh, yeah? What'd you have in mind?"

"Don't know." Caleb shrugged. He yanked off his shirt and stripped out of his pants while Andrew did the same mad dash to get out of his clothes. "Mostly I'm horny. I've spent the past hour looking at your porn. Plus, I was thinking about you looking at your porn." Caleb shuddered. He glanced down at his erection and palmed it. "I'm so damn hard, it hurts. What do you think, Doctor, do you have a cure for what ails me?" he waggled his eyebrows and asked in a campy tone.

Andrew snorted. "Oh, wow, that's terrible. Really terrible. I promise to make fun of you for it later, but right now, get your fine self over here." He climbed onto the bed and lay back, holding his arms open in invitation to Caleb.

With a wicked little grin, Caleb climbed onto the foot of the bed and started crawling up on all fours. He moved slowly, gazing at Andrew with heated eyes and occasionally bending down and nipping at skin. When he reached Andrew's testicles, he leaned forward and nuzzled the tender area.

"Mmm, love how you smell, Drew," Caleb mumbled. He lapped at Andrew's balls and then sucked them into his mouth, all the while making happy little mewling noises. Eventually, he licked a line up Andrew's cock and slid down the rigid pole.

"Ungh, yeah!" Andrew cried out, thrusting his hips up. "Flip around, Cae," he groaned. "Want to suck you at the same time."

It was a bit awkward, but Caleb managed to turn himself so he and Andrew were head to toe, all without losing his hold on Andrew's erection.

Andrew let himself revel in the pleasure he was receiving for a few more sucks, and then he rolled Caleb onto his back and crouched above him, straddling Caleb's face. He leaned on his elbows and lapped at the precum glistening at the tip of Caleb's cock, smiling when Caleb moaned around his dick. As much as he wanted to prolong the pleasure, maybe tease Caleb a bit, the scent of the body beneath him, the slurping sounds filling the room, and the exquisite heat and suction enveloping his cock made holding off the inevitable impossible. So Andrew slid his mouth down Caleb's erection, not stopping until he reached the base.

In this position, he could pump his dick down onto Caleb's mouth while he sucked his friend, so that was what he did. He rocked his hips, forcing his erection in and out of Caleb's mouth, pulling out more of those arousing moans and cries. And all the while, he slid his lips up and down Caleb's cock, sucking as hard as he could.

All too soon, Andrew's body shook and stiffened. He popped his mouth off the hard cock and cried out in pleasure as he pulsed down Caleb's throat.

"Drew!" Caleb shouted, and ropes of cum shot from his cock onto Andrew's face.

When they were done trembling from orgasmic aftershocks, both men melted onto the bed.

"I feel like a limp noodle," Caleb panted.

"Mm-hum" Andrew agreed.

"So, you wanna do it again?"

Andrew would have laughed, but he was too relaxed and sated. "How about we take advantage of our refractory period and get a snack. I'm starving."

"I'll go into the kitchen and scavenge for something you can eat," Caleb said. He patted Andrew's knee and got up. "You stay here and think nasty thoughts. With as hard up as I've been and as hot as you are, I'm not giving you more than a few minutes to recover, so buck up, camper." Caleb paused and grinned. "Get it? Buck *up*? Damn, I crack myself *up*. Ha! I did it again."

"You're a goofball, Cae," Andrew called out after his friend. Then he lay on the bed and smiled, feeling light and happy for the first time in months.

"I'M SORRY about this, Cae. Really I am," Andrew said dejectedly.

Caleb squeezed his bicep and then rubbed his arm.

"It's fine. I've got your car. I'll do a little shopping, maybe make some dinner, and then you'll be home. No biggie."

"I know." Andrew sighed. "It still sucks though. You're here to spend time with me and I have to work."

"I'm here all weekend. We'll have lots of time to spend together." Caleb smirked and waggled his eyebrows. "And I'll make sure that time sucks too, but in a much better way."

Andrew snorted out a laugh and ruffled Caleb's hair affectionately. "You're incorrigible."

Caleb gave him an air kiss and waved over his shoulder as he sashayed from the hospital entrance to Andrew's car. Andrew's gaze was glued to Caleb's ass the entire time, which was no doubt Caleb's intent in putting that little sway in his step. The man got off on driving him nuts.

Great. Now I'll be thinking about Caleb getting off all afternoon. He shuffled into the hospital, mentally cursing anybody and everybody he could possibly blame for making him pick up an extra shift.

"Dr. Thompson."

Andrew was too consumed writing his mental shit list to register his name being called.

"Dr. Thompson!" That was loud enough to get his attention.

He stopped and turned around, seeing Stanley Jacques, one of the attendings, rushing up to him.

"Hi, Doctor," Andrew said. "Do you need me for something?"

"No." The man shook his head. "Well, yes. Do you, uh, have a moment?"

Andrew pulled his pager off his belt, confirmed nobody was looking for him, and then nodded. "Sure, do you need help with a case?"

"Not right now, thank you."

Stanley led them to an empty office and waited for Andrew to walk in before closing the door. His face looked flush, and he was shifting from foot to foot, exposing his anxiety.

"What's going on, Dr. Jacques?"

"Nothing, nothing," he sighed and flopped down into one of the office chairs. "I'm sure it's nothing. It's just, uh…" Stanley dragged his hand through his receding hair. "Do you mind if I ask you a question?"

Andrew figured that was rhetorical, so he didn't answer. Sure enough, Stanley continued.

"Are you, um..." Stanley tapped his fingers across his thigh rapidly. "What I'm trying to ask is...ehm, what's your sexual preference, Dr. Thompson?"

"My sexual preference?" Andrew asked, raising one eyebrow. "Ah, I'd say it's often. Or at least, as often as possible."

The sarcastic remark was out of his mouth before Andrew could stop it. Man, he must have been channeling Caleb or something. The question seemed unusual, but innocuous. It wasn't as if Andrew had ever hidden who he was, so there was no reason for him to have been pissy to the other doctor because he asked about it.

He was about to apologize when the man started laughing. "Oh, to be young again." He got up from the chair and patted Andrew's back. "Good man, good man. I was just worried when I saw you outside talking with that..." Stanley's lips pursed, his nose wrinkled, and his eyes squinted. He looked like he'd just eaten a lemon. Or was painfully constipated. "When I saw you talking with that gentleman. Was he a patient or a patient's family member?"

He hadn't been outside with any patients or their families all day, so Stanley must have been referring to Caleb.

"That was my friend, Caleb. He's in town for the weekend."

Stanley's face lost some of the color he seemed to have

regained during the conversation. "Your *friend*? What do you mean by that?"

All right, either the conversation was bizarro or Andrew was too sleep-deprived to follow it.

"Uh, what do I mean by friend? Caleb and I grew up together. Our mothers were sorority sisters in college and—"

"Good!" Stanley almost shouted. Then he patted Andrew's back again and took a step toward the closed door. "You had me worried for a second there. I don't think I need to tell you that your friend comes off as a little..." He let the words trail off, but held up his hand and flipped it from side to side.

If Andrew stayed quiet, the attending would leave the room and the topic would be forgotten. But Andrew refused to live his life hidden. He grabbed the attending's arm to keep him from leaving the room.

"Stanley?" he said. "Caleb is my friend, but let's get one thing straight." He took a breath and continued, "I'm not."

"You're not what?" Stanley asked.

"I'm not straight. I'm gay. I don't see how that's any of your business but I..." *Don't want it to seem like I'm hiding anything, like I'm ashamed.* Andrew chose to keep his reasons for answering Stanley's question to himself. They were none of the man's business. Of course, neither was Andrew's orientation.

Stanley stumbled back to his chair and sighed. He dragged his hand through his hair again, more forcefully this time. Andrew considered telling him he should treat his remaining hairs with more care or they'd run away to join their fallen comrades.

"I was afraid of that," he said.

"What is that supposed to mean?" Andrew growled. He crossed his arms over his chest and stood tall, glaring down at the other doctor.

"I don't mind," Stanley claimed, as if he had some right to care one way or the other about Andrew's personal life. "But other people might not be so open, which could impact your career." His eyes met Andrew's and there seemed to be kindness and sincerity there, which struck Andrew as inconsistent with the topic of conversation. "Don't worry, I only figured it out because of your friend. You look normal, so I doubt anybody else will suspect. But just to be safe, consider asking your friend not to come here again. And make sure to send any other *friends* the same message. Otherwise, people might get the wrong impression."

Andrew didn't respond. After all, what was there to say? He was normal. And he'd make damn sure people got the right impression.

CHAPTER NINE

1996

"GET NAKED and bend over the sofa." Andrew nuzzled Caleb's throat. "I'll be right back."

Caleb watched Andrew's ass as he took Caleb's suitcase into the bedroom. Once that fine specimen was out of sight, he peeled off his oatmeal-colored light-weight sweater, kicked off his black loafers, and pushed his charcoal herringbone slim-fit trousers down to his ankles. He had his hands hooked in the sides of his matching herringbone jock when he heard Andrew moan behind him.

"Oh, Jesus, what are you wearing?"

Caleb turned around and rubbed his palm over the front of his jock. "New underwear. Do you like it?" he asked with a leer as he ran his fingers underneath the thin elastic waistband holding the barely there pouch. His favorite thing about losing weight had been getting a new wardrobe, which included things to wear under that wardrobe.

"I've never..." Andrew shook his head and gulped. "I've never seen anything hotter. Leave it on." That voice was deeper than usual, rough with desire.

He nodded, feeling thrilled that Andrew liked how he looked. Caleb dropped his hands from his waistband and braced himself against the arm of the couch, bending at the waist so his ass was elevated.

"Goddamn, Cae. You are so beautiful." Andrew glided his hand back and forth across Caleb's back, getting lower and lower. When that warm hand reached the curve of his ass, Caleb spread his legs and folded one knee underneath him, leaning it on the couch leg between his arms. That position exposed him further, and the feeling of cool air against his usually hidden area had him shaking and leaking.

Andrew's clothed body pressed against his, covering him like a blanket. Warm, soft kisses peppered his nape, strong hands massaged his shoulders and arms, and a hard dick thrust against his crease. Well then, turned out not every part of Andrew's body was clothed.

"We still okay going bare?" Andrew asked in a whisper.

"Uh, huh. Good on my side," Caleb confirmed.

"Me too."

The first time they'd had sex, condoms weren't even considered. Caleb didn't know whether that was because they were barely twenty, because they were both virgins, or because they were crazy horny. Whatever the case, that was how it had been.

They'd justified keeping up that arrangement with a deal—so long as they used rubbers with everybody else, they could continue going without when they were together. Andrew once told him he needed somebody in his life he could trust unconditionally. For Caleb's part, he knew what they were doing didn't make sense, but he didn't complain because it got him what he wanted—Andrew inside him with no barriers. Not his smartest decision, but not one Caleb was willing to change. Apparently, Andrew felt the same way.

Slick fingers massaged his rosebud, pushing inside steadily. Caleb's body relaxed under the gentle ministrations.

"Feel good?" Andrew asked, nuzzling the curve where his neck met his shoulder.

"Mm-hum." It felt great. Caleb loved being filled: fingers, tongue, cock, it all felt amazing.

"How do you want it, Cae?" Andrew pulled his fingers out and lined his lubed cock up with Caleb's opening. "Hard and fast or slow and gentle?"

Caleb pushed back as Andrew pressed forward, and that thick glans popped inside, making both men groan.

"Want it slow this time. Make it last."

"'Kay," Andrew agreed. He thrust forward into that tight channel, moaning at the heat gripping his cock. "Feels so damn good," he whispered.

Then he covered Caleb's hands with his own, twined their fingers together, and nipped Caleb's shoulder, his neck, his ear. Back and forth, he pulled himself out until just the head of his cock was inside Caleb, then he pushed his hot shaft back inside.

When they were together this way, moving slowly, gently, enjoying each other's warmth and touch, Caleb completely lost track of time. Their coupling stretched out, both men appreciating the journey without feeling a rush to reach their destination.

"Love being like this with you," Andrew said.

"Me too."

In and out, back and forth, Andrew rocked into him. Caleb knew the end was near when Andrew's pace quickened along with the hot breath blowing against his nape. Andrew's hand moved off his and slipped down to his jock, pushing the fabric to the side and allowing his hard cock to spring free. Then Andrew circled warm fingers around him and stroked in time with the thrusts in and out of his body.

"You close, Cae?"

Caleb undulated between the hand around his cock and the hard dick in his ass. It wouldn't take long now, not with those exquisite feelings on either end.

"Yeah, I'm with you. Go for it."

With an almost pained moan, Andrew increased his pace, moving faster in and out of Caleb's body and pushing Caleb's dick through his fist.

"Caleb!" Andrew cried out as his body shook and he stilled, buried deep inside Caleb as he shot.

The feeling of Andrew pulsing inside him, the sound of him gasping for air, the scent of their lovemaking, all of it combined to push Caleb over the edge, and he lost it, spilling over Andrew's hand.

"So good," he gasped. After a few moments, he straightened his leg and moved one hand back to caress Andrew's hip.

Andrew smiled. "Yeah. It always is," he said, and then Caleb felt a warm kiss on his nape. "I know we talked about going out to dinner, but what do you say we clean up and then eat takeout on the couch? That way we can cuddle and watch a movie."

"Sounds like a plan."

After another kiss to his neck and a regretful sigh, Andrew stepped back and gave Caleb room to move. He turned around just as his friend was pulling his scrub pants up from where they'd been draped at his ankles.

"Nice shirt," Caleb said with a smile once Andrew stood back up. It was a white long-sleeved T-shirt with "Closets are for Clothes" written on it. The thing wasn't going to win any fashion awards, but Andrew somehow managed to pull it off without looking ridiculous.

"Glad you like it, but it's coming off as soon as we get to the bedroom. That shower is calling my name." Andrew paused, tilted his ear toward the bathroom as if he could actually hear a sound, and then gasped. "Oh, do you hear that? It's calling your name too. Let's not keep it waiting."

He took Caleb's hand and pulled him into the bathroom, both of them laughing along the way.

"THIS IS one of the good times," Andrew mumbled into Caleb's hair.

They were lying on the sofa. Andrew sprawled across it lengthwise with Caleb on top of him, body wedged between Andrew's legs, cheek resting against Andrew's chest, head tucked underneath Andrew's chin. Andrew's arms were wrapped around him, one hand tangled in the back of his hair, the other massaging his lower back and ass through the soft pajamas he was wearing.

"Yeah," Caleb sighed and dropped a kiss at the base of Andrew's throat. "It's nice."

"I like to remember this stuff, you know?" Andrew's voice was quiet, his hands gentle as he stroked Caleb. "When things are crazy and I'm all pissed off...I pull out these good times and remind myself there'll be more of them."

It warmed him to know he was part of Andrew's happy place. It was only fair because Caleb's happy place consisted of a series of memories involving Andrew. Not for the first time, Caleb thought about how lucky they were to have such a close friendship, how lucky they were to have each other.

"Are they still giving you a hard time at work?" Caleb asked.

He could feel Andrew shaking his head. "No. Not really. Well, yeah. There are some doctors who avoid me like the plague. Literally. Like, I'm pretty sure they think they can get sick or something by sharing air with a faggot. But for the most part it's been okay. It helps that I'm the best surgeon who's ever been through that program."

Caleb chuckled. "Brag much?"

"Hey, it's true. I'm good at what I do."

Caleb kissed his way to Andrew's left ear and licked over the metal piercing before tugging at the lobe. "I know you are. I'm proud of you."

"You know, it turns out I'm not the only gay resident at the hospital. Now that the word's spread about me, a few people from other residencies and even some doctors on staff have approached me privately to tell me they're gay."

"It's a big hospital, Drew. Of course you're not the only one."

"Yeah, I know you've been saying that and it makes sense. It just sucks that it's so secret, you know? Between my family's connections and the size of my bank account, I'm not a good target for those assholes and they know it. But other people are scared of backlash, so they stay quiet."

"Doesn't seem right." Caleb shook his head. "They shouldn't be allowed to discriminate against people that way."

"No, it's not right," Andrew responded. "But there's no work protection for being gay, so they can do what they want. Plus, they're sneaky about it. They'll make up reasons why somebody should leave, or they'll make a person's life so miserable that they slink away in shame."

"Have you thought about taking a little bit of that trust money you're always bragging about and— Ow!" Caleb exclaimed when Andrew smacked his ass.

"I do not brag about my money!"

Andrew looked so affronted that Caleb actually felt a little guilty for the tease. He kissed Andrew's forehead and then cupped his cheeks and looked into his eyes.

"I was kidding, Mister Sensitive. Learn to take a joke."

"Sorry," Andrew sighed. "It's just"—blue eyes shifted to a spot on Caleb's shoulder—"that was one of the reasons Trey broke up with me."

"Shut the front door! What kind of an idiot breaks up with someone because he's loaded?"

Andrew immediately started cracking up. Big rolling laughs that jostled Caleb's body.

"Swear to God, Cae. That's one of the things I love most about you." He ruffled Caleb's hair. "Shut the front door," he repeated Caleb's words with a shake of his head as his laughter lightened to a chuckle. "You don't even try to butch it up a little."

"What do you mean? I'm totally macho!" Caleb said with an obviously fake frown. Then a bright smile took over his face. "No? Well, I'm definitely all sorts of fabulous. Now quit changing the topic. You were telling me about Troy and his vow of poverty."

"Oh no, *Trey* wasn't into poverty. Believe me. The man

went through money like water. At first I didn't think much of it, you know? I mean, I don't mind paying for dinner or shows or buying things for someone I'm dating."

"Wait," Caleb interrupted. "You're saying he was spending your money?"

Andrew blushed. "Well, at first it was just normal stuff. And I have more money than him so it's expected that—"

"Damn it, Drew! You can't let people take advantage of you that way."

"I know," he replied. "That's why I refused to pay for his vacation."

"I didn't know you were planning a vacation."

"Oh, I wasn't," Andrew said with a bitter laugh. "He was going to the beach with a bunch of friends. I wasn't invited, but he wanted me to pay for his trip. And get this, he asked me while we were in bed."

"In bed or *in bed*?" Caleb waggled his eyebrows on the second option.

"Both." Andrew paused and closed his eyes tightly. "God, this is so embarrassing." He took a deep breath and then continued. "He'd been talking about his trip all night, about how much better it is to fly first class, and about these great casitas at the resort and how expensive they were. I knew what he was getting at, but no way was I paying for him to go on a trip. I mean, we'd only been dating like six weeks or something. So, I didn't play into it at all, just let him talk."

"Good for you! He was being totally out of line."

"Yeah, I know. I know. Anyway, we started fooling around and I thought, okay, it's done, we've moved on. But, nope, I was wrong. He waits until we're like fully into it, you know, and then he says, '*Why don't you pay for my vaca?*'"

"Oh. My. God. You're telling me Drey asked that while you were cornholing him?"

"Cornholing?" One blond eyebrow raised and Andrew shook his head. "I'm not even going to ask. So he asks me to pay and I say I can't. So then Trey tells me that if I won't pay, the other guy he's seeing will."

"He was seeing someone else at the same time you were together?" Caleb asked incredulously. "His piece-of-shit factor just went up like a million points."

"Yeah, that was a surprise to me too. I actually thought about what you'd say if you were in that position, and I broke up with him right on the spot. So see, it was like a remote team effort, you were in the bushes while I was delivering the package."

"Hey," Caleb grumbled good-naturedly. "You may have been delivering your package, but I can surely guarantee you that I was not in any bushes." He shuddered dramatically and Andrew laughed. "In all seriousness, though, he orchestrated this entire conversation while you were fucking?"

"Afraid so." Andrew grimaced.

"That is not only incredibly tacky, but also wildly unarousing."

"Yeah, needless to say it cut the night—and our

relationship—short."

"Sounds like that was for the best, Drew." Caleb started playing with the new spike in Andrew's right earlobe. "Ray sounds like a user."

"Tr—oh, never mind. I don't remember how we got onto this topic anyway."

"I remember. I was giving you a suggestion on a way to spend your money. And it didn't involve vacations for philandering, money-hungry boyfriends."

"Let's hear your idea," Andrew chuckled.

"I was gonna say that you should start a gay medical students or doctors group at your hospital. Maybe if people realize they're not alone, it'll save them from having to hide. Plus, there's always strength in numbers."

"That's a great idea," Andrew said.

"I know!" Caleb responded emphatically. "I'm full of great ideas. That's why you've kept me around all these years. Lord knows it hasn't been because of my fat ass."

"Your ass is not fat. And I should know seeing as how you've been parading around my apartment in those barely there underwear all weekend."

"I haven't heard you complaining."

"Complaining? Do you think I'm an idiot? I'm going to buy you more of them." Andrew slipped his hand down the back of Caleb's pants and caressed the skin exposed by the G-string he wore. "And, Cae?"

"Uh-huh?"

"I've kept you around because I like how I feel when I'm with you. You're an amazing friend. Best ever."

Caleb leaned down for a quick peck.

"Right back atcha, Drew."

CHAPTER TEN

1997

"I WAS in a car accident."

"What?" Andrew yelled into the phone and shot up in bed. "Are you okay? Don't move, I'm on my way."

"Don't move?" Caleb snickered. "Drew, you live over two hundred miles away. Doesn't matter if you come by plane, train, or car, I'm pretty sure moving's going to be imperative at some point before you get here. Besides, I'm fine. There's no reason for you to rush over."

"What, are you nuts?" Andrew was grumbling and, based on the background noise, bumping into every piece of furniture in his bedroom. "You're hurt."

"I'm not hurt, Drew. Honest. Well, my pride might be a little wounded, but it'll recover."

"Yeah?" Andrew asked. "What kind of not hurt are you? Is it the bleeding not hurt or the broken bones not hurt?"

"It's the 'I ran a car into a street sign going ten miles an hour because I'm a shit driver and I was getting road-head' not hurt."

There was a long silence. "You, ehm." Andrew cleared his throat a couple of times. "You got into an accident because a guy was going down on you while you were driving?"

"Yeees," Caleb confirmed, drawing out the word.

"And you're okay, right? The car was going slow and you're, like, totally uninjured?"

"Yes, Drew. Totally uninjured."

Apparently that was all the assurance Andrew needed to let go because he started laughing hysterically.

"Go ahead, get it out of your system. Ha ha ha. Dumb Caleb hit a pole while his dick was hanging out. Ha ha ha," Caleb said in a monotone.

"Oh, come on." Andrew gasped for air. "You've got to admit that's hilarious."

"When you're hearing about it, sure. But when it's happening to you, it's just annoying. Like, really? We have to stop now?"

"That's what you were worried about?" Andrew asked before falling into another laughing fit. "You crash a car and you care about finishing the BJ? Way to have your priorities in order, Cae! Your ability to focus on what matters is truly inspiring."

"Well, what do you expect?" Caleb joined in Andrew's laughter. "I was all worked up and then bam! It's over."

"Bam!" Andrew barely got the word out along with the hysterical laugher. "Bam!" he said it again and gasped for air. "Like a car crashing... Bam!"

"Yeah, yeah. I know it's the funniest thing you've heard in your entire life; but chill before you hyperventilate."

Andrew didn't say anything for a couple of minutes as his laughter died down and he caught his breath. "Okay," he said. "I'm okay."

"Oh, thank God. Because I was terrified," Caleb replied.

"Well, I think it's safe to say you didn't injure your sarcasm. That remains perfectly intact. How's your, uh, passenger? Is he okay?"

"He's fine. I'm fine. The car's fine, save for a little scrape on the bumper. But, hey, bumpers are made for bumping, right?"

"Ppfff!" Andrew spat out. "Bumping...you know like *bow chica chica bow wow* bumping," he said before breaking out into more laughter.

"You've been on call for days, haven't you?"

"How'd you know?" Andrew asked when he finally stopped laughing.

"Just a wild guess. Get some sleep, Drew. We'll talk more later today."

Caleb was surprised when Andrew agreed without argument to hang up.

"'Kay. Night, Cae."

"Good night."

"Bumping, such a good one."

The line disconnected while Andrew was still chuckling. Caleb looked at the phone and shook his head as he smiled to himself, thinking of Andrew's face when he laughed. Nothing in the world was more satisfying than freeing his best friend from the stresses of life and watching him find pure happiness. It was even worth an aborted blow job and a scraped bumper.

"YOU LOOK like shit, Nate. Seriously, you've got to do something," Caleb said to his friend Nate Richardson as he poured a couple of mugs of coffee.

"I know. Believe it or not, I feel even worse." Nate's Southern drawl was thicker than usual, another indication of his exhaustion. "I actually waited a couple of hours before coming over here. Do the math and figure out how long I've been awake."

Caleb handed Nate a mug and joined him on the sofa.

"What's going on? Is it because of the accident you had this summer?"

"Yeah," Nate sighed. "But not in the way you mean. I'm fine, but Jake…" Nate blinked back tears. "God, I hate seeing him like this. It's like he's broken and there's nothing I can do to make him better. I feel so helpless."

Caleb set his coffee down, put his arm around Nate's shoulders, and pulled him in for a hug. "His parents recently died. It'll take him time to heal, Nate. I think that makes him human, not broken. Plus, I'm sure you're helping a lot."

Nate wiped his shirtsleeve across his eyes and shrugged. "I'm trying, but…" He sighed deeply. "Jake's always been the strong one, not me."

Never having met Nate's roommate, Caleb couldn't compare the two men, but he'd always thought of Nate as very strong and was about to say so when Nate continued speaking.

"Hey, are you, maybe, up for going dancing tonight? I think I need to get out of the apartment for a bit and you know, uh"—Nate's cheeks colored—"maybe meet someone to, uh, you know…"

Even though Nate was only a few years younger than Caleb, there was an endearing innocence to him that surfaced every so often, and this was one of those times. Caleb smiled knowingly.

"You need to get laid, Nate?"

"God, yes," Nate said loudly, and then blushed when he recognized the intensity of his response. "Sorry, it's just been so hard with Jake and—"

"Say no more." Caleb held his hand up. "I totally get out-of-control horny. If it wasn't for my frequent trips to Boston, I'd probably be crawling up the damn walls."

A knock on the door interrupted their conversation. Nate's eyes flicked to his wristwatch and he frowned.

"I thought I was the only person rude enough to barge into your apartment uninvited this early on a Saturday morning."

"Yeah, I pretty much thought the same thing," Caleb said with a wink. "I can't imagine who that would…" Realization dawned and he jumped off the couch and rushed to the door. "On second thought, I know exactly who it is."

He raised his voice as he flipped the deadbolts. "You have a key, Drew. What's with the kno…" His words trailed off when he opened the door to find Andrew holding a duffle bag in his left hand, two coffees from the place on the corner in his right, and a paper bag from Caleb's favorite bagel shop between his teeth.

"Thanks for breakfast." Caleb smiled and reached for the bag. "Seems like an awfully long trip for a food delivery."

Andrew's eyes moved over Caleb's entire body, clearly taking a visual index.

"I told you I was fine, Drew." Caleb rolled his eyes and walked backward into the apartment. He extended his arms to the sides before turning in a circle. "See, nothing's broken."

"I believed you. It's just, you were in an accident. You're my best friend. There's no scenario in which I'm not coming down here to check on you." Andrew dropped his duffle bag and set the coffees on the kitchen counter, which was just a couple of steps from the entryway. He put his hand on Caleb's shoulder and pulled him in for a hug. "You're really okay?"

The sound of a phone ringing had both men looking over to the couch.

"Oh, uh," Nate stammered as he dug his phone out of

his pocket. "This is Jake so I need to—" The phone was on his ear before he could finish his sentence. "Hey, everything okay?"

"That's Nate, the friend I've told you about," Caleb said quietly. "I'll introduce you as soon as he's off the phone."

"Dancing friend Nate?" Andrew asked. "The one who was in the terrible car accident over the summer?"

"That's the one," Caleb confirmed.

"Poor guy." Andrew ran his hands gently over Caleb's ribcage. "Anything hurt when I do this?"

"You've been here for two minutes and you're already giving me a physical exam," Caleb snickered.

"I just want to make sure you're okay. No need to be so ornery."

"Hey, I'm not complaining. As soon as Nate takes off, I'm happy to strip down so you can be *really* thorough. In fact, I'm thinking you may need to check for internal damage."

"Internal damage, huh?" Andrew cupped Caleb's ass and massaged the firm globes. "And just where do you think you ha—"

"I'm sorry to be so rude, but I need to go. My roommate called and..." Nate shook off the rest of his sentence and walked up to Andrew. He held his hand out. "You must be Andrew. I've heard a lot about you. I'm Nate Richardson."

"Nice to finally meet you, Nate." Andrew smiled warmly and shook Nate's hand. "Even if it's only for a minute."

"Well, you two can talk more tonight. We're going

dancing," Caleb announced.

"Oh, no, we don't have to go, Caleb. I'm sure with Andrew being in town you'll have other plans."

Caleb looked at Andrew. "You good with going to shake our groove thing tonight, Drew? Nate's on a manhunt."

"Caleb!" Nate looked positively horrified.

"We have *got* to teach you tact and manners, Cae." Andrew shook his head and smiled fondly at Caleb. Then he patted Nate's shoulder. "I'd love to go out tonight. You just got yourself a second wingman, Nate."

"WITH AS much as I've been hearing about this place, I figured it'd be more crowded," Nate said as he looked around the bar.

"It's pretty early. I'm sure it'll fill up later."

Nate shrugged. "Could be. I don't plan to be here later." The man's eyes darted to Andrew and he started stammering. "I mean, I didn't get much sleep last night and—"

"Let's dance." Caleb took Nate's hand and started pulling him toward the dance floor. He looked back over his shoulder. "Do you mind grabbing drinks for us, Drew? Nate, what do you want?"

"Oh, uh, vodka and cranberry but Andrew doesn't have to—"

"I've got it. Go on." Andrew waved the two men off with a chuckle and headed toward the bar.

He got their drinks and settled at a table with a view of the dance floor. As shy as Nate had seemed, Andrew was surprised at the unrestrained way the man danced. Finding company for the night wouldn't be a problem for him. A third man joined Caleb and Nate on the dance floor, and after a little while, Caleb stepped back and made his way to the table.

"Thanks," Caleb said when Andrew handed him his drink. He sat next to Andrew and squeezed his knee. "You wanna go out there and shake it?" he asked with a tilt of his head toward the bodies writhing to the thumping beat.

"Nah, I'm good," Andrew declined. "Your friend's really into it though." They both watched Nate grind against his dance partner. "Does he know that other guy?"

"Mm-hum. Well, he does now anyway, 'cause I just introduced them. The guy dancing with Nate is Tony Larkson. He's friends with some of my friends. Our paths have crossed for years."

"Well, he seems really into Nate. That's good, right? You said he wanted to meet someone tonight."

"Tony's really into whatever guy he thinks he can get into bed the fastest," Caleb said with a shrug. "And tonight, that's definitely Nate."

Andrew scowled. "He sounds like an asshole. You should warn your friend."

"Nah, he's not a bad guy, just kinda slutty. Besides, Nate's looking for the same thing right now."

Their conversation was cut short when Nate and Tony

stopped dancing and came to sit down. They took the two chairs at the opposite side of the table.

Nate was breathing a little heavily; his blond hair was sweaty and disheveled. "Is this mine?" He pointed toward the untouched drink.

"Yup." Andrew pushed the glass over to him with a smile and then looked at Tony.

"Hi. I'm Caleb's friend Andrew."

"Tony," the man replied with a nod.

The music was ridiculously loud, so Caleb and Andrew couldn't hear the conversation taking place across from them, but the substance became clear when Nate and Tony stood. Nate walked over and hunched down by Caleb's chair.

"I'm going to take off, Caleb. Tony asked me to go back to his place. Thanks for, uh..." Nate stammered and blushed. "Just, uh, thanks."

Caleb gave Nate a warm hug. "You're welcome. I hope you found what you need tonight. Call me when you get home tomorrow."

"Oh, I'm not spending the night with Tony." Nate looked surprised at the possibility. "Jake'll be home and I want to be with him. I just need a distraction for a couple of hours and a different kind of company, you know?"

The two men walked off arm in arm, and Andrew scowled after them.

"What's with the face?" Caleb elbowed Andrew's ribs without much force.

"Nothing. Your friend's just a little weird. The way he talks about that Jake guy, I'd think there was something between them, but he's out here prowling for tricks."

"Oh, yeah," Caleb agreed, his lips tightening in a frown. "Poor Nate. He's like hopelessly smitten with his roommate and, from what I hear, the guy is terminally straight."

"Sucks," Andrew said, suddenly feeling sorry for the other man. "I guess it's good he's putting himself out there tonight even if he doesn't expect anything to come of it. Still, I can't imagine this is a promising start to a relationship, especially with what you said about Tony."

"Nate isn't looking for a relationship. He's got his hands full with his roommate right now, dealing with stuff from their accident over the summer. Plus, like I said, he's got a serious thing for the guy. It's doubtful anybody'll have a real chance with Nate until he gets over Jake." Caleb set his empty cup down. "Anyway, he's barely twenty-one, so he has plenty of time to figure things out."

"I guess," Andrew said without much conviction. "Do you want to dance more or should we go home?"

"Home," Caleb replied. "What time do you need to leave tomorrow?"

"I have to go into the hospital at five, so I'll have to leave here pretty early. You're probably right about calling it a night. Sleep is imperative."

"Sex is imperative," Caleb drawled as they stepped out of the club. "Sleep didn't even factor into my decision-making process."

Andrew snickered. "Didn't I wear you out this afternoon? Damn, Cae, you're insatiab—"

Loud shouting and a commotion at the corner caught both men's attention.

"What's going on?" Caleb asked. He began walking toward the cluster of people.

Andrew grabbed his shoulder. "Wait, Cae. We don't know if it's safe."

"Someone needs to call an ambulance," a voice rang out.

"Screw them!" somebody else said. "They deserve what they got. Fuckin' haters."

The call for medical help was all it took for Andrew to change his mind about safety first. He waded through the mass of people and came upon an unexpected scene. Three men were lying on the ground, either unconscious or close to it, and a fourth guy was standing over them.

Despite being covered in dirt and blood, having torn clothes, and looking generally disheveled, the man was stunning. Fierce and scary-looking too, but the stunning was impossible to miss.

"Hi. My name's Andrew. I'm a doctor. Are you okay? Do you need help?" Andrew asked. Then he looked down at the people on the ground. "Do they?"

Green eyes zeroed in on him. The man spit a mixture of blood and saliva onto the sidewalk and then wiped his split lips with the back of his scraped, bloody hand before pushing his black hair out of his face. "I don't think you want to help these assholes. They were going after a couple of guys just to damage fags." He kicked one of the men in his side, causing him to whine and curl in on himself. "Isn't that what you said, tough guy? Not so impressive without your crowbars, are you?" He threw his foot backward and hit another of the men, eliciting what now sounded like sobs. "That guy you were aiming for is better on his worst day than you'll be in your entire life, you piece of shit."

Loud sirens sounded and an ambulance pulled up. EMTs came rushing out, shouting. "We need everybody to move. Come on! Move aside. Make room, people."

It looked like the man wasn't done with the fight quite yet, but the arrival of the emergency personnel didn't seem to leave him a choice. He stepped over the three bodies around him, crunching his boot over a limb here and there, no doubt intentionally, and began walking away.

"Wait!" One of the EMTs called out after him. "Sir, we need to take a look at your injuries."

"Nah, I'm fine, just a few bruises. Nothing a hot shower and some couch time with my roommate won't fix," he said. Then he left, moving slowly with his arm cradled across his ribcage.

"Damn, he is just as tough off the field as he is on it," one of the men in the crowd said in awe.

"You know him?" Caleb asked.

"I know of him. Jacob Owens. Some people say he'll be up for the Heisman."

Andrew leaned in and whispered in Caleb's ear, "That means college football."

"Really? Maybe I should start watching football 'cause that boy is H-O-T hot."

"Is that right? Well, feel free to go after him if he's so hot," Andrew snipped and crossed his arms over his chest.

Caleb laughed and put his hands on the sides of his friend's narrow waist, giving him a squeeze. "No thanks. You're the only hottie I want melting my Popsicle tonight."

Andrew relaxed and dropped his arms. "Good, 'cause I was looking forward to some quality time with you before I have to leave tomorrow. But here's an idea: if you're really nice to me, I'll get a football uniform next time you come visit."

"Oooh, role playing. Very kinky," Caleb said with chuckle. He kissed Andrew's cheek. "I like it!"

CHAPTER ELEVEN

1998

"THAT WAS the worst vacation ever," Andrew Thompson grumbled into the phone.

"What happened, Drew?" Caleb's voice—always caring, always interested, always there—soothed him.

Andrew kicked his feet up on the crowded desk shared by three of the doctors in his surgery residency, tilted his chair back, and covered his eyes with his forearm. His sleeve rode up, causing the gauze covering his skin to rub against his face and reminding him of his latest body mod. This one was a tattoo of two male symbols with the circular parts looped together, done in simple black ink.

"It's my own fault," Andrew sighed dejectedly. "I shouldn't have agreed to go to P-Town."

"Why not? P-Town's the best. We had a blast when we went, remember?" Caleb asked.

"Yeah." Andrew smiled for the first time in days. "I remember. Let's just say it wasn't nearly as fun this go-round. Well, at least not for me. DJ had a great ole time."

"What'd that shithead do, Drew?"

"You've never even met him, Cae, and already you're calling him names. Do you really think that's fair?" The words were barely out of Andrew's mouth before he winced. Damn it, why was he defending the guy who had just cheated on him?

"He hurt you, so he's a shithead. It's as simple as that," Caleb said roughly before sighing and gentling his tone. "Look, you don't have to tell me what happened, I can guess."

Andrew's laugh held no humor. "What does it say about me that you know my boyfriend cheated without me having to say a word?"

"It says that you've got shit taste in boyfriends, Drew. And that I know you well enough to have figured that out sometime over the past, oh, what's it been now? Ten years?"

"Depends on when you start counting, but being conservative, we can start with the summer when you actually remember meeting me."

"You're not going to goad me into changing the topic," Caleb replied. "Especially not by bringing up for the millionth time that fourteen-year-old me didn't immediately recognize fourteen-year-old you after we hadn't seen each other since we were eight. Now, back to shithead EJ."

"DJ," Andrew said.

"Whatever."

"It wasn't his fault, Cae. You remember what P-Town's like. Too many bars, too much drinking, too many hot guys walking around with practically no clothes on. I mean, what did I expect him to do?"

"You expected him to keep his dick in his pants or in you," Caleb practically growled. "That's not unreasonable. I don't remember either of us touching anybody but each other the whole week we were there. The thought didn't even cross my mind, and I seriously doubt you felt like I was holding you back from something or someone you wanted."

"'Course I didn't. But that's different," Andrew argued. "You're my best friend, which means you're not allowed to get sick of me and you have to be happy when I'm around. Boyfriends don't follow those same rules."

"Well, then I'm glad you kicked JD's ass to the curb."

"DJ," Andrew corrected.

"Whatever. Listen, when's your next forty-eight off?"

"Umm." Andrew thought through his work schedule. The hours sucked, but he loved the work too much to resent how much of his time it took. "I have next Tuesday and Wednesday off."

"Cool. I'll be there Monday night."

Andrew's stomach clenched with anticipation. Damn but he missed his friend. Still, he couldn't ask Caleb to just drop everything to come console him. Again. "You don't have to do that. I'm fine."

"Put the surgeon ego away, Drew. It's not all about you. I've been single for too long, and now that you're done with JT, my favorite toy is finally available."

"DJ," Andrew said reflexively.

"Whatever. The point is, I've got your dick on reserve starting Monday night all the way through until my flight takes off on Thursday. You might want to bring home some of that special hospital grade lotion because I predict serious chaffing by the time I'm through with you."

There was no way for Andrew to hold in his mirth. He smiled broadly. "I miss you, Cae. Glad you're coming for a visit."

"Miss you too," Caleb's voice came in a whisper, then he dragged in a deep breath and his tone lightened. "Okay, I've gotta go. If I don't find the right shade of green for this guy's den, he's going to unravel. I'm telling you, Drew, this whole working thing is incredibly stressful. Well, at least when it's about something that really matters, like the mood evoked by a person's home design. Plus, I figure you probably need to go too. Maybe take a splinter out from someone's knee or deal with a hangnail or something."

"Hardy har har. I'm focusing in neurosurgery and you know it. We don't deal in splinters or feet."

"Oh, that's right. You're literally a brain surgeon. Plus you have those gorgeous green eyes, the most perfect dick I've ever seen, and you can beat anyone around at both darts and pool. I think it's officially confirmed, CJ's a fucking moron."

Andrew was laughing hard enough that he had to wipe tears from the corner of his eye. "DJ," he choked out.

"Whatever."

ANDREW DIDN'T need to step into his apartment door to know Caleb was there. He could hear Elvis Costello crooning through the walls, and the scent of something fresh baked drifted from under the front door and filled the hallway air. He closed his eyes and took a moment to try to calm his racing heart and hold back the moisture that suddenly threatened his eyes.

What the hell was wrong with him? So he'd had another breakup. Really, they were so frequent at this point, it was almost impossible to take them seriously. Okay, so DJ cheated on him. In their hotel room. That he'd paid for.

Again, this was not the first time Andrew had dealt with that particular experience. He'd been through cheaters before and he was fine. He knew exactly what to do—just keep his chin up, concentrate on work, and time would heal the wound so he could get out there and try again.

But somehow, knowing that just a few inches of wood separated him from his best friend made it impossible for Andrew to rein in his emotions and gather his internal reserves. He'd been propping himself up for so long. And now, Caleb would take care of him, at least for a few days, so he didn't need to be strong.

With that realization, Andrew unlocked his apartment

door and strode inside. A few steps had him leaning his shoulder against the kitchen doorway and watching Caleb hum as he swung his hips to the music and chopped something on the bright orange cutting board that hadn't seen use since Caleb's last visit. Normally, he'd have stayed quiet and enjoyed the view. Caleb's rhythmic motion was a delicious treat. But his need to see those chocolate eyes focused on him overruled every other desire.

"Hey," Andrew said, hating how every bit of emotion was exposed in his voice with that one word. He cleared his throat, knowing the attempt was hopeless. He couldn't hide anything from Caleb, and there was no sense in trying. Besides, the last thing he wanted to do was hide from the one person who had always been able to see all of him.

"Hey, gorgeous! I didn't hear you come in." Caleb dried his hands on a towel and tossed it on the counter before walking over to Andrew and wrapping steady arms around his waist.

God, but did it feel good to come home to someone who cared about him, someone who knew him, someone who would always stand by his side. Every bit of energy drained from Andrew's body, and he bent down until his forehead rested on Caleb's shoulder. One slender arm stayed around his waist and the other stroked up his spine, rubbed his nape, and settled on the back of his head, petting his hair soothingly.

"Shhh. It's okay. I'm here now. Come on, let's get these

clothes off, take a nice hot shower, and fill up your belly. Then everything'll feel better."

Andrew wasn't sure whether his own responding sniffle was an aborted laugh or a soothed cry. "I'm pretty sure the only things in my fridge were soy milk and ketchup packets. What'd you make for dinner?"

Caleb pushed Andrew's sweatshirt over his head. "I stopped at the store and stocked you up. Tonight we're having tempeh loaf and a yellow beet and arugula salad. Plus there's a sweet potato pie cooling for dessert." Caleb looked at his T-shirt and chuckled. It was black with "One of Them" written on it in white block font.

"Where do you find these shirts?" Caleb asked as he dragged the garment up Andrew's chest and off his body.

"The Internet," Andrew answered. "It's amazing what you can find on there."

A kiss landed on Andrew's neck. "It sure is."

"You're joining me in the shower, right?" He didn't want to sound needy, but he hated the thought of being away from his friend at that moment. He needed Caleb's support, his warmth. He needed to feel like he really mattered to someone.

"'Course I am," Caleb confirmed. "I'll soap you up, rub away all the tension in your shoulders, suck your worries out through your dick, and then I figure you'll be relaxed enough to sit down and enjoy a meal."

"Mmmm, that sounds good." Andrew nuzzled Caleb's

neck for a few moments, and then he pulled back and curled his arm around Caleb's waist. "Come on. The faster we get in the shower, the faster I can taste what I'm sure will be the most delicious food I've had since the last time you were here."

"Oh, very nice. Flattery like that will get you laid, my friend."

"Hey, I'm getting laid regardless. That was fact not flattery; you know how hard it is to find a decent vegetarian meal at a restaurant. I swear, if I have one more version of pasta primavera, I think I'll lose my mind."

"That's why you need to learn to cook."

As soon as they got to the bedroom, Caleb bent down and untied his saddle shoes, setting them neatly next to his suitcase. Then he took off his Burberry plaid pashmina scarf, ivory light-weight sweater, and gray wool pants and placed them into a plastic bag.

Andrew stood and stared at him, feeling like he was watching his own private strip show. When Caleb had his thumbs in the waistband of his white mesh G-string, Andrew walked closer and trailed a single finger from the nape of his neck down his spine.

"Did you lose more weight?" he said. It wasn't a question, more like a diagnosis. He could clearly see that Caleb was steadily dropping pounds. Pounds he didn't have to spare.

Caleb turned around and Andrew raked his eyes

over his friend's chest and skimmed his fingers over Caleb's protruding ribcage. Caleb trembled and his cock hardened under those ridiculously sexy underwear, seemingly reaching for Andrew's touch, but Andrew wouldn't let his gaze drop below Caleb's belly button. Not until he addressed the situation with Caleb's eating issues.

"Yeah, I've almost completely eliminated carbs, and I doubled my cardio. It's made a major difference in how many guys are interested." Caleb dragged his eyes up and down Andrew's nude body, he leered at Andrew's hard-on arching, obviously trying to get the party started. "Like what you see?" His voice was husky with lust.

"It's you, Cae. I always like what I see when it comes to you. But no more weight loss, yeah? You were hot as hell thirty pounds ago. No reason to starve yourself."

Caleb chewed on his bottom lip. "So what're you saying? I'm too skinny now? I don't look good?"

The last thing he wanted was to make Caleb think there was something wrong with how he looked, particularly because the man was gorgeous, even if he couldn't seem to see it in himself. Andrew cupped Caleb's exposed ass cheeks and yanked him forward, bringing their erections together with only the thin layer of Caleb's underwear between them. "Does it feel like I think you don't look good?" he bucked his hips and let the feeling of his firm rod pressed against Caleb's lower belly make the answer to that question very clear. "Seeing you in those skimpy underwear you like is almost enough to make me lose it every single time. You're beautiful, Cae. Just the way you are now and just the way you were when you were more filled out. That's all I'm saying. So, I expect you to help me eat that delicious dinner you made, including the pie you baked."

Caleb's eyes searched his. He must have been satisfied that Andrew was being sincere because his tension eased. "'Kay. But before we can get to the dining portion of this evening's agenda, we need to complete the bathing unit."

"Bathing unit?"

"Yeah," Caleb replied as he wiggled out of his underwear and then grasped Andrew's hand and pulled him into the bathroom, letting go only to turn on the shower and adjust the temperature. "I'm bathing your unit, remember?"

He leered at Andrew over his right shoulder and wiggled his eyebrows in an exaggerated fashion.

Andrew smiled and slapped his ass. "Get in the water, you big goofball," he chuckled. "You're not the only one with raging hormones, and my water heater has a limited capacity. A cold shower would really put a damper on things, so no dillydallying."

Caleb didn't protest, sliding into the shower and immediately leaning back into the spray and letting it coat his brown hair.

"I'm going to do you a favor and pretend you didn't just channel an eighty-year-old woman. Who says dillydally?"

Andrew's mouth opened to reply, trade his own barb

in exchange for Caleb's latest sarcastic jab, but just then his friend turned around and a heated gaze pinned him to the tile wall.

"I want you." Caleb's voice had suddenly gone from playful to passionate, his chocolate eyes darkening until the pupils blended into the irises.

In his entire life, there had never been a single thing that had turned Andrew on as much as Caleb's face when he was aroused. Rosy cheeks, wide eyes, intense concentration focused on him, and pleasure that seemed to make Caleb glow from the inside. Damn but it felt good to know he could evoke those feelings in his friend. During those moments when they were alone together, Andrew felt like he was Caleb's whole world. And the feeling was mutual.

"Want you too, Cae." Andrew's voice shook with emotion. "You know how grateful I am to have you in my life, right? I mean, seriously, you're the best friend I could ever hope for."

Caleb nodded and wrapped his arms around Andrew's waist, pressing his face into Andrew's neck and squeezing him tightly. "I feel the same way, and that's never gonna change. Boyfriends come and go, but friends stick together, right? We'll never be alone."

"That's right," Andrew replied emphatically, feeling completely confident in the truth of his words. Sure, he hoped to one day find a man who'd actually want him, who wouldn't betray him, who'd be in it for the long haul. But whether that happened or not, he'd always have Caleb and Caleb would always have him.

It had been half a year since Andrew had been able to touch Caleb freely, not since he had started dating DJ. Deciding the time for talking was over, he let his hands explore that oh-so-sexy body. Caleb was thinner now, but no less familiar. Andrew was sure he could recognize his friend by touch alone.

"Mmmm. Feels good, Drew. Always so good with you," Caleb moaned.

"Uh-huh." Andrew brushed his lips over Caleb's throat, lapped at his chin, and trailed sucking kisses across his jawline until he reached Caleb's ear and tugged on the lobe with his teeth.

Their hips began moving together rhythmically, pressing their erections between them, allowing hot bodies to rub back and forth over hard flesh. Andrew groaned, cupped Caleb's ass, and yanked him even closer, increasing the speed of his thrusts. His head tilted back, and he huffed out quick breaths as he pumped his hips against Caleb.

"Close, Cae. Already so close. Damn, you make me hot."

Caleb trembled and pressed an openmouthed kiss against the base of Andrew's neck, following it with a desperate tug of teeth and sucking until Andrew was sure he'd have a deep, red hickey. Then he pulled back and licked at the sensitive spot. Andrew looked down and saw the expression on Caleb's face—pride, possession—and he shuddered and moaned. Apparently, Caleb wasn't the only one who enjoyed the outward sign of their union.

All thoughts fled Andrew's mind when Caleb dropped to his knees. A quick nuzzle to Andrew's hip and then Caleb was focused on the task at hand, seemingly wanting nothing more than to taste Andrew, to have his lips stretched by a thick cock, and help Andrew find release. One hand circled around the base of Andrew's erection and the other cupped his balls, rolling them gently. Caleb dipped his face down and his tongue joined the party, licking up and down Andrew's erection, swirling around the bulbous head, even darting into the slit at the top.

"Oh, sweet Jesus, that's good. Don't stop, Cae. Need this so much," Andrew blabbered almost incoherently.

"Won't stop." Caleb spoke against Andrew skin, sucked his way up the side of Andrew's cock, and then took that heated flesh down his throat until his face nestled in silky blond pubes.

"Yes, oh, yes." Andrew gripped Caleb's head, tangling his fingers in long locks, and held that precious face still as he looked down, watching his cock pump in and out of Caleb's warm mouth. "Gonna, Cae. Gonna. You ready for me to fill you up right now?" One more hard thrust and then Andrew's body arched, his face lifted toward the ceiling, and he pushed himself all the way into Caleb's mouth. "Uh, oh, yeah." He shook and panted as pure pleasure pulsed through his entire body and filled Caleb's mouth.

Once he was completely spent, Andrew's body folded in on itself, dropping him to the shower floor. He nuzzled Caleb's neck, wrapped his arms around that warm but too skinny chest, and sighed deeply.

"That sounded like a good one, ya'?" Caleb said. He held Andrew tightly, petting his heated skin.

"Oh, yeah. Great one." Andrew's tongue darted out and tasted Caleb's skin. "Give me a sec to get control of my body and then I'll take care of you."

Caleb's hands moved from Andrew's lower back up to his head and massaged his scalp. "I'm all set. Came when you did." He shrugged. "It's been way too long since I've had the pleasure of seeing you lose it, and you're so damn sexy. No way I could hold back."

"Mmmm, good," Andrew sighed contentedly. "Glad I can still do it for you that way. You ready to get out of here so we can eat and go to bed? I'm already looking forward to round two."

CHAPTER TWELVE

1999

IT WASN'T a snore. Not a whimper either. Just a sleepy little sound, and not a loud one at that. But it woke Andrew up. His arm was reaching across the bed and looking for warmth before his brain registered what his body already knew he wanted. Andrew's flight had arrived late the previous night, barely giving him enough time to say hello to his best friend before they tumbled into Caleb's bed and fell asleep.

He knew he had been tangled with Caleb when the night started, not that his exhausted mind could recall much from the previous night, but more because that was how they'd slept for years during their visits. Ever since the first day they'd discovered a mutual interest in adding a physical aspect to their multi-layered friendship, they'd shared a bed whenever they visited each other. When either of them was seeing someone, there wasn't sex involved, but there was still warmth, closeness, and friendship. Always friendship.

As soon as his fingers made contact with Caleb's skin, he heard another soft noise and then a warm body scooted toward him. Andrew helped close the distance and wrapped his arm around Caleb's shoulder, his fingers gently petting Caleb's nape.

"Mmmm," Caleb mumbled as he burrowed close, his face finding a resting place at the base of Andrew's throat and his leg wedging itself between Andrew's knees.

Andrew kissed the top of his friend's head and sighed contentedly. This was exactly what he'd needed—some time unwinding, letting go of the stress from moving his entire life to a brand-new city to start his neurosurgery fellowship. Of course, getting onto a plane right after said move hadn't exactly been conducive to that whole relaxation strategy. But, hey, the plane took him to Caleb, and Andrew was certain that Caleb's presence alone was enough to lower his blood pressure. The man was like a walking beta-blocker.

Of course, his heart rate certainly wasn't lower around Caleb. In fact, they often shared sweaty, passionate moments when Andrew was sure his heart would beat out of his chest and his lungs would explode. Just the memory of their shared pleasure was enough to arouse Andrew. His cock filled, and then that warm body wiggled against him, which just sped up the inevitable process. His body didn't care that it was the middle of the night—he was naked in a bed with Caleb, and he hadn't gotten laid in way too long.

Skilled fingers trailed across his chest, down his stomach, and circled his hard cock. "Horny?" Caleb spoke against the base of his throat, his voice husky with sleep.

Not seeing a point in denying it when Caleb held the irrefutable evidence in his hand, Andrew nodded. "Mm-hum. Didn't mean to wake you though. Go back to sleep and we can take care of that in the morning."

"I'll take care of whatever you come up with in the morning too, but right now I've got this bad boy to play with."

Andrew laughed. "Damn, Cae, is that cheesy porn dialogue the soundtrack in your dreams?"

A warning bite to his neck told him Caleb didn't appreciate his humor. "That line is a winner, believe me. You should hear the ridiculous things guys are saying to pick each other up these days. Last week a guy at Senses asked me if my father was a baker."

It was hard to follow the conversation with Caleb's hands roaming all over him, their bodies moving gently against each other, Caleb's hot breath blowing against his skin. But Andrew managed to hold on to some of his mental capacity, even as he returned the favor and cupped Caleb's ass, massaging the firm globes. "Baker?"

"Uh-huh," Caleb replied. "Because my buns looked delicious."

Andrew's laugh was instantaneous. "Well, I can confirm the accuracy of that guy's observation. You've got the tastiest ass around."

"M'kay. I'll be sure to mention that if I ever run into him again." Caleb's warm tongue traced his jawline and then soft lips nibbled on his lobe and around the curve of his ear, gently tugging on the three metal studs in the cartilage. "When'd you get the new piercings?"

"Oh, ah…" Andrew trembled at Caleb's touch. "A few months ago, I guess."

"Right around the time you stopped seeing Bob," Caleb mumbled.

"Rob."

"Whatever." Caleb licked, sucked, and gnawed on Andrew's throat, then pulled his mouth back and blew air on the damp skin.

"Oh, that's nice," Andrew moaned. With a squeeze to Caleb's hip, he rolled onto his back and dragged Caleb on top of him. "How about you climb up here and give me a taste of those delicious buns."

"Yeah, I'm the one with cheesy dialogue," Caleb scoffed. But he followed Andrew's suggestion, crawling over the firm body beneath him. He straddled Andrew's torso, planted a knee on each side of Andrew's neck, and braced his forearms against the wall.

Andrew gripped Caleb's waist and urged him down. His thumbs caressed slender hips, moved over to that tight ass, and eventually dipped into Caleb's crease. Caleb's forehead fell onto his arms, and he relaxed, letting Andrew take over his body.

Keeping his strokes slow, Andrew came progressively closer to the tempting opening. When Caleb was shivering uncontrollably, his desire undeniable, Andrew grasped his ass cheeks and pulled them to the sides, leaving him completely exposed. With a tug, Andrew urged him downward, and Caleb willingly complied, lowering until his skin made contact with Andrew's mouth.

Caleb's moan harmonized with Andrew's and then Andrew swiped his tongue over Caleb's rosebud, back and forth, over and over again. It didn't take long for Caleb to push down, clearly trying to get more contact with that slick muscle. Andrew didn't let him down.

Burying his face in Caleb's trench, Andrew flattened his tongue and tasted everything. He loved the feeling of Caleb shaking above him, loved hearing the aroused whimpers pouring out of Caleb, loved the scent of their combined sweat and arousal. With his tongue pointed, he pushed against Caleb's opening and entered the silky warmth.

"Jesus, yes," Caleb panted. "Don't stop. Feels so good."

Andrew had no intention of stopping, not even for long enough to pull his tongue out of his friend's ass and say so. Instead, he kept licking, kept tasting, kept fucking Caleb with his tongue. When he noticed Caleb moving his arm and taking hold of his own cock, Andrew followed suit, taking himself in hand and stroking.

"Uh, mmm," he moaned, one hand still gripping Caleb's hip so he could continue making love to Caleb with his mouth, while his other hand flew over his dick. The combination had him on the cusp of ecstasy within minutes. He planted his feet on the bed and thrust his hips up into his fist, completely letting go and allowing the pleasure to take him over.

Caleb started bobbing, pushing himself up and down against Andrew's face. "Oh, I'm right there. So close." His breath hitched, he froze for a moment, and then his pace picked up and he keened. "Ah, God, right there. Drew!"

Two more furious strokes and Andrew was shouting, his voice muffled by Caleb's body, his back arched, hips raised off the bed, and cock shooting seed all over his belly. When he had nothing left, his body melted, a languid feeling taking over his muscles and his eyes closing peacefully. Caleb scooted down until his head rested on Andrew's chest, tucked under his chin.

"That felt incredible," Caleb sighed contentedly. "Thanks."

"Mmm. Right back at you," Andrew replied. With the last bit of energy he had left, he dropped his hand off the side of the bed and reached around until he found a piece of discarded clothing, then he used it to wipe the semen off his body and Caleb's before dropping it back on the floor. "Night, Cae."

The soft snore told him Caleb was already in dreamland. Well, Caleb was asleep. Dreamland was where they'd both been minutes before.

"DID YOU tell your parents you're in the city?" Caleb asked, making sure to keep his voice even, not wanting Andrew to think he was implying either answer would be wrong. He knew his effort to keep the question light and casual failed when he saw Andrew's back stiffen.

"No, I just wanted a few days to relax." Andrew was no longer spooning food from the frying pan onto his plate, but he didn't move to sit at the table either. He just stood at the counter with his back to Caleb, his head bowed, and his hands clenched.

Caleb pushed his chair back, flinching at the high-pitched scraping sound the metal legs made against the brick floor. If Andrew wanted to see his parents, Caleb would drive to Somerset with him. If he didn't, no big deal. He walked over to the counter, picked the abandoned plate up with one hand, and gripped Andrew's elbow with the other.

"'Course you do. You've been working like a dog, finishing your residency, getting ready to start your fellowship, packing, moving. You're overdue for some serious R and R." He put the plate on the table, pulled Andrew's chair out for him, and waited for Andrew to sit down.

Once Andrew sat, his face was eye level with Caleb's groin. "Damn, Cae, your package looks amazing in those underwear."

"It isn't just the underwear," Caleb answered in an intentionally campy tone.

Andrew laughed, then rubbed his cheek against the smooth Lycra fabric of the low-rise boxer-briefs with stripes in alternating light and dark shades of green. It seemed as if he was about to peel the underwear off and taste what Caleb barely had hidden underneath, when he froze, likely remembering their topic of conversation. Nothing like thinking of his parents to kill Andrew's mood.

Picking up on Andrew's anxiety, Caleb softly stroked his cheek and kissed the top of his head before sitting back down. They ate in silence, but it wasn't uncomfortable. Caleb propped his bare foot on Andrew's chair and caressed Andrew's thigh with his arch. The connection felt good.

"This tofu scramble is delish," Andrew said as he smiled weakly at Caleb. "Thanks for putting green chili in it. I love spicy food in the morning."

"I know," Caleb replied.

Andrew squeezed his foot and gave him a smile, a real one this time. "Yeah, you do." The deep sigh signaled a coming shift in the conversation away from food and back to family. Caleb didn't say anything, just ate his breakfast and waited for Andrew to get it off his chest.

"All these years, I thought she should leave him. I've called him every name in the book for his lying and cheating." Andrew paused, looked down at his plate, and then raised his eyes, blinking them rapidly. "Is it weird now that she's finally done it that I wonder if maybe it was a mistake?"

"Why a mistake? Do you think it wasn't true? That he'd really stopped sleeping around?"

"No way." Andrew shook his head. "My dad isn't

capable of keeping it in his pants. It's just...I could never really tell if she was happy when they were together, but she's flat-out miserable now. She can't even hide it. And you know my mother's the queen of Put On a Happy Face."

Yeah, Lizzie Thompson had always managed to act like things were okay, but Caleb had never mistaken it for anything other than exactly that—an act.

"I had brunch with my parents a couple of weeks back, and your mother joined us." He hesitated and then continued, not wanting to be anything other than completely honest with Andrew. "I hear what you're saying and you're right, she wasn't as peppy as she used to be, but maybe that's okay. Is pretend-peppy actually a good thing?"

Andrew shrugged in response. He took a deep breath, closed his eyes, and shook his head. "Okay, enough parent talk. Tell me what happened with that guy you were dating."

Happy to take Andrew's mind off anything stressful, Caleb went with the change in topic. "Oh, God. I couldn't take it," he said. "I mean, he was cute and nice, but the sex was a pain in the ass."

Andrew snickered and Caleb rolled his eyes. "Seriously? That got a laugh out of you? I can't believe people let you cut into their brains when you're still stuck in the teenage years."

"Whatever." Andrew smiled broadly. "You liked me just fine when I was a teenager. Anyway, what was the problem in bed?"

"It was too much pressure. Like one night, we were fooling around, getting to the good stuff, and then he stops and says '*oh wait, I can't see you. I need to light the candles.*' He gets up, wanders around the house for at least ten minutes looking for a lighter, and then when he comes back into the bedroom, he takes another five minutes to light the, like, fifty candles he has sitting on every possible surface. I'm telling you, by the time he climbed into bed, I'd totally lost interest. No way was I getting it up."

Andrew bit his lip, clearly trying to keep himself from laughing. "So what'd you do?"

"I didn't want to fool around, but I didn't want to leave him hanging, so I said he could beat off and cum on my back. He refused, said it wasn't as meaningful," Caleb scoffed. "I climbed out of bed, got dressed, and went home."

"No, you didn't!" Andrew couldn't stop laughing now. "I can picture you rolling your eyes at some poor guy who was trying to woo you. He was being romantic, Cae. You didn't need to be so bitchy."

"You call it romantic, I call it orchestrated. Sex is supposed to be fun and messy and wild. That guy required mood lighting and theme music."

"Theme music?" Andrew asked hesitantly, as if he was afraid of the answer.

"Uh-huh." Caleb nodded. "He had a playlist he insisted on using for sexy time. And I call it that because that was the name of the playlist. 'Sexy time.'"

"He did not," Andrew said in disbelief.

"Yes, he did. Look, I took a picture." Caleb leaned his chair back, snagged his digital camera off the counter, and scrolled through the pictures before handing it to Andrew.

"Is that...?" Andrew's eyes widened in horror and he jerked them toward Caleb. "'I Wanna Sex You Up'?"

"'Fraid so," Caleb replied.

"Well then." Andrew cleared his throat and set the camera down. "Clearly this was not a match made in heaven. Tell me you at least let him down gently. And by gently, I mean tell me you didn't laugh in the poor guy's face."

"Oh, puh-lease! I am a master at breakups. I took him out to a really nice dinner, told him he was great but I was damaged, and then I introduced him to a cute accountant. Last I heard they were planning a summer trip to the Hamptons."

"Of course they are," Andrew chuckled. "What is this, the second ex you've set up in a happily ever after?"

Caleb swallowed down his last bite of breakfast and smirked. "Third."

"That has to be some kind of record."

"What can I say? Dating me might be emotionally draining, but at least my boyfriends can look forward to the breakup, because it's always sure to be a phenomenal experience."

"You're not kidding," Andrew laughed. "We should date just so you can break up with me and then set me up with someone. I can't seem to keep a boyfriend longer than a few months, and being your ex is, like, a surefire way to find a long-term relationship."

"Nah, that would never work," Caleb said, reaching for his water glass. "What reason would we ever have to break up?"

"Good point," Andrew nodded.

CHAPTER THIRTEEN

2000

"I'VE BEEN living here for a year, and I had no idea we have a vegan market. Tell me again how you heard of this store?" Andrew asked as he followed Caleb down a narrow aisle flanked by dozens of bins of legumes.

Caleb arched an eyebrow and responded dryly, "Google."

An elbow to the ribs got no reaction so Andrew pressed his chest to Caleb's back, rested his chin on Caleb's shoulder, and held onto his hips as they walked.

"I'm bored."

"Dear God. You have the attention span of a gnat. We've been in this store for ten minutes. Chill out and let me buy some food so I can make you proper meals while I'm here."

Andrew stayed silent for about sixty seconds. When they turned the corner to the next aisle, he swiped a few bottles of flower essence off the nearest shelf and pushed himself in front of Caleb.

"Watch this," he said as he walked backward and tossed the bottles into the air. "I can juggle."

Two bottles hit the ground within seconds and rolled under a shelf.

"Whoa!" Andrew exclaimed and barely caught the final bottle in his hand. "That was a close one."

With a long-suffering sigh, Caleb bent down and rescued the wayward bottles. "Well," he said as he read the labels. "It looks like you lost confidence and self-esteem." He put the bottles back on the shelf and then reached for the one in Andrew's hand. "Good news. You saved courage."

Andrew tilted his head back, opened his mouth, and made a loud roaring sound. When Caleb furrowed his brow and looked at him in confusion, he shrugged. "Courage. Lion. Roar."

"Right. That makes perfect sense."

If he didn't know Caleb so well, the statement may have come across as sincere. As it was, Andrew recognized it as classic snarky Caleb. He quickly moved behind his friend, pinched his ass, and then bounced around with his hands in front of him, as if he were warding off a counterattack.

"Nice," Caleb said with an eye roll and reached for a bag of unbleached organic flour. "You're six now. However did you manage to eradicate the past two decades of maturity without leaving a scar?"

Andrew stuck his tongue out, finally earning a smile.

"You're a goofball," Caleb said.

"Yup. And you love it." Andrew wrapped his arm around Caleb's shoulder and nudged their hips together. "So what're you making us for dinner?"

"A spinach and bean casserole with dumplings." Caleb stopped walking and looked at Andrew, moving one hand gently across his face and over the new bar in his left eyebrow. Caleb's expression was tender and his voice quiet when he kept talking. "Why didn't you tell me you were seeing someone?"

"I'm not," Andrew answered defensively, thinking of the hour they'd spent in bed earlier that day, right after Caleb had arrived. In fact, it was postcoital hunger that had ultimately led to this trip to the store. "You know I'd never cheat on anybody. If I were seeing someone, I wouldn't have—"

Caleb kissed him chastely, stopping the flow of words. "Of course I know that. I meant, why didn't you tell you me you *had* been seeing someone?"

Though he had no idea how Caleb had figured it out, Andrew had long ago stopped questioning his friend's insight. "It barely lasted a month. I didn't figure there was a point in saying something to you about Thad before he meant anything to me."

"Bullshit." There was no heat in Caleb's tone so Andrew wasn't offended. Besides, his friend was right.

"Look, it's getting to be embarrassing. How many times have I called you to whine about yet another breakup?

I figured I'd spare you the drama."

"I'm your friend, Drew. You don't need to spare me anything."

"Don't be mad." He dropped his forehead onto Caleb's shoulder. "This one got a text from his *girl*friend right after we were done in bed. He happened to be in the bathroom at the time, which is the only reason I figured it out. Can you see why I wasn't thrilled to tell you about that? It's embarrassing."

"To him," Caleb said. "It's embarrassing to *him*, not to you."

Andrew turned his back to Caleb, not wanting his friend to see his face. "When every guy I date doesn't think I'm enough, it might just reflect on me. Have you ever thought about that, Cae? At what point are we going to face reality and admit that I'm the problem here?"

"Hey." Caleb's hand squeezed his shoulder and then Caleb wrapped his arm around the top of Andrew's chest, pulling him back until his body rested against Caleb's. "I have thought about it."

"And?" Having his voice break on a one-syllable word didn't exactly add to his self-image at the moment. He dropped his chin to his chest and looked at the ground.

"And I think for some reason, you keep choosing guys who don't deserve you." Caleb managed to turn Andrew around. "Listen to me. I know you." He lifted Andrew's chin, forcing their eyes to meet. "I *know* you. You are more than enough in every possible way."

"MMM, THAT smells delicious."

Caleb turned around as Andrew walked into the kitchen, drying off his blond hair with a bath towel. He raked his eyes up and down Andrew's glorious body. Bare feet—narrow, long, with just a bit of light hair on the toes. White drawstring lounge pants Caleb had bought him for a birthday or Christmas, or maybe it was a just-because gift, either way he'd never had the good fortune to see Andrew wear them. No shirt, so his sinewy muscles were on display, along with his punk-ass tattoo. And no underwear, so his cock was clearly outlined underneath the thin, gauzy material of the pants.

"Caleb?"

Andrew was suddenly right in front of him, green eyes twinkling in amusement.

"Huh?" he asked distractedly, noticing how the light reflected off the metal in Andrew's ears.

Grinning, Andrew leaned over and kissed him softly, mouths meeting over and over again before Andrew grasped his lower lip between his teeth and tugged. "Dinner smells fantastic. Thanks for cooking." He received another delicious kiss. "As usual."

"No problem." Caleb threw his arms round Andrew's neck and pulled him close. "You know I love cooking for you." He pounced—licking and nibbling on Andrew's lips until he opened his mouth. With a moan, Caleb pushed his tongue inside.

Their heads tilted, lips slanted over each other, and Andrew snapped, pushing Caleb against the counter and rutting against him.

"So fucking hot, Drew," Caleb managed to pant out. He tangled his fingers in soft blond hair and yanked it, not aiming for gentle. Then he slammed his mouth back against Andrew's and thrust his tongue in and out.

"Ah, mnh." Andrew's moans and cries were deeply satisfying, and so was the hard dick pressing against him. He did that; he made his friend forget all about work and shithead boyfriends who couldn't recognize the best thing in the world when it was right in front of them. Well, Caleb wasn't a doctor or an Ivy League graduate, but he was sure as hell smart enough to know that Andrew was someone to be cherished, not betrayed. He shoved his hand between them, reaching for the button on his pants, and then he heard the doorbell.

"Oh, come on!" he exclaimed. He moved his hands up to Andrew's shoulders and leaned their foreheads together, breathing heavily. "You expecting someone?"

"I'm expecting whoever's at my door to be bleeding and in dire need of medical attention. Either that or they will be when I'm through with them," Andrew grumbled, but didn't move. When a loud knock sounded, Andrew kissed Caleb's forehead and pulled away regretfully. He walked toward the door and talked to Caleb over shoulder. "Sorry for the interruption, Cae. Promise to make it up to you just as soon as I get rid of...Tiff! What are you doing here?"

"Thank God you're home!" A disembodied voice filtered inside. "He's coming to pick me up in ten minutes and I can't get anything to look right." Caleb watched the owner of that voice walk into the apartment. Andrew's auburn-haired neighbor was tugging on her clothes nervously, chewing on her bottom lip, and shifting from foot to foot. "What do you think of my outfit?"

"Umm," Andrew responded, clearly unsure how to answer the question. "It looks good?"

Rolling his eyes, Caleb stepped toward the woman. She needed help and there was no chance in hell she was getting it from Andrew. If he wasn't wearing scrubs, the man alternated between ripped jeans and...ripped jeans.

He reached his hand out to the woman. "Hi, I'm Caleb."

Her head snapped toward him. "Oh! I'm Tiffany. Sorry, I didn't realize Andrew had company. I, uh, needed a second opinion on my outfit because I have this date and, uh..." She shook Caleb's hand quickly, looked back and forth between him and Andrew, and started walking back out the door. "I should go."

"Okay," Andrew replied.

"Don't be silly, we're happy to help," Caleb said with a smile at the exact same moment. Tiffany twisted her hair around her finger and chewed on her bottom lip.

With an eye roll at Andrew, Caleb marched over to Tiffany and looked her up and down. "So, tell me what you're going for here. Sexy? Sweet? Time-travel chic?"

"Uh, I don't know. I just wanted to look cute and..." Her brow furrowed as his words sank in. "Wait, are you saying my outfit looks dated? Damn it, I just bought this. I was in the mall most of the day, spent half my paycheck, and—"

"Hey, no worries. You've got all the bones of a good outfit there. The heels are super-hot. The skirt shows off your legs without being streetwalker short. And the blue spaghetti-strap shirt sets off your eyes." He pointed to the scarf tied into a huge bow around her neck. "It's just that gift wrap you've got going on there that screams 'Welcome back to the eighties.'"

Tiffany looked down and fingered her scarf. "Really? The sales person said the scarf made the outfit."

Caleb arched a brow in disbelief. "Did she see how you were planning to wear it? Because anybody who thinks that's a good look is visually impaired. She must have been looking at you in braille or something."

He reached over and tugged the knot loose. Then he took both ends of the scarf and wrapped them around her neck choker style, and let the ends drape along her back. "See that? Now we've gone from Julia Sugarbaker to Julia Roberts."

Tiffany rushed into the bathroom and looked at herself in the mirror. "Yeah, you think this looks okay? It's not too slutty with everything"—she waved her hands over suddenly exposed cleavage—"on display?"

Caleb leaned against the door and grinned. "No way, hon, you look just slutty enough."

She giggled and smacked his arm. "Caleb!"

"What?" he laughed. "I figure if this guy has you hot and bothered enough to spend all this time and money primping for him, the least he can do is actually get you hot and bothered." He waggled his eyebrows. "Know what I mean?"

She blushed and pushed past him to get out of the bathroom. "Something tells me he's not going to have any trouble in that department," she said shyly.

They walked back into the living room, where Andrew was still gripping the door handle. Suddenly, Tiffany froze. "Shit! You're half-naked! I...I didn't notice." Her head darted between Andrew and Caleb. "Did I interrupt something?"

"No," Caleb said, just as Andrew nodded his head affirmatively.

With another blush, she hurried toward the door. "I'm sorry, guys. Seriously, I didn't realize Andrew had company and I was in panic mode." She rushed out as quickly as she'd rushed in. "It was nice meeting you, Caleb. Thanks for your help."

"Good luck tonight, Tiff," Andrew called out after her with a laugh.

"Don't do anything I wouldn't do," Caleb added, leaning against Andrew's arm and looking out into the hallway.

"AND WHAT would that be?" Andrew asked as he closed and locked the apartment door. He backed Caleb against it and planted his hands on either side of Caleb's head, caging him in. "What exactly wouldn't you do, Cae?"

"Depends." Caleb grinned. "Are we talking with a date like Miss Tiffany's going on, or with you?"

With Caleb's back against the door, Andrew's chest mere inches in front of him, and Andrew's arms on either side of his body, Caleb had no ability to escape. The thought burned Andrew up from the inside. He ground his hips against Caleb's and licked a line up Caleb's neck to his ear.

"With me," he whispered hungrily.

Trembling, Caleb gulped. "Since when do we have limits with each other, Drew? Tell me what you want and I'll do it."

"I want to fuck your mouth," Andrew said into Caleb's ear as he continued to press his body against Caleb's. "I want to push myself so far down your throat that you can't breathe unless I decide to let you." He tugged on Caleb's earlobe with his teeth. "I want you on your knees and completely at my mercy."

He'd never even dream of talking to another man that way, of being so raw and aggressive with any of his exes. But it was different with Caleb. Their friendship was unconditional, unwavering, eternal. Andrew was more certain of that than he was of anything else in his life. Knowing he didn't need to make an impression, knowing he could put anything and everything out there without impacting Caleb's view of him or their relationship, was incredibly freeing.

"Make me," Caleb challenged, his brown eyes sparkling.

With a moan, Andrew grabbed both of Caleb's shoulders and pushed him to his knees. He shoved his pants down below his balls and gripped the base of his cock with his right hand. With his left, he held Caleb's head in place and painted Caleb's lips with his glans—upper first, then lower.

"Open," Andrew commanded as he tapped his cock against Caleb's closed mouth.

Caleb shook his head and kept his lips pressed together. The resistance just made Andrew hotter, which was no doubt Caleb's intent. He moved his left hand from the back of Caleb's head to his jaw and squeezed, encouraging those plump lips to part and let him in. As soon as he succeeded in creating an opening, Andrew fed his thick cock into Caleb's mouth.

"Ungh, that's good," he moaned, slowly sinking more of his length into that warm, wet cavern.

He cupped Caleb's cheek and held his face in place as he pulled back a little and then dipped in farther, continuing the in and out rhythm until his pubes were flush with Caleb's face. Caleb made a gurgling sound then swallowed around him convulsively.

"Oh, hell, that's hot. Take it, Cae. Fucking gag on it."
Andrew pulled out and then shoved back into Caleb's mouth
roughly, all the while looking down at heated brown eyes. He
stayed buried deep, grinding his groin against Caleb's face,
knowing there was no way for the man to take in air with
a cock lodged so far down his throat. All the while, Caleb's
expression contained no fear, only lust and trust.

"Fuck, yeah," Andrew grunted, dragging his dick out,
watching saliva escape Caleb's mouth and drizzle down his
chin. Then he twined his fingers into Caleb's brown hair and
held him in place as he ruthlessly jammed his cock back into
that opening.

With his eyes closed and his head tilted toward the
ceiling, Andrew acted on pure instinct, pumping in and out
of Caleb's mouth with abandon, pressing all the way against
his soft palate before sliding out and back in again. Suddenly
feeling an irresistible urge to watch Caleb's face as he fucked
it, Andrew opened his eyes. The dazed expression, swollen
lips, and spit-slick face that greeted him almost made him
lose control and pour himself into Caleb before he was ready.
Then he noticed that Caleb had managed to unbutton his own
pants and pull his dick out of what looked like a shiny red
G-string, and Andrew had to bite the inside of his cheek to
keep from spilling.

He pulled his cock out of that tempting mouth, and
Caleb whimpered, leaning toward him to get it back. A sharp
tug to the back of the man's hair kept Caleb in place, but his

eyes stayed fixed on Andrew's cock as his hand flew over his own.

"You want this?" Andrew asked while stroking his cock, Caleb's saliva helping his hand glide over heated skin. Caleb nodded and, unable to move his head because of Andrew's strong clutch in his hair, reached his tongue out. "Uh, uh, uh. Not until I'm ready." Andrew circled his fingers around the base of his dick and clubbed each of Caleb's cheeks with it, then his eyes, and eventually his chin. Each contact drew out a sound that was half moan, half whimper from the man kneeling before him.

Damn, the whole scene turned Andrew on like nothing else. There was no way he'd be able to hold his climax off much longer.

"I'm going to feed you my dick again, Cae. Going to fuck your mouth, choke you with it until you're desperate for oxygen. And then I'm going to come all over your face."

"Uh," Caleb moaned, his eyes clenching shut as he gasped. One shaking hand yanked on his own dick and the other grabbed Andrew's ass and pulled him forward. "Please," Caleb begged.

There was no point in denying Caleb, not when Andrew wanted the same thing, so he thrust his hips and fell into that sensuous mouth. Caleb moaned loudly around Andrew's length, stoking Andrew's arousal even further. He loved hearing Caleb's pleasure, loved seeing unwavering desire in those brown eyes. His gaze met Caleb's as he thrust in two more times, enjoying the incredible feeling of Caleb's tongue and mouth working him over. Then he pulled out, held Caleb's head still, and jerked off over his face, shouting his name as he painted his cheeks, lips, and even his hair with ropes of hot white ejaculate.

"Oh, God, yes!" Caleb shouted when Andrew's cum hit his skin. He groaned loudly, his entire body shaking as he found his own release.

Sinking to the floor, Andrew wrapped his arms around Caleb and pulled him onto his lap, hugging him tightly. "Damn, Cae," he panted. "Just damn."

"Best sex ever," Caleb gasped, struggling to drag air into his lungs.

"You say that every time," Andrew teased, caressing Caleb's damp cheek and looking at him fondly.

"It's true every time."

"Yeah," Andrew agreed and gave Caleb a soft, closemouthed kiss. "It really, really is."

CHAPTER FOURTEEN

2001

"DREW!" CALEB waved his arms over his head and shouted across the sea of holiday travelers. He saw the blond head turn and watched it weave through the crowd until Andrew's warm smile greeted him.

"Hey, hot stuff!" Andrew dropped his duffle bag and enveloped Caleb in a full body hug. "Damn but is it ever nice to see you." He nuzzled Caleb's neck and sighed deeply.

Caleb rubbed Andrew's back and let his friend rest against him. "How was your flight?" he asked quietly.

Andrew straightened and dragged his fingers through his already tousled hair. "Long, but not too bad."

Reaching over to Andrew's head, Caleb smoothed his hair. "I like the highlights. The lighter streaks add texture and volume."

"And here I thought it just looked cool." Andrew winked. Then his expression turned serious. "Are your parents mad that you're not staying with them for Christmas?"

Picking up Andrew's bag, Caleb began leading them

out of the Montrose airport. "My parents are fine. Should I even bother asking whether you checked any bags?"

"Nah, I'm only here for a week. One bag was plenty."

"Of course it is." Caleb chuckled. "I'll never understand how you can pack so light. Nice sweatshirt, by the way."

It was green with "Shh, nobody knows I'm gay" written on it. Caleb seriously doubted the veracity of that statement.

Andrew shrugged and pushed the sleeves of his sweatshirt up. A new tattoo caught Caleb's eye. It was simple, just the word "PRIDE" in black ink, but the letters were huge, covering Andrew's forearm from wrist to elbow.

Caleb stopped to trace the letters with one finger. "Hey, I forgot to tell you that I'm sorry about Braden."

"Aiden," Andrew replied and continued walking. "And you didn't forget. In fact, I believe you sent me a 'sorry about the orgy' card. So you're sure your parents aren't ticked off?"

"About me not staying with them? I'm sure." Caleb reached over and squeezed Andrew's arm. "Hey, the card was meant to cheer you up, ya'? I wasn't trying to be flippant; I really am sorry, Jayden...did what he did."

"It's Aiden, and I know, Cae. I appreciate it. Besides, you don't have any reason to be sorry. It's not your fault the guy decided to turn poker night with his friends into a game of smiles. Seriously though, your parents don't mind that you're not staying with them?"

"My parents are totally okay, Drew. It's not like I'm in another town. Our condo is in the same complex as theirs, and we're all spending Christmas together." He nudged Andrew's hip with his own as they walked into the parking lot. "So, is it too soon to ask how many guys were sitting around the table?"

Andrew laughed and shook his head. "Only you would ask that question."

"Hey, inquiring minds and all that." Caleb waggled his eyebrows and smiled wryly.

"Yeah, yeah," Andrew responded. "I think there were six of them. And two were nice enough to call and tell me about it after. Not nice enough to get up from the table, mind you, but, hey, at least they told me."

Caleb's jaw dropped open. "And he sucked all of them off?" He didn't know whether he should be disgusted or impressed. "Damn, Caden must have some serious stamina and a jaw of steel."

"Aiden. And yeah, he has stamina, but his technique sucks. No pun intended. You're sure your parents aren't mad, right? You'd tell me?"

"Yes, I'm sure! Since when have I ever held anything back from you, Drew? And what's with the big concern about my parents? Is your mom fussing about you not staying with her?"

They'd gotten to the rental car. Caleb opened the trunk and deposited Andrew's bag inside.

"Are you kidding me?" Andrew laughed. "My mother's thrilled that we're staying together. I think she has a not-so-secret dream that we'll start dating."

Caleb closed the trunk. "Yeah, I'm pretty sure my mom's in on that one. I keep telling her we like each other way too much to date."

Those tired green eyes sparkled with happiness as Andrew gazed at him. "You got that right." He cupped the back of Caleb's head with one hand and drew him forward for a kiss as his other hand settled on Caleb's lower back. "You're my favorite person," he added when their lips separated.

"Right back atcha, Drew."

"I'M GLAD you agreed to meet me for dinner, dear." Elizabeth Thompson patted the back of Andrew's hand with her french-tipped fingers. "I can't remember the last time we did this, just the two of us."

Andrew hoped he had been able to keep the guilt off his face and that his wince hadn't been too apparent. It had been years since he'd spent any length of time alone with his mother and that wasn't an accident. It was hard being with her, but he wasn't exactly sure why.

"Umm, Andrew?" He noticed his mother's hand tremble as she reached for her glass of Chardonnay. "There's, ehm, there's something I need to tell you."

"Go ahead," he said, feeling confused about what had her so nervous.

"I'm not alone on this trip." She pursed her lips tightly and Andrew was sure she'd be biting one if she didn't think it'd get lipstick on her teeth. His mother was a beautiful woman, but the amount of effort she put into looking just right made Andrew wonder whether she realized the smoke and mirrors were unnecessary.

When her words finally filtered into his brain, he stopped thinking about her obsession with her personal appearance and smiled broadly. "Oh, yeah? You're finally seeing someone?" He reached across the table and rubbed her forearm. "That's great, Mom. I can't wait to meet him."

"Actually..." She swallowed hard, looking nothing short of terrified. "You've already met him."

He furrowed his brow. "I have? When? What's his name?"

She closed her eyes and Andrew wondered why she didn't want to see his reaction to her revelation. He wasn't against his mother dating. Quite the opposite. He wanted her to be happy, to find someone who would appreciate her. Maybe even cherish her. It was the same thing he hoped to one day find for himself.

"Look, there's no easy way to say this so..." She took a deep breath and didn't open her eyes. "Your father and I have decided to reconcile. He's moved back into the house and we're going to remarry. He's at the condo right now, and he'll be joining us and the Lakes for Christmas dinner."

His mouth dropped open, his eyes widened, and he

stared at his mother. He couldn't formulate a thought, let alone a word. She sat perfectly still, her eyes still shut. A couple of long minutes ticked by.

"Is that supposed to be some kind of a joke?" he practically growled at her. "It's not funny, Mother."

"I'm not..." She finally opened her eyes, and he saw anxiety there, or maybe it was fear. "I'm not kidding. We love each other and we want to be together and—"

"He cheated on you, Mother! For years and with many different women. You gave him a million chances and nothing ever changed." He felt sick, literally sick. "What possible reason can you have for being with that man again? You don't need the money. Grandfather left you plenty. You're attractive, kind, intelligent. I know you can find someone else, someone who will treat you well."

"I don't want anybody else." Her eyes were wet now, her voice quiet but desperate. "Don't you see, honey, I've never wanted anybody else. Do you remember my friend Lanna? Her husband was in Tower One and now she's alone. But I don't have to be. Your father still loves me."

"Love? Mom, have you forgotten what that man—"

Suddenly sharp nails were digging into his forearm and his mother was glaring daggers at him. "Your father. *That man* is your father, Andrew. And you'd be well served to remember it and treat him with respect."

He shoved his chair away from the table and threw his napkin onto his plate. "Damn it, Mom!" he hissed. "You think the way he acted was respectful? The sneaking around, the mistresses? How can you ask me to respect him? How can you respect him? Hell, how can he respect himself?"

"I can ask you to respect him because he is your father. And if that isn't good enough, I'll remind you that I'm your mother, Andrew. Now calm down. We're in a restaurant and people are going to stare."

All those years encouraging her to stand up for herself, trying to save her from a bad marriage—and here they were, back to the same place. Strangely, she didn't seem unhappy. Well, not less happy than she'd been since the divorce. Did that mean she was making the right decision? That his father's infidelity should be forgiven, or at least ignored? Was that the only way for his mother to find happiness?

Feeling inexplicably drained, he slumped into his chair. He didn't know what to say, what to think. The only thing keeping him from melting down completely was the knowledge that he'd be going home to Caleb at the end of the night, so he didn't need to figure this out on his own. He licked his lips and pasted a smile on his face.

"How's your salad, Mom?"

She blinked in surprise and then Andrew saw her relief before she schooled her features.

"Oh, it's delicious, dear. How is your dinner?"

He shrugged and looked down at his grilled vegetable plate, wondering why a four star restaurant couldn't manage a single protein that hadn't been killed. Tofu was sold at every supermarket; was it really so difficult to grill some? "It's fine."

"Good. That's good. Your fellowship will be done this summer, right? Have you chosen a permanent position?"

"Yes. I took a job with a neurosurgery practice in Emile City. I'm moving in June."

His mother nodded agreeably, took a small bite of her salad, and continued asking meaningless questions and listening to his answers with unaccountable interest. Small talk. That was where they were. With as tired as he felt, Andrew figured he had no room to complain.

DINNER WITH his parents ran later than Caleb had anticipated. He rushed back to the condo he was renting with Andrew for the week and hoped his friend was still awake so they could spend some time together. Their plan had been to order in and catch up during Andrew's first night in town. But Elizabeth Thompson had called while they were driving in from the airport and practically begged Andrew to meet her for dinner.

With his friend occupied, Caleb figured he should spend some time with his own parents, which meant joining them for dinner at Cosmo's. Between the extra wait to get seated, the busy kitchen, and his parents' decision to order the tasting menu, the meal took twice as long as he'd expected. It was close to midnight by the time he tiptoed into the condo.

"I'm awake, Cae," Andrew called out in the dark. "No need to keep it down."

Caleb flicked on the switch and blinked his eyes to adjust to the light. Andrew was sprawled across the couch, one hand across his forehead and the other holding a giant coffee cup on his chest. Caleb took off his jacket and hung it on the peg by the door before starting to walk over.

"That vat of coffee is going to keep you up all night, Drew."

Andrew sat up and set the cup down on the coffee table. Then he reached his hand out to Caleb.

"Nah. It's decaf, so it's big but not effective."

Caleb snickered. "Sounds like a lot of guys I know." That should have earned him a laugh or at least a smile, but instead Andrew sighed dejectedly. Something was wrong.

"Drew?" Caleb quickened his pace and joined Andrew on the couch, straddling his lap with a knee resting next to each of Andrew's hips. He cupped the sides of Andrew's face and brushed his thumbs across his cheeks. "What's wrong? Is it your mother?"

"Yes. Maybe. I don't know." Andrew buried his face in Caleb's neck. "She's getting back together with my dad, which should suck, but she seems happy about it. Or as close to happy as she ever is. And it doesn't make sense, but it does, you know? Like I don't understand why she's doing it, but then I totally get it. So now I'm sitting here wondering whether every decision I ever made was wrong. I mean, it always seemed right, but I'm alone like she was and..." The sound leaving Andrew's throat could be described as nothing other than a tortured sob, and Caleb's chest ached in sympathy.

"Oh, Drew." He kissed Andrew's forehead and wrapped him in a tight embrace. "You're not alone. You'll never be alone." Caleb could feel Andrew's heart racing, his breath huffing against Caleb's skin at a too-rapid clip. "Do you want to talk about it?"

"Yeah, but not now. I don't want to think anymore. Help me," Andrew begged brokenly.

"Shh," Caleb whispered. He swayed them gently from side to side and trailed soft, calming kisses across Andrew's jaw and down his neck. "Let it go, just let it go. I'm here and I'll take care of you, babe."

Andrew nodded and took in a deep breath, his entire body shuddering before he seemed to melt against Caleb. They were pressed completely together—from groin to face—so Caleb knew Andrew wasn't hard. But he also knew exactly what his friend needed to stop that brilliant mind from spinning. He slid down Andrew's body and settled himself between long, muscular thighs.

He was reaching for the button on Andrew's jeans when he felt a tug on his hair. He looked up, but didn't stop undressing his friend.

"I'm not sure I can get it up right now," Andrew confessed. "My mind's all over the place."

With Andrew's zipper down, Caleb was able to reach

into the opening of his boxer briefs and caress his warm flesh.

"You let me worry about that, okay? Just lean back and relax."

Andrew nodded once, seemingly relieved. Then he leaned back and closed his eyes.

Caleb pulled Andrew's cock out and stroked it gently as he suckled the tip. "Mmm, love how you taste, Drew." The tense body trembled then Andrew's fingers wove through his hair.

There we go.

He continued to suck and stroke with one hand while he used the other to cup Andrew's balls through the fabric of his briefs. Though he could have moved back long enough to undress Andrew, or at least lower his briefs and pants, there was something erotic about doing it this way—him kneeling at Andrew's feet, both of them clothed, with only Andrew's hardening prick exposed.

And there was no doubt that it was hardening. Caleb could feel the hot flesh in his mouth expand with every suck and moan. He looked up and met Andrew's eyes, letting him see how much he enjoyed this act.

"Oh, damn, Cae," Andrew groaned. One finger traced Caleb's stretched lips. "So hot."

That's right. He knew what Andrew needed. Knew just how to arouse him, how to empty his mind from everything other than heat and need and pleasure.

When those heavy balls drew up close to Andrew's

body and early seed slicked Caleb's tongue, he popped off the thick cock.

Andrew's hips shot off the couch, chasing his mouth. "Ungh," he moaned. "Cae..."

"I'm coming," Caleb assured him.

He stood and unfastened his black slacks, letting them drop to the floor as he watched for Andrew's reaction to his underwear. Perhaps underwear was overstating it. It was more a series of elastic straps—one around his hips, another around his thighs and just below his ass cheeks, and a third circling his cock. That was it, no fabric at all keeping anything hidden.

"Holy shit!" Andrew gasped. His eyes were wide and glued to Caleb's dick.

"I got them for you," Caleb said as he stepped out of his pants and pulled his lavender cashmere sweater over his head, leaving himself wearing only the jockstrap while Andrew remained clothed. "I've had them on all day. Been waiting until we were alone so I could show you. Do you like them?" he asked coyly.

There was no doubt about the answer to that question when Andrew whimpered and grabbed the base of his own cock, clearly trying to stave off his orgasm. "Get that fine ass up here right now, Cae." Andrew's eyes seared into him. "Before I explode."

Yeah, that was the idea. Caleb climbed onto the couch and straddled Andrew again, kneeling above him as he pushed Andrew's rigid cock through his own spread legs before lowering himself. Hot flesh dragged along his ass, eliciting moans from both of them. Desperate hands tangled in his hair, and Andrew yanked him forward, crushing their mouths together in a hungry kiss.

Caleb gave as good as he got, sucking Andrew's tongue into his mouth and writhing against his friend. He reached behind himself and grasped his ass, spreading it open so Andrew's erection could settle between his firm cheeks.

"Yes! Oh, damn," Andrew moaned and thrust his hips, pushing himself through that warm channel.

"That's it, Drew. Feel it. Feel me," Caleb whispered into Andrew's mouth, gripping his lower lip between his teeth and tugging on it. With one hand behind him, he kept Andrew's dick in place as he bounced in his lap. His own cock was rubbing against a flat stomach, the silky hairs adding sensation. He felt incredible.

"Oh, Cae, yeah. So good. Almost there. Almost the—" Andrew bucked and shook as liquid heat sprayed on Caleb's back. That was all it took to send him over edge, crying out Andrew's name as he came.

"Mmm." Andrew nuzzled his neck before kissing him tenderly. Hooded green eyes met his, Andrew looking relaxed and sated.

Deciding morning would be soon enough to talk about Andrew's conversation with his mother and the resulting self-assessment, Caleb climbed off Andrew's lap and pulled him away from the couch.

"It's late. Let's get in the shower and go to bed."

Andrew followed willingly, plastering himself to Caleb's back as they walked into the bathroom. "You think you can leave these on in the shower?" Andrew mumbled against the back of his neck and fingered the waistband of the barely there jockstrap.

"I think wet elastic will make me chafe," Caleb laughed. "Besides, it's not like you can get it up again tonight anyway."

"Oh, I don't know about that." Andrew turned Caleb around and cupped his soft cock and balls. "You inspire me, Cae. Always have."

Caleb snickered. "Well, that's good to hear. Because I love morning sex."

The grin he got in reaction to that comment was nothing short of wicked, and Caleb found himself wondering what memory inspired it. Lord knew they'd had some wild mornings together over the years. And evenings. And afternoons.

A groan distracted him from his thoughts. Well, a groan and the hand stroking his miraculously hardening flesh. "Get into the shower, Cae," Andrew rumbled as he tore his own clothes off. "I'm pretty sure we both have another round in us before morning."

Caleb stumbled in his haste to get into the shower. No way was he turning down that offer.

CHAPTER FIFTEEN

2002

"'LO?"

"Hey. Sorry I'm calling so late but your message said to call back tonight, and my phone died so I just got it."

"No worries, Cae. I'm the PSOC tonight so my phone's been ringing on and off. Believe me, hearing from you is like a ray of sunshine compared to the other calls I've been getting."

Caleb wondered if he was supposed to know what that meant and his brain was just too tired to remember. "PSOC?" he asked.

"Poor Sucker On Call."

"Fabulous," Caleb laughed. "Doctor humor. So what was so important it couldn't wait until tomorrow?"

"I met someone." Andrew sounded like he was bouncing.

Caleb smiled and settled into his bed, ready to hear about the latest man that caught Andrew's eye. He found it endearing how Andrew always jumped in with both feet and never gave up, no matter how many times he'd been screwed over.

"Oh yeah? That's great. Tell me about him."

"His name is Drake. He's thirty-three, about your height, black hair, brown eyes. I don't know much else yet. We've only been out once, but I think there might be something there."

Of course Andrew thought there was something there. Andrew *always* thought there was something there.

"What does he do?"

"Oh! It's perfect. He's a flight attendant. He said his travel schedule makes relationships hard, but I told him I don't mind because I work so much anyway."

"That's what you said, huh? On the first date?"

There was a long pause before Andrew answered. "Yeah. Was it too soon for me to say something like that? Will he think I'm getting too serious too fast?"

"From anybody else, yeah it would have been too soon to start talking relationship," Caleb answered honestly. "But you don't do casual, Drew. There's no point in hiding it and pretending to be somebody you're not."

"You think so?" The worry in Andrew's voice was clear.

Caleb nodded, and then he remembered that his friend couldn't see him. "Yes, I do."

"Cool. You'll meet him when you're in town next month." He paused for a moment. "I know you'll like him, Cae. He's great."

Privately, Caleb thought the odds of Andrew still seeing this latest guy in a month's time were about fifty-fifty, but he didn't want to dampen his friend's excitement. "I'm sure I will."

"ARE WE meeting him at the restaurant?" Caleb yelled out so Andrew could hear him from the other room. He'd been in the bathroom for ten minutes, finger-combing modeling clay into his hair in an attempt to achieve a just-rolled-out-of-bed look.

"No, we're picking him up at his place and we'll drive over together. That way only one of us has to stay sober."

"Ah, so it's going to be that kind of night, is it?" Caleb snickered. "Sounds like fun."

He walked out of the bathroom and froze when he met Andrew's scorching gaze. Green eyes dragged up and down his body.

"You look good." Andrew's voice was husky.

"Thanks," Caleb answered, trying to keep his breathing even and hoping his sudden erection wasn't obvious in his slim-fit jeans. He straightened the collar on his gray button-down and failed in his attempt not to check out Andrew's package.

It was always difficult when either of them was dating someone. There was no way to turn off the attraction or the memories of how good it could be between them. But Andrew deserved to have a boyfriend—they both did. So if there was a guy around interviewing for the job, they could keep their libidos in check. After all, their friendship consisted of more than just sex.

Even if it was good sex. Really good sex. Hot, down and dirty sex.

Caleb cleared his throat and walked toward the door. "You ready to go?" he asked. When Andrew didn't answer, he looked over his shoulder. "Drew?"

Andrew's gaze snapped up from its perch on his ass and he blushed. "Sorry, those jeans are distracting. What'd you say?"

Shaking his head, Caleb opened the door and walked outside. "Nothing. How far away does Drake live?"

"Not far. He's in EC West too."

"Good, 'cause I'm starving."

"Yeah, me too." They got into the car and Andrew backed out of the driveway of his little rented bungalow. "How're your parents? Anything new?"

"They're good. Dad's working, Mom's shopping. Nothing new."

"I don't see how she has room for more things," Andrew said skeptically. "Their house is big, I'll give you that, but it's not as if there's any empty space in there."

"She gives a lot away to her charities. Half the stuff still has tags on it. We all have our quirks, right?" Caleb figured there were worse things than his mother's shopping habit. "How's your mom?"

"She's fine," Andrew said. "It's working for them."

"And your dad? Have you talked to him?"

Andrew chewed on his bottom lip and shook his head. "Not yet, but she keeps nagging me to do it. We'll see."

They pulled into a nice apartment complex, and Caleb followed Andrew to a unit on the second floor. After ringing the doorbell, Andrew began to fidget. "Do I look all right?" he asked as he smoothed down his T-shirt. This one was bright blue and it had a rainbow across it with the words "Taste the Rainbow" underneath it in a cursive font.

"You? Yeah. That shirt...not so much."

"Bitch," Andrew responded.

"Hey, you say that like it's a bad thing!" Caleb poked his ribs.

They were both laughing by the time the door opened.

"Hi!" A happy voice had them looking away from each other. Caleb saw a flash of black hair before a body separated him from Andrew. He watched the other man lean up and kiss his friend, then a hand was shoved in Caleb's face.

"You must be Caleb. I'm Drake." Caleb shook the man's hand even though he suddenly felt light-headed. "Come in, come in. I just need to grab my jacket."

Drake rushed back into the apartment and disappeared down the hall.

"You all right, Cae?" Andrew sounded concerned.

"Yeah, I'm fine. My blood sugar's probably low or something."

Andrew rubbed circles on his back and led him inside. "Let's sit down for a minute." He steered Caleb to the sofa, which only made matters worse.

"Oh my God." Caleb honestly thought he might throw up.

"What's wrong?" Andrew sounded panicked.

"I'm pretty sure that's a Florence Knoll," Caleb gulped. "But it's been reupholstered in neon-orange velour."

"Christ, Cae! You scared me."

"You should be scared. That horrifying use of no-quality fabric in a classic piece of furniture is so appalling chances are high someone is going to call the police and report a crime. Did your boyfriend do this? Because I think he could be facing jail time."

"Caleb..." Andrew's tone held a warning note. "Be nice."

He bit his tongue and sat down. Then he spotted the picture on the wall in front of him.

"So...ehm..." Caleb cleared his throat. "I take it Drake's a bottom?"

In the huge image, Drake was bent in half, with his legs spread and his ass to the camera, and he was pushing a dildo into himself. His torso was twisted so his face was visible and he had what Caleb assumed was meant to be a sultry expression. The picture was in black and white, probably in an attempt to look artistic. But the photographer was no Mapplethorpe, and besides, who the hell put naked sex pictures of themselves in their living room?

Andrew followed Caleb's line of sight and blushed. "Drake used to date a photographer. Let me go see if he has something for you to munch on right now so you don't pass out or bite someone's head off. I didn't realize how hungry you were."

Caleb looked around the great room, hoping to purge the disturbing image on the wall from his brain, and immediately regretted it. His gaze landed on a glass étagère filled with pictures of Drake with all sorts of men. Like a moth to the flame, he couldn't stop himself from walking over to get a better look.

Some of the people in the pictures may have been Drake's friends, but the body language in most of the shots made it clear there was more to it. Hell, the man had his hand down the front of a guy's pants in one picture, and in another, a different guy was licking his neck.

"Why are you standing up?" Andrew was suddenly at his side. "Here, I brought you a protein bar. That's all Drake had in his kitchen, but I checked and there's no whey in it."

Caleb couldn't believe they were talking about whether there was dairy in food when there were pictures of Andrew's boyfriend in various states of undress with any number of men. He wasn't sure if he wanted to strangle Drake for being a slut or Andrew for having such incredibly poor judgment in his dating choices.

"Andrew tells me you're a photographer," Drake said, making Caleb realize he was back in the room. Fucker was like a ninja tornado. "As you can tell, I'm obsessed with pictures."

"I'm obsessed with getting the hell out of here," Caleb muttered under his breath. An elbow to the ribs had him glaring mutinously at Andrew. "What the hell, Drew?" he hissed, rubbing the abused spot on his side.

Andrew ignored him completely. "You ready to go, Drake? I think we need to get some food into Caleb. He doesn't do well when he's hungry."

"Yeah, sure."

Caleb let Andrew pull him out of the apartment and into the car, but he refused to engage in Drake's attempts at conversation. After he didn't do more than grunt in response to any of Drake's questions, Andrew smoothly took over the dialogue for the rest of the drive. They walked up to the restaurant in silence, which would have been uncomfortable if Caleb wasn't so busy being pissed.

"Uh, I made a reservation, but..." Andrew looked back and forth between the hostess stand and them. There was a long line in a small space, so all three of them couldn't go wait. But it was clear Andrew didn't want to leave him alone with Drake. Caleb couldn't blame him. He wasn't sure what he'd do to the little slut if he had half a chance.

"Go ahead, Andrew. We don't mind waiting out front." Drake smiled sweetly at him. "Isn't that right, Caleb?"

Was this guy serious? "That's right. I don't mind at all." Caleb glared at Drake. "Go ahead, Drew."

Andrew shifted from foot to foot nervously before finally walking away and leaving the two of them in a quiet spot at the corner of the building.

"Damn, man." Drake rounded on him. "I've never been accused of being a sweetheart or anything, but you turn being an asshole into a competitive sport."

Caleb couldn't believe the nerve of this guy. "You're calling me an asshole? I'm not the one whose apartment is a shrine to promiscuity!"

"Are you serious?" Drake asked incredulously. "That's your problem? So what, now I'm supposed to apologize for liking sex?"

"Noooo," Caleb drew out the word like he was talking to a small child. "Liking sex is fine. You're just not supposed to like it with people other than your *boyfriend*."

"Oh, that is such bullshit. Are you listening to yourself? I'm dating Andrew and suddenly every guy I've ever been with has to be forgotten?"

"You don't have to forget them, but there's no reason to throw them in Andrew's face. They're in the past and he's supposed to be your future. It hurts him to see you with other guys!"

Caleb expected Drake to yell back. After all, they were having quite an escalating back and forth. So he was surprised when Drake's expression softened, along with his volume.

"Did Andrew say that to you, or are you superimposing your own views on our relationship?"

Great. Now he was being psychoanalyzed.

"Oh, wait, I'm sorry," Caleb said deadpan. "Were you saying something? I nodded off there for a second."

"Oh, for shit's sake, turn down the bitchy. I get it. You're all up in my face standing up for your friend. Point made and taken. But you may want to talk to Andrew about our relationship before you keep making an ass of yourself. It's not like we're exclusive."

Caleb was bug-eyed. "I can't believe you just admitted it like that."

"Admitted what?" Drake looked genuinely confused.

"Did you just tell me that you're cheating on Andrew?"

"No. Cheating implies that we're exclusive, which, as I just said, we're not."

"Does Andrew kn—"

"Our table's ready." Andrew interrupted. "Drake, do you mind giving us a minute?"

"No problem." Drake smiled at him and Caleb knew it was genuine this time. "I care about Andrew. I'm not lying and I'm not hiding anything." He leaned up and kissed Andrew's cheek and then walked away.

"I should have told you, huh?" Andrew asked sheepishly.

"I'm not sure exactly what I haven't been told, but, yeah. Drew, what the hell?"

"We have an open relationship."

"An open relationship?"

"Yes."

"I don't understand," Caleb said.

Andrew raised one eyebrow and gave him a lopsided grin. "You need me to explain the concept to you, Cae?"

"I need you to explain how my friend who has spent the past decade looking for a partner just suddenly decided he wanted a fuck buddy."

"It isn't like that."

Caleb wrapped his arm around Andrew's shoulder and cupped the back of his neck. He stroked the smooth skin with this thumb in a gesture so familiar it had an automatic calming effect on both of them. "Then tell me how it is, Drew. Explain it to me."

Andrew dropped his forehead against Caleb's. "I still want a partner, but you know how it's always been for me, Cae. How many times I've tried the whole monogamy thing and had it fail. I think maybe it isn't meant to work that way. At least not for me. So I'm looking for something different in a partner this time."

"Oh, Drew." Caleb stroked Andrew's cheek. "You're going to find someone who cherishes you, who doesn't want or need anybody else, and—"

"You don't know that, Caleb!" Andrew snapped then took in a calming breath. "I thought I knew what I wanted, but now... Look, you know what happened with my parents. I just...I need to try it this way."

Caleb never thought he'd see the day Andrew gave up on finding Mister Right. The man had always been so committed to the search, so unwavering in what he wanted out of life and the man he hoped would someday share it. And now...well, at least Andrew's fear of turning into his father hadn't come to fruition. It seemed he'd chosen his mother's path instead. Caleb felt like his heart was breaking.

Andrew rubbed his hands up and down Caleb's arms. "Try to understand, Cae. Please don't hate me."

"You know I could never hate you. Not ever."

"I know," Andrew nodded. "I know." He straightened up and wiped his hands on his pants. "We can talk more later, but Drake's waiting inside and he's leaving on a flight tomorrow. Can we please try to rescue this night? I really think you two'll hit it off. Don't make him suffer because I was too chickenshit to give you the backstory. Please give him a chance, Cae. For me?"

There was no way Caleb could refuse that request. He'd never been able to refuse his friend anything. So he squared his shoulders and gave Andrew a reassuring nod, even though he wasn't sure he was physically capable of being in a good mood at that moment. "Okay, let's go in there."

They walked into the restaurant side by side and sat down. Caleb smiled weakly at Drake and reached for his water glass, hoping to buy himself another couple of seconds before he had to make nice. Just then a woman tried to squeeze behind his chair and knocked him forward, causing the water to splash over his hand. Unfazed, she kept right on going without so much as an "excuse me."

Caleb glared at her and noticed her too-small shirt. It was decorated with rhinestones spelling "Jesus is my personal trainer."

"I bet that's pretty cheap," he muttered.

"Yeah," Drake agreed. "But by the look of things it isn't very effective."

Caleb laughed so hard he was sure he'd have been spitting out his water if he'd actually been able to take a drink.

"I think you and I are going to get along just fine," he said to Drake, almost feeling like he meant it.

When he saw Andrew beam at him, he knew he'd do anything he could to get there.

CHAPTER SIXTEEN

2003

"YOU WERE supposed to call me last night when you got home." Andrew couldn't manage a sufficiently accusatory tone when his tongue felt three times its normal size. Maybe he should have stopped at three mojitos, but Drake had been flying all over the bar, having such a great time, and Andrew was having fun watching him. Well, at least the parts he remembered were fun.

"Quit shouting, Drew, damn. This newfangled telephone technology means you can talk at a regular volume and the person on the other end will hear you just fine."

"It's too early for sarcasm, Cae. And my eyes hurt too much to yell. You're probably still drunk from last night." Andrew placed a pillow over his eyes, plunging himself into complete darkness. He sighed in relief.

"Hi, Mister Pot. I see you've met Mister Kettle," Caleb said.

Andrew grunted in response.

"Oh, and by the way, I'm not hungover and I did call

you when I got in last night," Caleb added.

"Nuh-uh."

"Yuh-huh."

"Nuh-uh."

"I refuse to do this," Caleb said. "Check your call history when we hang up. I called you."

Andrew was silent for a few a beats, trying to figure out whether Caleb could be right about the phone call. Considering how much he'd had to drink, he decided chances were pretty high.

"Sorry. Guess I was so drunk I don't remember talking to you."

"It's not that you don't remember," Caleb laughed. At least Andrew thought it was a laugh. At the end there, it sounded more like a pained moan. "It's that you didn't know you were talking to me. I don't think I've ever heard you so out of it."

"Yeah," Andrew sighed. "I've gotta stop trying to keep up with Drake. The man's like a machine."

"There's probably a raunchy joke there somewhere," Caleb replied. "But I feel too shitty to come up with it."

Hearing that Caleb wasn't feeling well had Andrew reaching for focus in his fuzzy brain.

"What's wrong? Was it a bad date?"

"Well, let me put it this way: the best part of my night was that 'ahh' moment when you take off your skinny jeans and you can feel your dick again."

Andrew chuckled, but the resulting throb in his temples made him regret it.

"Hey, if he got your pants off, the night wasn't a total loss."

"*I* got my pants off. When I got home. *Alone.* Like I told you last night, I feel like shit."

"What're your symptoms?"

"Oh, so you've whipped out the doctor hat? Sexy."

Andrew snickered. "Right. 'Oh, baby, tell me your symptoms.' It's the hottest line around. All the phone sex operators are using it."

"I know you can't see me, so I'll give you a play by play. I'm sticking my tongue out at you. And if I had just a little bit more energy, I'd pick up my hand and flip you off."

"That's scintillating. Thanks for the update. Now tell me what hurts."

Andrew waited, figuring he'd just set Caleb up perfectly for some biting remark or a dirty joke. When neither came, he began to worry in earnest.

"My stomach. I think I might have the flu or something. Last night it just sort of hurt a little, but now it's worse and I'm pretty sure I'm gonna throw up."

Andrew shot up in bed, all concerns about the too-bright morning light forgotten.

"Where exactly does it hurt, Caleb? And what do you mean it hurt a little and now it's worse? How much worse? Can you describe the pain?"

"Uh, it's my lower stomach, I guess."

"Left side? Right side? Middle? Where does it hurt?" Andrew was out of bed, digging a pair of jeans and long-sleeved T-shirt out of his dresser.

"Right side. Well, it's the right side now. Last night it was like the middle of my belly. Maybe something I ate had chicken stock. I asked the waiter twenty questions, like always, but I swear those people lie half the time." He stopped talking and groaned miserably. "I'm pretty sure I'm gonna hurl soon, so maybe it'll pass."

"Maybe," Andrew agreed as he tucked his wallet into his pocket and looked for his tennis shoes. "I want you to put your hand over the area that hurts, just rest it there gently." He heard the sheets shifting. "You doing it, Cae?"

"Yeah."

"Good," he nodded, not that Caleb could see him. "Now press down hard and move your hand back up quickly."

"Ow! Shit, that hurt. Feels like someone stabbed me. Ow, ow, ow," Caleb whimpered.

"Caleb?" Andrew had his keys in his hand and he was almost to his front door. "Caleb, I need you to get dressed and go to the hospital."

"What? Why? It's just food poisoning or maybe the flu. No reason to get hysterical."

"You could be right. But it sounds like it could be your appendix, and I can't tell without examining you. I'm getting into my car now, and I'll take the first flight out, but if you've been hurting since last night and it's appendicitis, we don't have time to wait until I get there."

"I don't wanna get up."

As worried as he was, Andrew couldn't hold back a soft smile in response to Caleb's whiney voice. It was adorable, such a contrast to his friend's usual snarky attitude. Of course, the snark was pretty hot.

Great. I'm a total pig. Andrew shook off his wandering thoughts.

"I know you don't feel up to moving, but you don't have a choice. I'll stay on the phone with you while you get dressed and get a cab. I'll be there as soon as I can, Cae."

"Fine, fine. I'll go to the hospital. But you don't need to fly up here. I'm sure it's nothing, and you have patients tomorrow."

Right, like he was going to be able to concentrate on anything with Caleb being sick.

ANDREW HAD his phone open and was dialing Caleb before the plane got to the gate. Three failed attempts to get an answer later, he was calling Caleb's mother.

"Andrew?"

"Hi, Barbara. I'm—"

"I'm glad you got my message, dear," she interrupted.

Barbara had called him? When? Why? What did she

say?

Andrew shook his head. He needed to calm down or get some sleep or something. The answers to all those questions were probably waiting for him on a message on his phone.

Or he could pay attention to the woman talking in his ear.

"He's fine, but I'm sure he'd feel better if you were here. Do you think you can make time to come in?"

Yeah, that explanation didn't help at all. He unfolded himself from the tiny airplane seat and remained hunched over, waiting for his turn to cut into the aisle and walk off the plane.

"I'm at Kennedy, Barbara. My plane just landed. I tried to call Caleb, but he didn't answer. Are you with him?"

"You're here? Oh, that's wonderful. Yes, I'm with Caleb at University Hospital. The surgery went well and he's resting."

For the first time in his life, the thought of surgery made Andrew light-headed. And considering his line of work, it was a very frequent thought.

"Surgery?" he asked in a strained voice. "What surgery?"

Were the people in front of him somehow regenerating? He swore there hadn't been nearly as many of them when they'd boarded. He fisted the hand not holding the phone in order to keep himself from pushing through the crowd.

"The one to remove his appendix. Did you get my message?"

Oh, damn. He had been hoping for mild food poisoning or a cold. Andrew finally managed to squeeze himself off the plane and immediately started running.

"I'll be there as soon as I can," he huffed into the phone as he sprinted through the airport in a desperate effort to get to Caleb.

ANDREW HAD been in Caleb's hospital room for about ten minutes when Barbara walked in holding a coffee. Years of rearing went out the window when he didn't get up from his chair. It was rude, and he'd been raised better, but there was no way he could bring himself to move even an inch away from his friend.

"I think it's making him feel better," he explained with a tilt of his chin toward where his hand was petting Caleb's hair.

Barbara didn't seem to mind. She just walked over to him, kissed his cheek, and smiled down at him fondly.

"How is it that we haven't seen each other in close to two years? We really can't let it go that long again. You look gre—" Her eyes darted from the piercings in his ears, to the bar through his eyebrow, and finally to the tattoos on his forearms, visible because his shirtsleeves were pushed up. Her brow furrowed as she focused on the fuzzy squirrel on his T-shirt with a comment bubble next to him proclaiming "I like nuts." "Ehm, did he wake up while I was gone?"

Andrew chuckled. One of his favorite things about Caleb's family was that they didn't blow smoke. Oh, Barbara's approach was much more subtle than her son's. It didn't involve snippy comments or eye rolls, but she didn't feed anyone bullshit. She thought he looked weird, and she wouldn't say otherwise. Andrew appreciated that honesty.

"He was sleeping when I got here. I don't think he was able to get much rest last night, and then there's the anesthesia from the surgery. He'll probably be out for a while."

Barbara's gaze flicked from Caleb's face to Andrew's hand, which was still moving gently over messy brown hair. If Caleb had been awake, he would have been demanding hair product and a mirror. The man was persnickety about being out of the house without his hair just so.

Truth be told, Andrew preferred Caleb's hair like this—soft and slightly disheveled. And he loved knowing he was the only person who got to see Caleb this way. The only one who knew the stripped-down version of the always immaculately put together man.

"How long can you stay, dear?"

"Hmm?" Andrew looked away from Caleb's sleeping face to focus on Barbara. "Oh, umm, I'll stay as long as he needs me. The surgery was laparoscopic, so his recovery shouldn't take more than a week or two."

Okay, so he'd reviewed the chart when he'd gotten to the hospital. And he'd done a quick exam of the incision points. He went back to analyzing Caleb's sleeping face. His features were relaxed, seemingly not in any pain.

"And there's not an issue with you being away from work unexpectedly like this?" Barbara asked.

He shook his head. "No. The other doctors in my practice are covering for me. We do that for each other. Last month, I covered for a guy whose wife had a baby. That's the benefit of being part of a group."

"Yes, but Caleb isn't your wife." Barbara's tone was so odd it had Andrew turning away from Caleb to look at her, but her expression was inscrutable.

"I've known Caleb longer than that doctor has been married to his wife. Both his current wife and his ex-wife combined. Family is family. Don't worry, Barbara. I'll make sure Caleb's back on his feet before I leave."

ANDREW WAS on his hands and knees, face lowered to the ground, trying to plug a new DVD player into the AV jack in Caleb's television. "You're sure I can put everything in this hole?" He heard the beginnings of a laugh from behind him and then a groan.

"Quit it, Drew," Caleb panted. "It hurts to laugh."

He looked over his shoulder and furrowed his brow. "What? What'd I say?" The couch pillow that hit his face had him grinning. "Oh, you know you love me. Quit your whining."

After he had everything hooked up, he climbed to his feet and walked into Caleb's kitchen. "You want some juice, Cae?" He didn't wait for an answer, just poured Caleb a glass of cranberry juice and grabbed a banana for himself.

"So," he said as he settled on the couch next to Caleb and handed him the juice. "This is a pretty big banana. Do you think I'll be able to get my mouth around it?"

"You're ridiculous," Caleb said with a dramatic sigh and an accompanying eye roll.

"*Hilarious.* I think the word you're looking for is hilarious. And thank you."

Andrew rested his hand on Caleb's stomach and explored gently, making sure he was healing.

"Whatever. So did you join that rugby team yet?"

A few of Andrew's colleagues played in a men's rugby league. They'd been nagging him to join their all-physician team, apparently convinced that his young age would trump his complete lack of experience with the sport.

"Not going to happen." He shook his head. "If I want to donate blood, I'll do it the old-fashioned way. Not that I can donate blood, mind you, because I'm a man who's had sex with another man, even once, since 1977. Assholes."

"Are we still talking about your future rugby teammates?"

"Ha ha. So what happened with that guy you were dating? Not the one from the other night, the other guy from before that." It seemed like Caleb had been jumping from one man to the next lately. They rarely made it past the first date and those that did were usually set loose within a date or two after that. Andrew wanted his friend to find what he had with Drake—someone steady in his life, a boyfriend. Well, maybe not exactly the same thing he had with Drake, but Andrew wouldn't let himself think about those aspects of his relationship.

"Oh God, it was awful," Caleb groaned. "He took me to a karaoke bar. Went on and on about how he used to sing with this garage band in high school and then he gets on stage and belts out 'You're The One That I Want.' When he was doing the John Travolta lines, it sounded like he was strangling cats. Then he got to the Olivia Newton-John verses, and it should have been embarrassing that he was doing both roles, but truthfully, by that point I was just grateful because my ears started bleeding so I didn't have to hear the rest of the song."

"You're exaggerating!" Andrew said, trying to keep a straight face, but unable to hold back a chuckle at Caleb's animated description.

"No, I'm not." Caleb shook his head. "When he was mercifully done with the song, the entire room started clapping. Not to show appreciation, mind you, but to thank him for stopping."

Andrew was now laughing so hard, tears were rolling

down his cheeks. He eventually managed to get himself under control. "Okay, so he's a bad singer." A bit more laughter escaped. "There are worse things. You've got to give people more of a chance."

"Funny you should say that," Caleb responded. "Because I did. It was our third date, so I figured I should go back to his place after the bar. He had the dining room table all set, like with chargers, stemware, candles, the whole bit."

"That's nice," Andrew interrupted. "How can you possibly find fault in that?"

"Yeah, it would've been nice if we'd been eating dinner at his place. But we'd gone out to dinner before karaoke. He just keeps his table set like that all the time. Like he's living in a model home or something."

Andrew bit his lip to keep from smiling. He didn't want to encourage Caleb's pickiness. The man was never going to find someone if he expected perfection. That was a hard lesson to learn, one Andrew reminded himself of more often than he'd have liked. "Well, at least he cares about making sure his place looks nice. You of all people can appreciate that."

"Uh-huh. There's a nice-looking house and then there's your name in neon lights over your bed. I sort of froze when I walked in and saw that, and he gave me this, like, totally smarmy look and said, '*Nice, right? They're festive. Just like the party in my pants.*'"

There was no way for Andrew to hold back the

horrified gasp.

"Yeah, I know," Caleb said in response to his friend's reaction. "I gave up at that point. Just hightailed it out of there."

"I'm sorry, Cae." Andrew caressed Caleb's cheek. "You've had the worst dating luck lately."

"Ah, no worries." Caleb stretched out and rested his head on Andrew's lap. "Bad dates make good stories. Even with the lack of sex, I figure it's a net gain." He wiggled as if trying to find a comfortable position and his eyelids drooped. "Besides." He yawned and closed his eyes. "Why do I need a boyfriend when I have you?"

CHAPTER SEVENTEEN

2004

"'LO."

"Hey. Why do you sound like death warmed over?" Caleb asked even though he already knew the answer.

"Went out last night. Drank too much."

"Andrew," Caleb sighed and tried to collect his thoughts. He didn't want to get into another fight about Drake. Truth was, he didn't even blame Drake anymore. It was going on two years into Andrew's relationship, and Caleb could finally admit that his hostile feelings were rooted in jealousy. He'd always been the person Andrew could turn to for everything, and he hated that Drake now shared any part of that. "What're you doing?" Caleb finally said, sadness evident in his voice.

"I don't know what you mean."

Great. Now Andrew was digging in his heels. Caleb could imagine him sitting on his sofa with his arms crossed over chest defiantly. Maybe even pouting.

"I mean," Caleb started, trying as hard as he could

not to sound sarcastic or angry or anything else that would instigate a fight. "I thought you and Drake were going to stay in last night and watch the *Sex and the City* finale. How did that turn into going out drinking? Again."

"I don't know. We watched the finale, and then Drake said it was too early to call it a night. Said he wanted to party, so we went out."

Of course, that was what happened. It was what always happened. Caleb tried to phrase his next sentence without blaming Drake, knowing that was a surefire way to veer off topic.

"It seems like you're partying an awful lot lately, Drew. Too much."

"Too much?" Andrew laughed bitterly. "Wonderful. You tell me I party too much, and Drake tells me I'm too uptight. I can't win for losing."

Caleb held his mouth closed so tightly his jaw ached. It was pointless; he couldn't hold back a jab about Drake.

"What is this, junior high school? He's pressuring you into drinking now?"

"It isn't like that, Cae. Drake isn't making me do anything. How many times do I need to explain it to you?"

Andrew sounded so damn tired that Caleb almost regretted pushing the conversation. But he was too worried about his friend to let it go.

"Apparently, at least once more," Caleb said. "Seeing as how he's telling you you're uptight unless you drink yourself sick."

"That's not what he says. It's just...it's hard to keep up with him and—"

"Why do you need to keep up with him? Again, this isn't junior high. We're adults and—"

"Caleb!" Andrew raised his voice, which was unusual enough to stop Caleb mid-sentence. "If you're going to ask me something, then you need to let me finish explaining."

"Sorry," Caleb whispered.

"'S okay. Anyway, what I was saying is that he likes to party and, I didn't tell you this before because I knew you'd add it to your reasons to hate Drake list, but—"

"I don't hate Drake," Caleb said without much conviction.

"Right. You two are best friends. That's why you plan your visits when he's out of town and you get that I-just-ate-something-nasty look on your face whenever his name comes up."

"I'm trying, Drew. Honestly, I am. I just don't like how much you've been drinking and partying lately, and the cheating thing still pisses—"

"He doesn't cheat. We have an open relationship."

Caleb rolled his eyes, took in a deep breath, and then rolled them again for good measure. He knew for a fact that the relationship was only open in one direction. Regardless of the title, Andrew wouldn't fool around with someone while he had a boyfriend. And both Caleb and Andrew had had the blue balls to prove it during every one of their visits over the past two years.

"Fine," Caleb conceded to avoid an argument.

"Okay." Andrew let out a breath before he continued. "Don't make me regret telling you this, but Drake's not just drinking. He's using meth. A lot."

"Oh, Drew."

"I know. I'm trying to get him to stop, but when I explain the damage he's doing to his body with it, he laughs me off. Says I'm uptight and I shouldn't worry so much. So I figure if I go out with him and have fun, he'll think I understand and then he'll listen to me."

"I get what you're trying to do," Caleb said, even though he didn't actually mean it. Andrew's logic didn't make sense to him. "But sacrificing your liver doesn't seem like the best approach here."

"Yeah, well, what do you suggest, Cae? Meth tears people apart and he's already immunocompromised from the HIV. If he doesn't think I understand, how am I going to save him?"

"It's not your job to save him!" Now Caleb was yelling. He took in deep breaths to calm down. "He's an adult, Drew. He is responsible for himself."

"Yeah, like that matters. Look at my parents. We both know being an adult doesn't mean shit as far as good decision-making. Not that they listen to me either."

"Drew," Caleb sighed once again. "It's not your

responsibility to fix your parents' problems. You tried everything you could, but they have to make their own decisions."

"Right. I tried to save them and failed. My father's still a cheating shit and my mother's still married to him. So far, I'm having about the same streak of success with Drake."

All right, the conversation wasn't getting them anywhere. Caleb tried to think of a different approach.

"If what you're doing isn't working, then there's no point in continuing it, right? If Drake isn't pushing you to drink so much—"

"He's not," Andrew insisted.

"Good. If he's not pushing you to drink so much, then you can stop. You can still party with your boyfriend without making yourself sick. And you can keep talking to him about the drugs."

"You really think that'll work?" Andrew asked desperately. "You think he'll listen to me and stop?"

"I honestly don't know what he'll do. But what I do know is that it's all you *can* do."

"I'M PRETTY sure Drake isn't taking his meds," Andrew said as soon as Caleb answered the phone.

"That's good, right?" Caleb asked. "You've been trying to get him to stop taking drugs for months."

"I'm not talking about the meth, Cae. I'm talking about his antiretrovirals."

"Oh, why do you think he isn't taking his medication?"

"Well, uh, I stay over at his place sometimes and I, uh, needed something from his medicine cabinet once, and when I opened it, I couldn't help but notice—"

"This conversation will be exponentially less painful if you cut the crap, Drew. You were snooping through your boyfriend's medicine cabinet and..." He trailed off, waiting for Andrew to complete the story.

"Fine. I was snooping. I've been looking at the dates on his prescription bottles and counting his pills. He isn't taking them."

"Excellent. He has no problem shooting up or smoking or whatever the hell he does with street drugs, but pills his doctor prescribes are too much trouble. Have you considered smacking some sense into him, Drew? Because I think your boy's not right in the head."

"You know what? The sarcasm isn't helping me so cut it out. This is serious. I don't know what to do."

Caleb picked up the nearest object, a bowl he'd made in a ceramics class, and threw it against the wall. The loud crash was deeply satisfying.

"What was that?" Andrew asked.

"Nothing. Okay, so you know he isn't taking the antiretrovirals in his medicine cabinet. But what if that's an old prescription and he has new meds that he keeps somewhere else?"

There was silence for a few moments, and Caleb assumed Andrew was considering that possibility.

"Where else would he keep his meds, Cae?"

"Not everybody keeps medicine in the medicine cabinet. At the end of the day, that's just a name. Hell, lots of houses don't even have medicine cabinets. I just did a remodel last month where we pulled them all out and replaced them with hand painted mirr—"

"I've searched his entire bathroom and his kitchen," Andrew said the words in a rapid clip, clearly trying to get the confession out there.

Okay, so Andrew had already considered the possibility of a newer prescription. Not a surprise.

"What about his Dopp kit?" Caleb suggested.

"Why would he keep his meds there?"

"Because he's a flight attendant so he travels for work all the time. Maybe it's easier to remember if he just keeps his meds in the Dopp kit all the time. Did you look there?"

"No. But I can. I mean, he's on a trip now and I don't usually stay at his place, but I'm sure when he's back I can come up with some excuse and—"

"Or you could just ask him," Caleb suggested gently. "I don't understand why you're being stealthy about this, Drew. He's your boyfriend. Doesn't two years together mean you have a right to know about his health?"

"Probably, it's just...Drake's really into having his own

space and privacy and..."

Andrew sounded so defeated that it broke Caleb's heart. He hated how insecure Andrew was in his relationship, how worried he was about saying something wrong and upsetting his boyfriend. Blaming Drake would be satisfying, but Caleb didn't actually think it was Drake's doing. Andrew's ego had taken such a battering over the years of cheating boyfriends. Add that to his deep-seated desire to maintain a long-term relationship, and the man was always on edge, worried he'd do or say the wrong thing and lose yet another boyfriend.

"Okay," Andrew suddenly said. "I'll do it. I'll talk to him about what's going on with his antiretrovirals."

"CALEB?" ANDREW said, his voice hoarse.

"What's wrong, Drew? What happened?"

"It's Drake...he...he..." Andrew cried softly.

So Drake ended things. Damn it! Caleb should be pleased; he wasn't a fan of Andrew's relationship. But no matter what, Caleb wanted Andrew to be happy, and he knew happy meant avoiding another breakup and holding onto Drake. What on earth could the man have found fault with? Andrew did everything he wanted and practically worshiped the guy. Caleb took in a breath to start a rant about Drake being an ungrateful asshole and Andrew deserving much better when Andrew's sobbing stopped and he finished his sentence.

"Drake's in the hospital. I don't think he's going to make it."

"Shit! What happened?"

"I don't...pneumonia... I...I need you, Cae."

Caleb looked around his apartment to see if there was anything that needed to be done before he left. It was a pretty small space, and he kept it immaculate at all times. Not surprisingly, nothing was out of order.

"I'll take the next flight out, Drew. Text me the name of the hospital, and I'll be there as soon as I can."

It was the middle of the night by the time Caleb arrived at the hospital in Emile City. He found Andrew sitting in a small waiting room outside the intensive care unit. His friend was slumped in his chair, forearms across his knees and chin dropped down on his chest.

"Drew?" Caleb said when he walked in.

Hazy green eyes looked up at him and quickly filled with tears. Caleb rushed over and stood in front of Andrew. Immediately, Andrew leaned forward, resting his forehead on Caleb's chest.

"Shhh," he murmured quietly as he pet Andrew's hair. Eventually, Andrew calmed down and straightened in his chair. Caleb sat next to him.

"What's going on? Tell me what happened."

Andrew cleared his throat and nodded. "Well, I hadn't

seen Drake in what seemed like forever. He had a trip for work, and then he went out of town to visit some friends. After that he had another work trip. Anyway, when we talked on the phone, I noticed that he didn't sound right."

"What do you mean, not right?"

"He was coughing a lot, almost wheezing. Sometimes, he seemed tired." Andrew shrugged. "He wasn't right. It was obvious, so I told him to go see his doctor and he freaked, just like he did when I tried to talk to him about not taking his antiretrovirals. He replayed that whole 'just because he has a doctor for a boyfriend doesn't mean he wants to be treated like a patient all the time' argument."

"Like I said when you told me about that originally, caring about your boyfriend doesn't mean you're treating him like a patient." Not wanting to speak ill of Drake when the man was in the hospital, Caleb bit off any further comment. "Go on," he said.

"Well, he, uh, refused to talk about being sick, and then I tried asking him again about whether he was taking his medication and he refused to talk about that too. He didn't take my calls for the past week. And then..." Andrew squeezed his eyes shut. "His sister called to tell me he was in the ICU. Turns out he'd been home for a few days. He thought he had a cold. She went to see him and ended up calling an ambulance when he passed out."

Andrew turned to the side and buried his face in Caleb's neck. Caleb wrapped his arm around Andrew's shoulder and held onto him.

"He has pneumonia? That's what you said on the phone, right?"

"Yeah," Andrew nodded. "But it's serious. You know he hasn't been taking care of himself, his immune system's shot, he didn't go to his doctor when he should have. Apparently, he's coinfected, which I didn't realize."

"Coinfected?" Caleb asked.

"Yeah, he has Hep C too." Andrew swallowed thickly. "The prognosis isn't good, Cae. I don't think there's anything I can do to save him."

"HOW IS it you only have two suitcases?" Andrew asked. "You pack more when we go on vacation for a week."

Caleb looked over his shoulder to where Andrew was sitting on the bed in his guestroom, now Caleb's bedroom. His friend had dark circles under his eyes, his skin was pale, and he was nervously chewing on the side of his lower lip.

"My entire apartment is boxed and on the way here. I figured with a moving truck bringing the big items, it made no sense for me to lug anything other than what I'd need for the next week or two on the plane. Everything else will be here soon."

"The movers are on their way?" Andrew asked.

"Yup," Caleb assured him for the third time since he'd

arrived back in Emile City. He'd stayed for a couple of days after Drake's funeral, and then he flew home, packed up his life, and moved to be closer to Andrew. Much closer, actually. He was moving into Andrew's house.

With his last shirt hung, Caleb closed the closet door and walked over to the bed. He sat right next to Andrew and put his hand on his friend's knee, giving it a light squeeze. Andrew leaned into him for a second, then he stiffened and stood. He walked to the door.

"I'm, uh, going to turn in. It's been a long day."

"Drew?"

"Yeah?" Andrew stopped in his tracks and answered without turning around to look at Caleb.

"You don't have to sleep alone."

Andrew didn't answer right away. He stood just inside the bedroom and didn't move a muscle. Then his entire body seemed to fold in on itself, and he walked out, answering Caleb once again without facing him.

"Yeah, I think I do, Cae. Good night."

CHAPTER EIGHTEEN

2005

ANDREW WALKED into the kitchen to find Caleb hunched over the table with a slew of photos and papers spread in front of him. The man's ass was tipped up, the muscular globes evident under the well-fitting trousers.

"What're you doing?"

"Umm, just going through my proposal for David Miller's house remodel. Getting this project would be a total coup. Not only is his remodel great, but he's a major referral source because he's like the top Realtor in EC West. So if he likes my work, it could really spread my name out there and help me get my design studio off the ground."

"David Miller?" Andrew grumbled.

"Uh-huh," Caleb replied distractedly as he shuffled some pictures around.

"Black hair, blue eyes, all muscle-bound. That David Miller?"

"Yeah. Hey, can you hand me that portfolio case?" Caleb pointed to a cocoa leather Gucci case sitting on the counter.

"Sure," Andrew said, reaching for the case. "Here you go. So he's some sort of super-Realtor? David Miller, I mean."

"Yeah." Caleb nodded. "He's supposed to be the best. Totally brilliant at getting houses sold or finding buyers the perfect place. Actually, I think it'd be good for me to set up a time for all three of us to grab dinner. It doesn't make any sense for you to be renting, and I'm sure David can give you some good ideas about what's out there to buy." He started picking up papers and photos and slipping them into the portfolio.

"I thought you liked this house," Andrew grumbled. "I don't see why we need your fabulous Realtor to get involved."

"I do like this house, Drew, but it's silly for you not to buy. You can afford a house, so why throw money away on rent?" He stopped talking and chewed on his bottom lip as he took a final inventory of his documents. "Okay, let's see, I have the floor plan, the furniture layout, color samples, a picture of myself beating off to a photo spread in *Elle Decor* magazine." Caleb winked as he said the last one, then got everything gathered and zipped up the leather case. He straightened and beamed at Andrew. "I think I'm set to show David I'm the best designer for the job."

"Are you sure you're angling for a job, Cae? It sounds to me like you might be after something more personal with Mister Brain-Brawn Combo Punch."

Caleb ignored Andrew's rude tone. It was par for the course lately. He had practically worn through his copy of *On*

Death and Dying trying to figure out how to help Andrew heal.

"David and I already tried the dating thing. It lasted about five minutes," Caleb said.

"When did you date David Miller? How come I don't know about this?"

Caleb rolled his eyes and took a final look at his proposal. "We had lunch together last week. I didn't mention it because it could barely be classified as a date. Like I said, a few minutes into it we realized there was no chemistry, and we started talking shop. Good thing, too, because I need a job more than I need a date."

Confident that he had all his materials ready to go, Caleb glanced at Andrew. There was an odd look on his friend's face. It seemed like relief or maybe even a smidgen of happiness. But then it was gone before Caleb could be sure, and he chalked it up to wishful thinking. He hadn't seen Andrew happy since before Drake died.

"You don't *need* a job, Cae. We're not exactly hurting for cash."

"*I'm* not hurting for cash. *You're* rolling in it," Caleb teased. "But that's beside the point. I *want* a job. Working is important. Plus, I like what I do. There're lots of shiny fabrics and glitter and stuff."

"David Miller is going to use glitter in his house remodel?" Andrew asked skeptically.

Caleb looked fondly at Andrew. The years hadn't completely washed away his charming naïveté. "Well, maybe not so much, but I'll work on it." He tugged on the shirtsleeves of his pale-blue dress shirt and flattened the front of his narrow-cut black trousers. "How do I look?"

Andrew's eyes raked Caleb's body from top to bottom and back up again. Now, that look Caleb recognized. It was pure, unadulterated lust, and it made heat surge through Caleb.

"You look good," Andrew said, his voice rough and husky.

If Caleb thought he had so much as a chance of getting his friend into bed, he would have postponed the meeting with David. He hadn't gotten laid in an embarrassingly long time, and he was painfully horny. But he knew it was hopeless. Andrew had been completely hands-off since the day Drake died. Or, more accurately, he'd been completely hands-off with anybody except Drake since the two had started dating, and the man's death hadn't done a thing to curb the trend.

Some open relationship that had turned out to be. Just as Caleb had predicted, Drake had slept around and Andrew had remained faithful, was still remaining faithful. Sometimes it made Caleb want to tear out his hair, but he tried to hide his frustration and remain supportive.

"Thanks, Drew." Caleb put his empty hand on Andrew's shoulder and leaned up to kiss his cheek. "I'll see you later. Wish me luck."

"COME ON, Drew. It's just drinks. Two hours, max," Caleb wheedled.

"Uh-huh." Andrew kept his face buried in his book and didn't move from his semi-permanent position on the retro tweed couch Caleb had recently purchased. It was extra-long, which was perfect for Andrew's tall frame.

"Drew, come on!" Caleb pulled the book out of Andrew's hands and set it on the antique walnut sofa table. "You can't spend all your time either at work or in this house. Going out and doing something social will be good for you." Andrew didn't respond. Just lay on the couch and looked up at the ceiling. Caleb sighed. "Drew? Are you listening to me?"

"Yeah, I heard you. And I'll give it a lot of thought. Promise. Right after I'm done washing my hair. Oh, and if there's nothing on TV, of course. Can you pass me the remote?"

Caleb passed an orange silk throw pillow directly to Andrew's face.

"Very nice," Andrew said from underneath the pillow, his voice muffled. "You're really Mister Maturity."

"Yeah, well, do you see these shiny new shoes I walked in here wearing? I can walk right back out in them."

"Who's stopping you, Dorothy? Go ahead and clap those heels together."

After counting to ten and then counting again, Caleb took a deep breath and made sure to keep his voice calm and supportive. "Look, Drew, the last thing I want is to complicate our friendship with feelings, but I'm worried about you."

"Sounds like a personal problem to me," Andrew responded.

"Andrew Thompson!" Caleb lost his temper and raised his voice, which was rare. He stalked around the sofa and straddled Andrew's hips, picking the pillow up off his chest and smacking him in the face with it while glaring into his eyes. "Don't you dare take that tone with me. You are either going to get your ass off this couch and go out with me tonight or you're going to give me a damn good reason why you're not. I'm done letting you hide from the world."

"Here's a reason, Mister Mom. Being a third wheel on your date isn't my idea of a good time," Andrew said dryly.

Caleb raised his face to the ceiling, growled in frustration, and then took in yet another calming breath. He was aiming for calming, anyway, but not so much accomplishing it. "For the millionth time, I am not dating David Miller."

"Look, Cae, I know how much time you've been spending with David the past few months."

Andrew clicked the new metal ball in his tongue against his teeth and Caleb furrowed his brow. Something about that piercing niggled at Caleb. It wasn't that he didn't like Andrew's body mods; in fact, he found them hot as hell. But there was just something off about this one.

"I get that you're trying to keep your relationship from me so I don't think about Drake," Andrew continued. "But it's okay." His tone sounded anything but okay. "You can have a boyfriend without feeling guilty that mine died."

Caleb's jaw dropped. "I'm to the point now where I can't tell if you're being passive-aggressive or delusional." He cupped Andrew's cheeks and bent down so they were mere inches apart, and then he talked quietly, carefully enunciating every word. "Listen to me very carefully, Drew. David Miller and I are. Not. Interested. In. Each. Other. He's my friend and my client. I've been spending a lot of time with him because I'm helping do a substantial remodel on his house. That's my job. You won't be a third wheel because I am not now, nor will I ever be, dating David Miller. In fact, David has a new boyfriend. Raul. Nice guy. He's a doctor, so you two will have a lot to talk about if he's there tonight."

He stood up and pulled on Andrew's arm. "You will now get up, take a quick shower because you stink, put on something at least halfway decent, and join me for an evening of fun with friends." Caleb made the demand through gritted teeth.

"They're not my friends," Andrew muttered under his breath as he stomped into the bedroom.

"They'll be your friends as soon as you meet them and give them a chance, you annoying, stubborn ass!" Caleb called after him. "Now go shower before I strangle you!"

"Jeez, Cae." Andrew looked at him over his shoulder with wide eyes. "There's no reason to get violent."

"Urgh!"

Caleb flopped down on the sofa and then bolted up

when he realized he was flattening his hair after having spent fifteen minutes getting it to stand in a just-got-out-of-bed look. Deciding that staying vertical was safer, he stood and paced back and forth across the living room. He needed to find a way to get Andrew to join the land of the living, and he was plum out of ideas. Forcibly dragging the man into social situations seemed to be the only hope, so that was what Caleb was going to do.

"I'm ready." Andrew shuffled out of the bedroom. His blond hair was still wet and barely combed. He wore loose jeans and a baggy navy hoody, both with tattered hems, and his red All Stars. "So, Cae, how do I look?" he asked defiantly.

Well, he didn't look dressed to go out, that was for sure, but Caleb met his eyes and answered honestly.

"You look gorgeous, Drew." He rubbed Andrew's upper arm briskly and tugged on his elbow. "Come on, our friends are waiting at Two of a Kind. It'll be a fun night. I think someone even said something about karaoke."

Andrew's entire face lit up. "I kick ass in karaoke!"

Oh, wow, did it ever feel good to see Andrew smile. Caleb grinned at him. "I know. You rock it. What're you going to sing?"

"Hmmm, this is a critical decision. Let's not rush it. Preliminarily, I'm thinking something by Madonna."

After an animated discussion that lasted all the way to the bar, Andrew still hadn't chosen a song for his evening karaoke debut. To Caleb, it didn't matter. He felt lighter than he had in months walking into Two of a Kind because his friend seemed truly happy. Andrew wasn't sulking or snapping at him, and he was even smiling. A real smile that reached his eyes. It took tremendous effort for Caleb to keep himself from pulling Andrew into a tight hug and telling him it was good to have him back. But the last thing he wanted was to risk ruining the delicate recovery Andrew seemed to be making.

"Caleb Lakes!"

Caleb heard his name being called moments after they walked in the door. He turned to his left to see bright blue eyes locked on him.

"Clark! Hey," he responded and smiled at the incredibly nice man walking toward him. Creamy skin and strawberry blond hair on a perfectly shaped body made Clark look like the all-American boy from either the fifties or the Victorian era.

"Clark, this is my roommate Andrew Thompson." Caleb wrapped his arm around Andrew and rested his hand on the small of Andrew's back, encouraging him to step forward. "Andrew, this is Clark Lehman."

"Ah, so you're the famous roommate," Clark said with a wide smile. "It's great to finally meet you."

Andrew put his left hand on Clark's shoulder and reached his right hand out to shake Clark's. "It's nice to meet you too, Clark."

A strapping man with shaggy dark hair joined them. He wrapped his arms around Clark's belly and pulled him away from Andrew and against a broad, muscular frame. If Caleb didn't know Noah, he might have been nervous in the face of the man's knee-buckling scowl. But, as Caleb expected, once Clark was in Noah's arms, his expression softened. He nuzzled his partner's neck.

"Hi, Noah," Caleb said with a chuckle. "Andrew, this is Clark's partner, Noah." Caleb pointed to Noah and then he grasped Andrew's hand and pulled him up against his side as he finished the introductions. "Noah, this is Andrew."

Noah raised one eyebrow and smirked. "Caleb talks about you all the time, but we were starting to wonder whether you were real. Honestly, you're harder to meet than those girlfriends from Canada guys often seem to meet in Niagara Falls."

Clark smiled fondly up at Noah. "I think what Noah means is that we're glad you had time to join us tonight."

"Thanks for inviting me. I've been looking forward to meeting Caleb's friends," Andrew said.

Caleb turned his face and whispered in Andrew's ear, "Bullshit. You haven't so much as asked the name of a single friend I've made in the six months I've lived here."

Andrew shifted so they were cheek to cheek, each of their mouths next to the other's ear. "It's not bullshit. I've wanted to meet them. Anybody important to you is somebody I want to meet."

The night was going better than Caleb could have hoped. He kissed Andrew's cheek and then turned toward his friends. Noah gave him a strange look.

"So, where are we sitting? Are David and Raul here yet?" Caleb asked.

"David's here," Clark replied. "He's saving a table in the corner for us. I think he went out with Raul last night, which means he's flying solo tonight."

"So frickin' weird." Caleb shook his head and laughed. "I don't understand why these guys put up with David. It's like he's intentionally pushing them away."

"I'm guessing it's because of his horse dick," Noah said. Clark's head snapped in his direction, and he pursed his lips disapprovingly. "What?" Noah asked. "Don't tell me you haven't heard Tim and Frank talk about David's cock. From what I understand, it's legendary."

Clark just sighed, shook his head, and continued walking, leading them to the table. Andrew and Caleb followed him. Noah fell into step on the other side of Caleb and gave him a knowing look.

"So Andrew's your *friend*, huh?" he said quietly enough only Caleb could hear him over the music.

Caleb furrowed his brow, confused by Noah's tone. "Yeah. My best friend since we were kids. And now he's also my roommate. Why do you ask?"

Noah's eyes dropped to Caleb's hand, which was still twined with Andrew's. "No reason," he said.

CHAPTER NINETEEN

2006

"I NEED to get roaring drunk tonight," Andrew said as he threw his keys into the copper bowl by the front door. He walked into the living room, flopped onto the sofa, and rubbed his eyes with the meaty part of his palms. "This day has been for absolute shit."

"What happened?" Caleb asked from the hallway.

Andrew shot up and blinked at Caleb. "Caleb! You're here."

"Umm, yeah. Who were you expecting?"

Caleb sauntered over to the sofa, hips swaying. The responding pull in Andrew's groin honestly surprised him. He would have sworn he was way too tired and stressed out to get it up. Of course, Caleb had always managed to evoke arousal in him, so he shouldn't have been surprised at his body's familiar reaction.

After walking up to him, Caleb stood in front of the sofa, directly in Andrew's line of sight. The tight pants the man favored made his cock and balls obvious, and for a crazy minute, Andrew thought about bending forward just a couple of inches and mouthing that bulge through the fabric. It'd been so long since he'd had a man in his mouth, even longer since he'd tasted Caleb. He swallowed back his moan, closed his eyes, and tried to focus on the conversation.

"I, uh, wasn't expecting anybody. I was talking to myself, I guess." Andrew licked his lips. "It's late. I figured you'd be out."

The sofa dipped and Caleb's hand caressed his knee.

"Talking to yourself, huh? It really must have been a doozy of a day. Wanna talk about it?'

"I don't know." Andrew shrugged. "It was just work stuff."

"Did you lose a patient?" Caleb asked, concern evident in his voice.

"Almost. He was Larry's patient, not mine, which was the real issue. He had several comorbidities, which complicated his surgery. Anyway, things weren't going well and I had to step in to take over. By then, the patient was worse off than he'd been before Larry cut into him." Andrew rubbed his eyes again and sighed. "We got through it and I think he'll be okay, but the reality is that Larry doesn't have enough experience doing the Thompson procedure in the frontal lobe to have taken on this patient."

"Umm, I may be missing something here," Caleb said. "But seeing as how you invented the aptly named Thompson procedure, why weren't you doing it? I thought complex patients flew in to Emile City specifically to have you operate on them."

"They do. This patient did. But you know how it is, Cae. Once they meet me, sometimes..." Andrew shrugged. "It's not like I give a shit, mind you, but I don't exactly fit the image people have of a surgeon. Most people overlook it because I'm damn good at what I do, but this patient decided he'd rather have someone who looks more distinguished operate on him."

Caleb traced over Andrew's piercings gently—the bar in his eyebrow, the ring in his left ear, the spike in his right one, and the studs running up the cartilage.

"I like how you look, Drew." Caleb's voice was husky. He leaned forward, his breath ghosting over Andrew's cheek, his lips. "Always have."

They were so close together now, almost connected. Andrew's mouth watered at the memory of his friend's taste.

"Cae, I..." he panted.

"Yeah?"

Somehow Caleb managed to get closer, his body turned to the side, both hands resting on Andrew's knees. Though he wasn't making actual contact, Caleb moved his lips along Andrew's jawline to his ear, his hot breath driving Andrew to the brink.

"I want... I..." Andrew panted and blinked his eyes furiously. "Let's...let's go out," he finally said. "I don't want to talk about my day anymore."

Andrew knew he should get up, knew he should pull away. But how could he move apart from those chocolate eyes that could see inside him? Caleb always made him feel so *real*. It was heady and wonderful and he didn't want it to stop.

"We don't have to talk," Caleb whispered.

Andrew gnawed on his lips and stared at his friend, feeling his pulse race. Caleb moved closer, tilted his head to the side, his eyes fluttered shut and then—

"I can't," Andrew said, jumping to his feet. He wiped his clammy palms on his scrub pants. "I'm going to grab a quick shower and then we can go out, okay?"

He didn't wait for an answer, just turned on his heel and headed for his bedroom.

"Drew, please wait," Caleb called out, forcing him to stop midtrack. "Is it..." His friend paused and Andrew could hear him breathing rapidly. "If you have...something, we can still...damn, this shouldn't be so hard." Caleb sounded defeated.

Andrew turned around, not wanting to force Caleb to keep talking to his back. That seemed to give the man the strength to continue.

"Look, obviously, I know Drake was positive, and if you got infected when you were with him, if that's why you don't want to...with me," Caleb sighed, "I'm saying it's okay, Drew. We can be careful. You don't need to stay away from me."

"It's not that." Andrew shook his head. "I'm negative. Drake and I always used rubbers. I've been tested."

"Then why?" Caleb asked, his voice breaking on the second word.

"Because," Andrew said, blinking back tears and hating himself for getting emotional. "I'm a fucking mess, Cae. Just..." He shook his head and pressed his lips together, not sure how to continue, not sure how to explain the tornado of feelings and thoughts that swirled in his mind.

Suddenly, Caleb was right there in front of him, his hands strong and sure, rubbing Andrew's back.

"Shhh, 's okay. Go shower," Caleb said softly. "We'll go out and take your mind off your day."

CALEB GRABBED a few grocery bags from his trunk and ran into the house as quickly as possible. It was late September, and it'd been raining on and off for days. Right then, it was coming down hard, so he was soaked and shivering by the time he walked into the foyer. He toed off his wet shoes and padded through the house, heading into the kitchen to put away the groceries. After that, he had an appointment with a steaming hot shower.

"Damn, Cae! What in the hell are you doing?"

He pulled his face out of the refrigerator and looked at Andrew, who was standing in the doorway.

"Putting away the soy milk," he said, aiming for a sarcastic tone in response to the obvious question, but losing the impact due to his chattering teeth. He was even too cold to roll his eyes. Who knew that was possible?

Andrew stormed over and yanked him away from the refrigerator. "Your lips are blue and you're soaking wet," he said, worry laced through his voice. "We need to get you out of these clothes." He started tugging on Caleb's sweater and the long-sleeved shirt he wore underneath, pulling them both up over his chest and head.

"I've been trying to get you interested in taking my clothes off for years, Drew, and you're saying all I had to do was walk through a little rain?" Caleb tried to keep his tone light, but he wasn't sure if he succeeded. He pushed his wet hair out of his face. "I wish I would've known it was this easy. We could've been fooling around all this time."

The words were like a cattle prod, sending Andrew stumbling away from him. Caleb gasped and held his palm against the middle of his chest. There was no way for him to hide the pang of hurt he felt at Andrew's reaction.

"Come on, Cae. You know I'm interested in..." Andrew dragged his eyes over Caleb's shirtless body. "You know it's not a matter of me not being interested."

Two years after Drake's death, Caleb wasn't sure he knew much of anything. Andrew was better than he had been, true enough. He socialized with their friends, smiled occasionally, and didn't bite Caleb's head off at every opportunity. But it was all on the surface. Caleb knew Andrew well enough to recognize that deep down, he was still hurting, still depressed, and, of course, he was still unwilling to have sex with Caleb or, as far as he knew, anybody else. Though he wasn't completely sure of the reason, Caleb suspected it had to do with more than Drake's absence.

He slowly approached Andrew, keeping their eyes locked together. The other man's expression was panicked, but he seemed rooted in place, like he was captured by Caleb's gaze and couldn't move away. When he got close enough, Caleb raised his hand and gently stroked the side of Andrew's face, melting a little inside when Andrew leaned into the touch and shivered.

"Sure, I can tell you're physically interested," Caleb said. "But you won't let yourself act on it. When you were with Drake, I understood—"

"When I was with Drake," Andrew's voice sounded thick, and his gaze seemed almost pained. He swallowed and then continued talking. "When I was with Drake, you wouldn't let me come near you."

That was an unexpected commented. And it didn't make sense.

"Well, yeah, I mean..." Caleb licked his lips and furrowed his brow. "You had a boyfriend. We don't ever fool around with each other when we're seeing somebody. That's our rule."

"Yes, that was our rule," Andrew said slowly, maybe

even carefully. "But Drake and I had an open relationship."

Caleb failed to understand why that mattered. A relationship was a relationship. Of all the people he expected to understand that concept, Andrew was at the top of the list.

"But you still had a boyfriend," he said. "You know I don't mess with guys in relationships and…" Caleb was confused at the turn the conversation had taken. Andrew would never have cheated on Drake, open relationship or not. Would he? "Drew, did you mess around with other guys when you were with Drake?"

"No." Andrew shook his head, confirming for Caleb that the world hadn't just gone completely topsy-turvy.

Caleb would've expected Andrew to be offended at the question about his fidelity. But instead of looking angry, Andrew just seemed tired.

"I don't…I don't understand what we're talking about," Caleb said, meaning every word. Somewhere along the way, he'd lost his grip on their discussion and now he was completely lost. It was a foreign feeling in a conversation with the man he knew better than anyone, and not one Caleb had ever expected to experience.

"We're not talking about anything," Andrew sighed. "I'm hungry. Do you want me to start dinner while you change out of those wet clothes?"

"Drew?" Caleb whispered.

The single word was a question, a pleading, and a show of support all in one. Andrew shook his head in response, not uttering a sound. After several long moments, Andrew cleared his throat and plastered on a smile that wouldn't pass for real in any scenario.

"Yeah, you're right. My cooking's a disaster. How about cereal for dinner? That's always good."

"Whatever you want, Drew."

Based on the shiny green eyes and the quick nod Andrew gave him, Caleb knew his friend understood he wasn't referring to cereal. Though, it looked like that'd have to be enough for now.

"DREW?" CALEB called out as soon as he walked in the front door. "I have bagels and coffee." He tossed his keys in the bowl and walked into the kitchen. "I'll start toasting them. You want peanut butter on yours?" he asked but didn't wait for an answer.

Andrew always wanted peanut butter on his bagel. The man actually ate the stuff from the jar with a spoon. And somehow he didn't have an ounce of fat on him. Bastard. Lean, sexy bastard.

"Oh my God!" Caleb gasped the instant Andrew walked into the kitchen. "What'd you do to your hair?"

"Nothing much. Just ready for something new." Andrew rubbed his palm over the nearly non-existent hair on both sides of his head. "Do you like it?"

Something new was "take a little extra off the top, please" not "give me a mohawk." A blue mohawk. Caleb blinked his eyes rapidly, hoping the image in front of him would somehow change. It didn't.

He'd always loved Andrew's blond hair, loved how it looked, loved how silky soft it felt when he combed his hands through it. Now it was shaved and dyed and spiked and...

"Oh, yeah. Looks great, Drew."

He licked his lips and opened the refrigerator, taking longer than could possibly be justified to find the Tofutti Better Than Cream Cheese, but needing to hide his face from Andrew. There was no way for him to school his expression fast enough to prevent Andrew from knowing that his hair, in fact, did not look great. At least not to Caleb.

It was silly, really. Caleb knew that. But Andrew was blond. In his earliest memories, he remembered playing with that platinum-blond eight-year-old and then getting reacquainted with the golden blond fourteen-year-old version of the same boy. He was so attached to Andrew's hair that he'd been known to complain when the man cut it even a little short, and Andrew always laughed and said he'd keep it shaggy for Caleb because he had to look at Andrew more than anybody else.

Caleb sighed. Well, this was most definitely a change for the worse as far as the hairstyle Caleb favored on Andrew, but it was a change Andrew apparently wanted. Caleb reminded himself that it made no sense to feel like the man's choice to cut his own hair was somehow an indictment of Caleb or their friendship. With that thought squarely in mind, he gripped the cream cheese, closed the refrigerator, and sat at the table, where he'd already placed the toasted bagels and peanut butter.

"So, let's eat and then I have something exciting to talk to you about," Caleb said. "At least I think it's exciting. I'm pretty sure you will too."

He looked at Andrew and then quickly flicked his eyes away from the disturbingly unfamiliar image, smiling weakly. He'd get used to the hair in a few days. It'd be fine. And until then, he'd concentrate on other things, like spreading peanut butter on a bagel and his new idea for Andrew. He would not think about shorn, dyed hair.

It was just hair. He wasn't this shallow. But it didn't feel like just hair; it felt like something more. Caleb shifted uncomfortably in his chair.

"Wow, hurts to sit on a hard chair, ya'? It really must have been some night with your moped."

"Huh?" Caleb looked up from the plate and stared at Andrew in confusion. "What moped? I drive an Audi." A piece of information Andrew already knew.

That question garnered Caleb a loud, but seemingly angry, laugh. Maybe staying up all night putting the finishing touches on the business plan he wanted to give Andrew had been a bad idea. The lack of sleep was making him paranoid.

"The kind of moped I'm talking about drives *into* you."

"Drew," Caleb sighed and pushed Andrew's plate toward him. He then started spreading cream cheese on his own bagel. "I'm tired, 'kay? I've been up all night. I don't understand what you're talking about."

"All night, huh? Go moped."

"Stop it," Caleb pleaded. It was like they were back to the pissy version of Andrew who'd bitten Caleb's head off at every opportunity for a good year after Drake died.

"I'll stop it when you stop hiding him. With all the sleepovers you've been having, it's insulting to my intelligence to keep pretending I don't know about him at this point."

"Who's him?" Caleb asked, feeling completely dumbfounded.

"Your moped," Andrew answered. "The guy who's good enough to ride all night but too embarrassing to admit to in public."

There were so many things wrong with that nasty barb that Caleb didn't have a clue how to respond. Instead, he pushed his chair back and stomped over to the counter, where he'd left the file folder containing what he'd hoped would be Andrew's salvation. Caleb couldn't seem to heal Andrew's guilt over not having saved Drake, so he had hoped creating a venue to save other people with the same diagnosis would help Andrew.

He held the file so tightly his knuckles turned white, and then he wheeled around and flung it across the table, sending a few pages flying.

"I was at a coffee shop, working on this last night, Drew. Same thing I've done a lot of other nights lately." He breathed rapidly. "What is it, you ask?" he said, even though Andrew hadn't asked anything. The man's eyes were wide and his head was bobbing between Caleb and the file in front of him. "It's a business plan for an HIV center. Complete with information on a few buildings in EC West that are currently available, some grant options that'll help fund it, and detailed information about the kinds of services you can offer. I've talked to similar centers in other cities, and I think it's doable."

"An HIV center?" Andrew repeated more than asked.

"Yeah. A place guys can go to get tested without stigma. A place that can provide educational outreach and counseling. A place that can give guys ideas about how to stay healthy with the disease—diet, traditional medicine, alternative medicine. You'll need to put in the money at first, but if we start small, it won't bankrupt you. After that..." Caleb shrugged. "There are grants. People in other cities do fundraisers." He took in a deep breath and tilted his chin toward the folder Andrew now held. "Like I said, it's all in the folder."

Andrew blinked rapidly, seemingly unsure how he should respond to Caleb's angry rant. This wasn't how Caleb had planned to present his idea. He needed to calm down so he could talk intelligently about this project. A hot shower seemed like the perfect solution, so he turned around and walked toward the door.

"Cae, I..." Andrew's voice was soft, sad.

"I'm going to take a shower, and then I'll be back to talk about the HIV center." Caleb looked over his shoulder. "Oh, and Drew? About that moped comment, I've never ridden anyone except you. But just to be clear, if I meet a guy I'm interested in enough to, uh, go for a ride, I sure as hell wouldn't hide him. That's not who I am."

"I know you're not. I'm sorry. I..." Andrew's brow furrowed and he stopped talking for a moment. "What do you mean you haven't ridden anyone except me?"

Caleb couldn't help it, he smiled. That question was typical Andrew, and there was no way for him to hold on to his anger when his old friend was shining through. There they were in the middle of a knock-down fight, they literally had a proposal on the table that was meaningful and life-altering, and Andrew wanted to know about his sex life. Or, in this case, lack of sex life.

"You know how short my relationships have been," Caleb explained. "I've never wanted to bottom with anyone I didn't know that well. And the guys I've been with were tops so..." He shrugged and let the thought trail off. "Anyway, it's not like I was going without for all that long. Don't forget, you and I were getting it from each other pretty regularly until..." The last thing he wanted to do was mention Drake, so he stopped explaining and pushed the conversation forward. "I'll take a shower and come back to talk about the HIV center. Take a look at the information while I'm gone."

CHAPTER TWENTY

2007

"HEY! IT'S Bert and Ernie!" Noah Forman's booming voice called out to Caleb and Andrew.

They were on the dance floor, bodies swaying, moving with the music. It was fun, but being so close to a gyrating and sweating Andrew was driving Caleb's libido through the roof. He needed to take a break and seeing Clark and Noah walk in seemed like as plausible a reason as any.

"I'm gonna go grab a drink and say hi to Clark and Noah," Caleb shouted into Andrew's ear so he could be heard over the thumping beat. "You want anything?"

"Nah, I'm good for now. I'll catch up with you in a bit."

With a nod, Caleb walked off the dance floor and made his way to the bar where his friends were sitting.

"Hey, Eli!" He gave a tight hug to the brown-haired man who looked too young to be in a bar, but was actually well past the legal age. "You get carded tonight?" he asked.

Green eyes twinkled and Eli grinned. "Nah, they remember me from last time."

"Noah, Clark," Caleb said as he raised his chin in their direction. Clark was sitting on a barstool and Noah was standing behind him, his arms wrapped possessively around Clark's chest. "I didn't know you two'd be here tonight."

"Last minute thing," Clark explained and scooted over one barstool to make room for Caleb. "We wanted to get out of our apartment."

"We really need to buy a house, angel," Noah said to Clark. "How're you liking your new house, Caleb?"

Caleb sat down.

"Technically, it's Andrew's house, but we like it. Great street, big trees in the back. Plus, we love EC West."

"Let me remind you that we've been to your place," Eli said. "You can't tell us Andrew's the one who knows how to combine midcentury modern with classic antiques to create that classy eclectic vibe you have going."

Caleb laughed. "I'm responsible for the décor. I just meant that Andrew owns the house. He's the one who paid for it."

"Hey, you can either earn it, win it, or marry it," Noah said. "Seems to me it's your house under option number three."

"Andrew and I are friends, Noah. We're not a couple." Caleb rolled his eyes. How many times had he had this conversation with Noah? For some reason, it'd become more painful lately. His stomach twisted with a feeling of loss and longing.

"How're things with the HIV center coming along, Caleb?" Clark smoothly changed the topic, likely noticing Caleb's distress. "Is it still going to open this month?"

Caleb nodded. "Yup, Andrew set a goal of opening in January, and we'll be opening in January, even if it's eleven fifty-nine on January thirty-first. He's all over it, making sure nothing gets off schedule. He has staff lined up, equipment ordered, pretty much everything done. Now he's moved on to the triple-checking part. I had to drag him out of the house tonight for some forced relaxation."

The words may have sounded like a complaint, but Caleb smiled to show he had no problem with Andrew's commitment to the new HIV center. If anything, he was happy about how things were going. It seemed like Andrew had latched onto the project and found some inner peace as a result.

The bartender walked up and Caleb leaned over the bar. "I'll take a bottle of water," he called out.

"Caleb, man, drinking water in a bar is like praying while you're getting head," Eli drawled. "Both things are great on their own, but they don't go well together."

"Oh, I don't know about that." Caleb winked at Eli. "I've had quite a few guys call out to God while I was going down on them."

He took the bottle of water from the bartender, twisted off the top, and gulped half of it down.

"I can attest to that," Andrew said from behind him.

"Caleb's mouth is like a religious experience."

Caleb swiveled around to face Andrew. He rubbed the lean, muscular chest through a damp T-shirt. This one had a picture of a man with a bulging crotch holding a wrapped box, and it said "Nice Package." Caleb shook his head—Andrew and his T-shirts. Originally, Caleb knew, Andrew had worn them to prove some sort of "I'm queer, I'm here, get used to it" point. But now he thought his friend actually liked the hideous things.

"You all done dancing?" Caleb asked.

"Oh, no. Hold on just one fucking minute," Noah practically shouted. "Did Bert just say you'd gone down on him, Ernie? When did this new development start? What happened to the whole platonic friendship bit?"

"Ah, okay, first, why am I Bert? I thought Caleb was Bert," Andrew protested. His hand was balled up and he pointed his thumb in Caleb's direction. "And B, I'm the one who taught Toothy McTooth over here how to suck cock without drawing blood. So the development isn't exactly new."

"So says the man whose gag reflex used to start at his gum line," Caleb growled at Andrew and planted his hands on his hips. "And you damn well know I'm not Bert!"

"Uh, oh. I think they're having a domestic," Eli pointed out in a stage whisper. "Again."

"Hey, hey," Clark said calmly, putting a hand on each of their shoulders. "There's no reason to fight over this. Last

I heard, neither of you was fond of Noah's Sesame Street nicknames."

"Aww, why're you stopping them, Clark?" Eli complained. "They're about one good barb from fucking against the bar. That would be totally hot."

Caleb deflated. Noah's ridiculous nicknames really were a dumb reason to argue. He smiled sheepishly at his best friend. "You can be Ernie."

"Nah, forget it." Andrew gave Caleb a sweet smile. "I think I'll be Kermit the Frog. He likes to sing."

"Kermit's a Muppet, but he's not on Sesame Street," Noah said to Andrew, as if this was an important revelation. "If you're going to be Kermit that means Caleb has to be—"

"Let me just warn you right now, Noah"—Caleb glared at Noah as he spoke—"if you call me Miss Piggy, I don't care that you're a black belt, I'll find a way to make you pay."

"THANKSGIVING OR Christmas?" Caleb asked, apropos of nothing.

"Uh..." Andrew looked up from the medical journal he was reading and twisted his head around to see if someone had come over without him noticing and was now standing in their living room. Nope, just him and Caleb. He blinked at his friend in confusion. "If you're expecting me to take part in this conversation, I'm going to need a little more than that non sequitur."

"When do you want to go to New York? For Thanksgiving or for Christmas?"

"We're going to New York?" Andrew asked.

"Yes. I haven't celebrated the holidays with my parents since I moved here. That's three years running, Drew. There's no way I'm telling them we're not coming again this year. So, decide if you want to do Thanksgiving or Christmas with our parents, and I'll take care of the rest."

Andrew knew full well why Caleb hadn't spent the holidays with his parents in all that time. It was because Andrew hadn't wanted to go and Caleb wouldn't leave him behind while he was getting his shit together after Drake's death. Not that Andrew had pushed him to go, of course. It wasn't like he was all that selfless.

"Okay, yeah, I can handle a holiday with your parents. Umm, let's do Thanksgiving, I guess, because I already have the time off. But that's next week. Will it work for your parents or do they need more notice?"

"They'll be thrilled, no worries," Caleb said and stood from the armchair where he'd been curled up reading a magazine. Andrew loved evenings like this, the two of them at home, quietly spending time together. "I'll make a Tofurkey for us. Everything else will be catered."

"Your mother is having dinner catered for four people?" Andrew laughed. "Is it really that hard to make some mashed potatoes and green beans?"

"Good question, Drew." Caleb raised one eyebrow and crossed his arms over his defined chest. Caleb's time at the gym seemed to be having an impact. He was thin, but had visible muscles. Andrew found himself wondering whether Caleb still favored those sexy as hell underwear he used to wear. "Is it really that hard?" Caleb asked.

Andrew was sure the question wasn't about the state of his dick, which was in fact hard due to the thoughts about Caleb's body. But he had no idea what Caleb wanted to know. When he didn't respond, Caleb started tapping one foot impatiently.

"Uh, I don't, uh...what'd you say?" Andrew stuttered.

"When was the last time you made mashed potatoes, Drew? Or green beans? Or, say, anything?"

Andrew blushed. "I'm not good in the kitchen."

"You'd be fine in the kitchen if you wanted to be. It's just not your thing, which is fine. It's not my parents' thing either. Hence the ordering in."

Caleb didn't seem mad, which was good because Andrew felt like he'd been uncomfortably close to somehow being stuck making Thanksgiving dinner. Not that he would have made it himself. He'd have ordered in. The irony of that thought made him chuckle. Huh, that may have been Caleb's point.

"Oh, and Drew?" Caleb added, sounding nervous all of a sudden. He sat next to Andrew on the sofa and tucked one leg underneath his ass. "It won't be just the four of us. Your parents are coming too."

"No. Uh, uh. Absolutely not," Andrew said vehemently and shook his head. "I have no desire to spend Thanksgiving duking it out with my father while my mother vacillates between cowering and defensive. Honestly," he snorted. "What kind of way is that to spend a holiday?"

"Traditional?" Caleb asked hopefully, a wry grin on his face.

"You're a regular laugh riot, Cae. The answer's still no."

"Drew," Caleb sighed.

He took Andrew's hand between both of his and rubbed Andrew's wrist with this thumbs. The tender touch felt so good, so right, and the urge to kiss Caleb suddenly rammed into Andrew with the force of a Mack Truck. He was having trouble breathing, his heart was racing, and he thought maybe it wouldn't be so bad for him to give in to his desires just this once.

Andrew was tired of staying away from the man next to him, wasn't even completely sure why he was doing it anymore. Originally, it was because of guilt and then self-loathing. But now...it'd been so long since he'd had intimate human contact and to have it with Caleb... Andrew shivered at the thought.

"Hey, it won't be that bad," Caleb said soothingly, clearly misunderstanding the source of Andrew's physical reaction to their conversation. "I'll be there the whole time, and when we go to bed at night, we can laugh at all the crazy things our parents say."

Well, it looked like they were going to spend Thanksgiving with their families. Andrew nodded.

"All righty then," he said. "Let the awkward times roll."

AS IT turned out, there were two impediments to the plan for them to laugh together in bed at night. First, the Lakes' house was big enough to have multiple guest rooms, so it didn't make sense for them to share a room. Well, not unless Andrew said, "Hey, Barbara, I want to do your son tonight. Mind if we bunk together?"

But the second impediment was the bigger problem. By the time they got to New York, Caleb was dating someone. And with that craptastic development, the whole shared bed, banging Barbara's son idea was out the window anyway. To be replaced with the not-nearly-as-enjoyable lonely bed, banging-your-head-against-the-wall reality that was Andrew's life.

He wasn't sure how it happened. One minute he was planning to seduce Caleb—the seduction plan was him mauling Caleb when the man came home from work and, hopefully, not coming in his pants within seconds. And the next minute, Caleb was calling him to say he wouldn't be home for dinner because he had a date. A date.

Andrew told himself the reason he was upset was because he was horny, and Caleb dating someone was effectively a cock-blocker. Upset may have been an understatement. He wanted to either punch someone or curl up in the corner of the room crying. It was a real toss-up. Yeah, sure, it was just because he was horny.

"See, the trip wasn't horrible. Definitely not as terrible as you'd built it up to be," Caleb said to him as he pulled his suitcase into their house.

"Yeah, it was fine," Andrew acquiesced.

His father had obviously gone out of his way not to instigate a fight. And his mother hadn't seemed miserable, which was always a plus. But as important as those two factors, another critical component of the no-screaming-thus-successful Thanksgiving meal was that Andrew just plain didn't give a damn.

He had spent almost every second of the trip thinking about Caleb, wondering whether his friend would be willing to fool around even though he was dating someone, then hating himself for wondering, and then wondering again. All that time focused on Caleb meant he didn't have the energy to get into it with his parents, which was for the best.

"I'm glad you agree," Caleb beamed. "Because I told my mom we'd be back next year. It can be like a tradition—Thanksgiving in New York. What do you think?"

"Won't Nick mind going to New York for Thanksgiving?" Andrew asked and then mentally slapped himself for giving Caleb that idea. After that, he sighed internally at the realization that he wasn't done with the whole obsessing-about-Caleb-dating bit. Honestly, what was wrong with him?

"Nick? You mean Nick Gallaway? Why would he come to New York for Thanksgiving?"

"Uh, because he's your boyfriend," Andrew stated the obvious.

"When have I ever had a relationship last a year, Drew?" Caleb asked but didn't wait for an answer before he continued speaking. "That's right, never. And I can tell you after having dated the guy for two weeks that my unblemished record isn't going to be broken with Nick. It's doubtful the guy will still be in the picture a month from now."

"Then why are you with him?" Andrew asked. "If you know it isn't going anywhere, why bother?"

Caleb smiled fondly at him, those brown eyes warm and sentimental. "I know for you dating has always been a search for someone permanent, but for me..." Caleb shrugged and his face darkened. "I've been single a long time and I'm horny. That's reason enough to date Nick for now," Caleb explained, his voice quiet, almost pained. "Looking for someone permanent isn't realistic for me. I mean, come on, do you actually think there's a man alive who wouldn't drive me nuts or go running in the opposite direction after a few months?" Caleb shook his head, his expression clearing, and then he laughed at what he seemed to consider an absurd idea as he rolled his suitcase down the hall to his bedroom.

"Yeah, there's me," Andrew whispered hoarsely. But by then, Caleb had left the room, and Andrew was standing alone, absorbing the powerful truth of his realization.

"TELL ME again why we're walking when we have two perfectly serviceable cars parked in the garage?" Andrew asked.

Caleb rolled his eyes. "We're walking because it's New Year's Eve, and if Seth and Eli's party is even halfway decent, we'll both be too plastered to drive home. Honestly, Drew, their house is two blocks away. We walked farther than this to get bagels when I lived in the City."

Andrew wrapped his arms around himself and rubbed his biceps. "But it's cold," he whined.

"Oh. My. God. It's December thirty-first, of course it's a little chilly. But we're in Emile City, not Manhattan. There isn't even any snow on the ground."

When Andrew just looked at him with pathetic puppy dog eyes, Caleb sighed and cradled his arm around Andrew. His friend sighed softly and melted against his side.

"There, is that better?" Caleb's voice was noticeably gentler. It was impossible to stay snarky when there was a warm, cuddly Andrew pressed up against him.

"Mm-hum," Andrew whispered. "Thanks, Cae."

"Welcome," he said and then cleared his throat

because it suddenly felt very scratchy.

It didn't take long for them to get to the party and start having fun with their friends. It wasn't a rowdy scene, just the usual suspects wearing clothes that were a bit more festive than on other days and enjoying each other's company. Noah and Clark didn't show and weren't answering their phones, so everybody figured they'd decided to spend the evening in bed enjoying each other's company in a more intimate way.

David Miller came to the party with Jonathan, his new but already hot-and-heavy partner. The man was stunning and sweet, but seemingly shy. He stayed glued to David's side and said very little. Caleb figured since he'd been helping the couple redo their kitchen, he'd spent more time with Jonathan than anyone else in the room, which made it his responsibility to help get the man out of his shell.

"Hey, Jonathan. How are you?" Caleb asked.

A simple question, not controversial, but it still made Jonathan blush.

"I'm fine. Good. I'm good," he stammered.

David smiled at Caleb gratefully and leaned down so his mouth was next to Jonathan's ear. "I'm going to go get us a couple of drinks," he said. "You keep talking to Caleb. I'll be right back."

"Awesome!" Caleb smiled wickedly and snatched Jonathan's hand, pulling him to the couch. "He's gone, now I can ask you totally inappropriate questions about your sex life."

He hadn't been aiming for quiet, so Caleb wasn't surprised when David stumbled and shook his head. Still, he walked away, giving his partner time to bond with his friends.

"I was just kidding about the inappropriate questions," Caleb said to Jonathan once they were sitting. "Unless you're willing to tell me all the dirty details, in which case I was completely serious."

"Oh, uh..." Jonathan didn't seem to know how to respond.

"I'm just kidding." Caleb patted Jonathan's knee. "I'm not so good with boundaries when I've been drinking," he explained.

"How much have you had to drink?" Jonathan asked.

"Um, let's see." He looked at his watch. "I've been here about three hours so that makes, umm, two glasses of wine." Caleb winked and chuckled. "Okay, you caught me. I'm not so good with boundaries when I haven't been drinking either."

That comment had Jonathan smiling and then laughing so hard he had to grip Caleb's shoulder for support. Caleb grinned. The man was a sweetheart, really.

"Uh oh," Jonathan said and tore his hands off Caleb, the smile suddenly dropping from his face. "I didn't know you and Andrew Thompson were together. Sorry."

"We're not together." Caleb furrowed his brow in confusion about Jonathan's apology.

"Uh, does he know that? Because if looks could kill, I'd be a goner right now," Jonathan said, his eyes darting to a spot over Caleb's shoulder and then down to his lap where he had started pulling a thread on his jeans.

Caleb twisted his torso and looked in the direction where Jonathan had been staring. Sure enough, Andrew was standing there, glaring at them. When Caleb met his eyes and raised one eyebrow in question, Andrew turned around and joined a group of guys in another part of the room.

"That was weird," Caleb muttered.

"Maybe he has a crush on you," Jonathan suggested.

"Nah. We're best friends, have been for years. We even live together. I'd know if Andrew was crushing on me."

Caleb felt a pulling in his groin in response to the idea that Andrew wanted him. He sighed. Hopeless, that was what he was. Just hopeless.

"Oh. So you guys just don't have chemistry together, or what?"

"What do you mean?" Caleb asked.

"Is that why you aren't together? Lack of chemistry?"

"No, no. Our chemistry is just fine."

Their chemistry was actually more than fine: it sizzled. Even with years of no intimate contact between them, Andrew was still the inspiration for most of Caleb's erections. That was one of the reasons Caleb had ended things with Nick. He wanted Andrew, and trying to pretend otherwise by dating someone else hadn't worked. Of course the other reason he'd ended things with Nick was that the guy was a prick.

"So why aren't you together? You said he's your best

friend, right? And the chemistry's there, so I take it that means you've, uh, you know."

"Yeah, I know." Caleb grinned at the unexpected turn of events. Here he'd threatened to prod into Jonathan's sex life and the opposite was happening. But, hey, he didn't have anything to hide. Plus, Jonathan seemed to be coming out of his shell, so Caleb saw no reason to stop the conversation. "Andrew and I were each other's first... First everything, actually."

"And then what happened?" Jonathan leaned forward, his eyes wide. "Did you break up?"

"No." Caleb shook his head. "We were never *together* together."

"Why not?"

"Well, I guess maybe it was because we lived in different cities back then. We were going to school. It's not something we ever talked about." Caleb was speaking quietly, more to himself than to Jonathan, remembering those years, remembering how he'd felt about Andrew. Then he snapped back to the present and cleared his throat. "Ehm, we were so young. Barely eighteen. You know how it is at that age. Nobody knows what the hell they want."

"I did," Jonathan said so quietly Caleb wasn't sure he'd heard the words correctly. Then silver eyes met his and Jonathan spoke more clearly. "Well, you're not eighteen anymore and you're living in the same city, same house even. So why aren't you *together* together now?"

Caleb didn't respond. He just stared, his mouth hanging open at the obvious question. Shouldn't he have an answer to that? And what did it mean that he didn't?

"God, I'm sorry," Jonathan apologized, seemingly thinking Caleb was angry based on his silence. "I'm sure you have your reasons and it's none of my business. It's just, you both seem so nice. Even if Andrew does have all those weird piercings." Jonathan leaned closer to Caleb and whispered, "I've never been with a guy who has an apadravya. What's it like?"

"An apadravya?" Caleb growled. "What in the hell is that?"

"Oh, God. I need to just stop talking." Jonathan was flustered. "It's just you...you...you said you guys had chemistry. I thought that meant you two were fucking. I'm an idiot."

"You're not an idiot," Caleb said in a regular tone, wanting to kick his own ass for stressing poor Jonathan out. "But what's an apadravya?"

"It's a bar pierced through..." Jonathan looked from side to side and leaned close to Caleb again. "It's pierced through the head of your cock."

Caleb suddenly felt a little light-headed, but it wasn't because the thought of Andrew's dick being pierced scared him. It was because all the blood in his body seemed to have pooled in his own cock in reaction to the vision he had in his head of Andrew—nude and hard with a metal bar through his dick.

He groaned. How did he not know about this piercing? When was the last time he'd seen Andrew naked? They'd gone swimming together over the summer, maybe even during the fall, and his dick hadn't had any jewelry back then. Speaking of seeing Andrew naked, how did Jonathan know about the piercing?

"I haven't seen it," Jonathan said hurriedly, and Caleb wondered how the man seemed to have read his mind. "Andrew mentioned it when David and I saw him a couple of weeks ago. That's how I know. Honest. Listen, uh…" Jonathan looked wildly around the room. "I think David needs me so… it was nice talking to you."

The man was up from the couch and bolting as far away as possible before Caleb had a chance to respond. He should have felt bad about that. After all, he'd likely scared Jonathan away with his none-too-welcoming response to the news of Andrew's new piercing. But Caleb couldn't focus on Jonathan at that moment. The only person on his mind was Andrew.

He had long ago figured out that each of Andrew's body mods had been a reaction to an asshole boyfriend cheating on him. But Andrew hadn't dated anybody since Drake, so why had he recently gotten a piercing in his cock?

Caleb chewed his bottom lip and went through his mental Rolodex of Andrew's piercings and tattoos. He could literally name the ex that went with every single one. Every single one except the apadravya Andrew had gotten sometime over the past couple of months. Well, the apadravya and the stud in his tongue.

That damn tongue piercing had gotten Caleb hard for months. He remembered how difficult it had been for him to concentrate on David Miller's remodel project when all he'd wanted to do was lay naked in bed while Andrew licked him like an ice cream cone. His only saving grace had been Andrew's unbearably grouchy mood at that time. It seemed like he was looking for reasons to start fights, and if he couldn't find a reason, he'd create one. Like his accusations that Caleb was dating David despite Caleb's constant denials. None of it had made sense, and Caleb had chalked it up to part of Andrew's healing process.

Suddenly, Caleb thought of another type of change Andrew had made since Drake died—the blue mohawk. He still hated the damn thing just as much as he had the first day he'd seen it. That day flashed through Caleb's mind. He had come home to tell Andrew his idea for an HIV center and Andrew was acting oddly belligerent and accusing him of having a hidden boyfriend.

Caleb gasped as realization dawned. He got up from the sofa and stormed over to where Andrew was having a conversation with a group of guys. They needed to talk and no way was he patient enough to wait. It was time to go home.

CHAPTER TWENTY-ONE

2008

NEITHER MAN had been paying attention to the time when they'd left the party. It had all been sort of a blind rush. Caleb was quiet on the way home, his thoughts bouncing around in his head. And Andrew had his doctor's hat on, assuming the pallor of Caleb's complexion and his insistence that they leave the party early meant something was wrong medically. So walking in the front door and seeing the entryway clock reading five minutes after midnight was unexpected. Unexpected but not unwelcome. At least not to Caleb.

He closed and locked the front door and then pressed his chest to Andrew's, pushing the man through the entryway and down the hallway.

"Give me a kiss, Drew," he whispered hoarsely as he moved his hands to Andrew's shoulders and began kneading them while they continued walking toward his bedroom. Not that Andrew likely knew that was their intended destination.

"What?" Andrew asked, green eyes blinking in surprise.

"It's New Year's. Tradition and all that," Caleb said, veering them into his bedroom. "Kiss me."

When the back of Andrew's knees hit the bed, his plump lips separated in surprise. Caleb decided to take that as an invitation. He leaned up, cupped the back of Andrew's head, and pulled him down.

Their lips met in a kiss that started out as soft and searching and turned into a scorching meeting of tongues and teeth with both men doing everything they could to get closer to each other. To Caleb, it felt like Andrew was trying to eat him alive, and he knew without a doubt that he wanted to be consumed by the man pressed up against him, the man who'd given him his first kiss, the man who'd been his best friend and so much more for two decades.

Caleb pulled away just long enough to shove Andrew's sweater up and over his head and tear off his own shirt. Then he dove back into the kiss and sucked on Andrew's tongue as they both grappled with each other's buttons and zippers.

Though he wanted skin to skin contact, there was no way Caleb was willing to move apart long enough to get there gracefully. Andrew must have finally managed to unfasten his pants, because Caleb felt them being shoved to the floor. He hissed with pleasure when a big, warm hand wrapped around his dick.

At some point during the frantic kiss, Andrew managed to reverse their positions. He rubbed his hands up and down Caleb's arms and then landed on his shoulders and, with a gentle pressure, encouraged him to sit on the edge of the bed. But sitting meant creating a separation between their bodies and the last thing Caleb wanted was to let Andrew go. Not tonight. Not ever. Andrew was his now. Maybe at some level he always had been.

"I WANT to suck you, Cae," Andrew whispered into Caleb's mouth.

He tried once again to encourage Caleb to sit, but the man was having none of it. At least not yet. Andrew figured if he did his job right, his friend would be weak-kneed in no time.

Friend, Andrew scoffed internally.

Like it was perfectly normal to crave the taste of your *friend*'s dick to the point where you're sure you'll lose your mind if you don't get it. Like *friends* spend entire days thinking about each other and feeling their hearts warm with pleasure and ache with need. Whatever he and Caleb were, Andrew knew *friends* didn't quite cover it.

He worked his way down Caleb's nude body, layering kisses, nibbles, and gentle sucks over the smooth, pale skin. When he reached Caleb's nipple, the man shuddered and gasped. Needing to see more of that reaction, Andrew swirled his tongue around the perimeter of the tiny nub before pulling it into his mouth and sucking hard.

"Drew!" Caleb shouted out, his chest arching and his hand cupping the back of Andrew's head and pulling him closer. "Damn, that metal feels incredible."

Andrew smiled internally at the pleasure his tongue piercing was giving Caleb. This was his first opportunity to test out the erotic aspects of his body art.

With a final suck, Andrew popped off that nipple and feasted on the other one. Lapping at it, tugging it between his teeth, and sucking it into his mouth. Eventually, he moved from Caleb's nipples to his ribs and then to his belly. With a hand on each of Caleb's hipbones, he once again encouraged the man to sit. This time, Caleb didn't protest, he just crumpled onto the bed and spread his legs wide, making room for Andrew between them.

Moaning in approval, Andrew kneeled between Caleb's thighs and aimed straight for his balls: swiping his tongue over the hot skin, nibbling on the area behind them, and then going back to the hot orbs and sucking them into his mouth. Caleb cried out in pleasure, rocking his body and grasping Andrew's ears like handles.

"Want you," he gasped.

Andrew wanted him too. He wanted to taste. He took Caleb's glans into his mouth and sucked hard, poking the tip of his tongue into the slit, searching for flavor. His entire body shook with pleasure as he reacquainted himself with the man beneath him. It felt so right that Andrew wondered how he'd gone so long without.

Pushing his stretched lips farther down around the hard cock resulted in Caleb calling out his name and bucking his ass up off the bed. Andrew didn't stop him. He drizzled saliva from his mouth to help ease the journey and bobbed up and down the hard flesh.

"I can't..." Caleb thrust up into Andrew's mouth once again. "Can't stop, Drew. Can't...ungh!"

Andrew didn't want Caleb to stop. He wanted a mouth full of seed. So he continued sucking hard on Caleb's crown and wrapped his hand around the rest of the man's cock, stroking it in time with his mouth.

"No...no," Caleb panted. "Not like this. Don't want to come like this." He tugged on Andrew's hair to get his attention and then pleaded with him. "Want you to fuck me. 'S been so long. Need it so bad. Please, Drew."

Andrew squeezed his eyes shut and groaned at Caleb's words. Just the thought of pushing into the man's tight heat was enough to bring him to the edge.

"God, Cae," he panted. "Need you too."

His breaths were harsh as he stood and made quick work of removing his pants, socks, and shoes. Caleb took the opportunity to crabwalk backward on the bed, his eyes remaining fixated on Andrew's body. He reached to the side and fumbled with the nightstand drawer before finally giving up on blind searching and turning his head. By the time Andrew crawled up the bed, Caleb was spread eagle and clutching the lube.

"You going to let me fuck you bare, Cae?" Andrew asked, his voice so rough it was barely recognizable.

He was on all fours, balanced above Caleb's prone form, their eyes locked together.

"Is that what you want, Drew?" Caleb's pupils were dilated, his cheeks red. The man was the picture of arousal, which made it impossible for Andrew to think. Or maybe it made it impossible for Andrew to stew over all the what-ifs that had occupied his mind for years. Either way, he found himself answering on instinct, not intellect.

"So much. I..." Andrew licked his lips. "I need to know you trust me."

Caleb reached his hand up and cupped the side of Andrew's face.

"You wanna know what I think you need, Drew?" Caleb asked gently. Andrew blinked and swallowed. Then he gave a barely perceptible nod. Caleb smiled at him, his expression full of understanding and affection. "I think you need to know that *you* can trust me."

Andrew furrowed his brow. "I don't understand."

Taking his distraction as an opportunity, Caleb somehow managed to reverse their positions, and before he knew it, Andrew was lying on his back with Caleb propped above him.

"Brendan," Caleb said as he bent forward and tugged the ring in Andrew's left ear between his lips. "Trey," he continued while he circled the spike in Andrew's right ear with his tongue. "DJ," he whispered and ghosted his hand over the huge tattoo of intertwined male symbols on Andrew's left forearm.

"I don't..." Andrew blinked furiously. "What're you doing?"

Caleb didn't answer. He just smiled in that same warm, comforting way and kept listing names. "Rob," he said and then lapped at the studs along the perimeter of Andrew's right ear. "Thad," he tugged on the bar in Andrew's left eyebrow. "Aiden," he said and then bent down and trailed kisses along the Pride tattoo on Andrew's right forearm.

Once he'd covered the tattoo in kisses, Caleb looked at Andrew expectantly. "Do you understand what I'm saying, Drew?" he asked.

The only thing Andrew understood was that Caleb had just named off his ex-boyfriends in chronological order. And he'd said their names accurately, something the man had refused to do back when Andrew was dating them. Or maybe Caleb's insistence on name-butchering only kicked in post-breakup. The thought of post-breakup behavior made the answer to Caleb's question click in Andrew's mind.

"Getting those done makes me feel better," Andrew explained. "The metal, the ink...they make me feel like my body is strong and beautiful, even if it's not enough to satisfy my exes."

Caleb leaned down and pressed his lips against Andrew's.

"They're idiots," he murmured. "You're enough. More than enough. You're everything, Drew," Caleb finished on a sigh, his voice so quiet it was barely audible.

A couple of light kisses later, they were both licking at each other, and then Caleb gripped Andrew's jaw and peered into his eyes. He darted his tongue out and jiggled the ball pierced through Andrew's tongue.

"Wanna tell me about this one?" he asked, clearly referring to the stud in Andrew's tongue. Then he reached one hand between them and stroked Andrew's hard cock. He moved his thumb over the steel barbell in Andrew's glans. "And this one?"

Andrew rolled his lips over his teeth and shook his head.

"Okay." Caleb leaned down and kissed his forehead tenderly. "'S okay."

Then Andrew watched as Caleb straddled his body and kneeled above him. He picked up the bottle of lube and spread the slick fluid over his own fingers, then reached around behind himself. Andrew couldn't see those slender digits impale the tight hole, but when Caleb gasped and his eyes rolled back, Andrew understood the reason.

With a trembling hand, Andrew picked up the slick. He coated his own fingers and stretched his arm, reaching behind Caleb, and then pushed his finger in alongside Caleb's.

"Ungh," Caleb grunted, the erotic sound causing Andrew to feel a pulling in his own groin.

He pumped his finger in and out of Caleb several times, grasping Caleb's nipples with his free hand and twisting them. It wasn't long before Caleb's entire body was moving: his eyes closed, mouth hanging open, and body rocking up and down on their joined fingers. The vision was hot as hell, but eventually it wasn't enough. Andrew pulled his finger out, spread slick over his rigid cock and encouraged Caleb to move forward with a tug on his hip.

Brown, hazy eyes blinked open. Caleb looked down and saw Andrew's large hand stroking his own erection. He licked his lips.

"Yeah," Caleb moaned. "Want that."

"It's yours, Cae. All yours." Andrew meant those words more than he thought Caleb realized. He'd give everything he had to Caleb, everything he was, if only his friend would want to take it, to take him.

"Yeah," Caleb whispered as he rose to his knees and positioned Andrew's cock at his opening. "You are."

It was hard to speak after that because Caleb was bearing down, pushing his tight, silky heat over Andrew's cock, surrounding him with pleasure. Andrew held on to Caleb's hips, helping him move up and down. He planted his own feet on the bed and snapped his hips, adding force to their movements.

"Yes!" Caleb shouted. "Like that, Drew. Hard. Want it hard."

With a roar, Andrew flipped them over. He kneeled on

the bed and grasped Caleb's thin frame.

"Turn over," he grunted. "Hands and knees."

Caleb scrambled to comply, gripping the headboard and tilting his ass up in invitation. Andrew wrapped his hand around his cock and rubbed it over Caleb's opening for a few seconds before pushing himself back inside.

"Mmm, yes," he moaned. He tilted his head back and swallowed several times, his throat working. Once he felt like he wasn't going to lose it way too soon, Andrew clutched Caleb's hips and pulled out slowly before slamming home.

Caleb flattened his palms against the headboard and met his thrusts, pushing his ass back as Andrew shoved forward.

"Harder, oh God, Drew...harder!" he begged.

With a loud grunt, Andrew complied, pumping in and out at a furious pace. He curled his fingers around Caleb's waist, wedged his thighs between the man's spread legs, and snapped his hips. Oh, God, he couldn't last. There was no way to restrain himself in the face of pleasure this intense. He tilted his head back, clenched his eyes shut, and licked his lips.

"I'm there, I'm there, I'm there," Caleb stuttered, and Andrew felt the man's ass convulse around him.

"Oh, God! Yes, yes! Cae!" Andrew shouted.

He clutched Caleb's hips tight enough to leave marks, pushed in as deep as he could, and pulsed inside that warm cavern, coating Caleb's insides with his release. Then he folded himself over Caleb's back and kissed his nape. Caleb turned his head and kissed the side of Andrew's arm. The tenderness of the moment, the connection between them, threatened to overwhelm him.

"I missed this so damn much," Andrew said huskily as his hand reverently caressed Caleb's flank.

"I missed this too," Caleb responded. "I missed you, Drew."

Andrew was quiet for a few heartbeats and then he pressed his mouth next to Caleb's ear and whispered, "Yeah, me too."

But did Caleb miss him in the same way? Did Caleb crave more than friendship? And was it possible to change the nature of their relationship after two decades? Not knowing how to ask those questions, Andrew rested his lips on the back of Caleb's sweat-slick neck and inhaled his scent before trailing openmouthed kisses from the top of his vertebrae to his hairline and back over to his ear.

"What do we do now?" he asked eventually, the simplicity of the words belying the complexity of the question.

"Well," Caleb said. "I guess that depends."

He squirmed beneath Andrew until Andrew straightened his arms and made enough room for Caleb to roll onto his back. Then he met Andrew's gaze.

"Are you ready to tell me about this one?" He moved his thumb over the apadravya in the crown of Andrew's cock. Then he stretched his neck and kissed Andrew, licking at Andrew's lips until they opened and then lapping at the piercing in his tongue. "And this one?" He moved one hand to Andrew's head and tugged at the blue mohawk. "How about this one?"

Andrew suspected that, just like always, Caleb already knew the answers to those questions. It was uncanny, really, the way Caleb knew him, and it probably should have been frustrating, not being able to hide even embarrassing shortcomings. But Andrew wasn't frustrated. Being with someone who knew him so completely, sometimes even better than he knew himself, and yet still wanted to be around him... It wasn't frustrating, it was exhilarating and freeing.

"I was jealous," he admitted.

Caleb gave him a barely perceptible nod, but otherwise stayed quiet, clearly waiting for him to continue. Andrew dragged in a deep breath.

"Well, the tongue, I thought you were dating David Miller, remember? And it bugged me. I wasn't really sure why at the time, just thought it felt wrong. You moved here to be with me, and then you were spending all sorts of time with him." Andrew shrugged. "I didn't like it. But I felt like a silly kid, you know, like I wanted to stick my tongue out at you in frustration. So I pierced it.

"The mohawk..." Andrew thought back to when he'd shorn off most of his hair and dyed the rest. "I was pissed, unreasonably pissed, because I thought you were dating someone and keeping it from me. I figured you knew how I felt when I thought you were with David so you didn't want to tell me about whoever he was, and you were sneaking around instead. And I knew how much you like my hair blond, so—"

"Drew," Caleb interrupted. "I didn't sneak around on you."

"I know. It's not like you had some obligation to tell me who you were dating. Like I said, I was mad, but it wasn't reasonable."

"I'm not apologizing for dating somebody. I'm just saying, whatever else I've ever done, I've never lied to you. I would never lie to you. The only guy I've dated since I moved here, other than that one barely date with David Miller, was Nick Gallaway."

Andrew scowled. "I hated that you were dating Nick. Hated it. And not just because the guy's a real prick." Andrew added the last sentence with a wicked grin. "It hurt every single time you were out with him. That's why I got the apadravya. I wanted something I'd really feel, you know?"

"You should have told me," Caleb whispered. "Why didn't you say anything?"

"What could I have said?" Andrew asked. "I don't like your boyfriend so you should dump him."

"No," Caleb shook his head. "But you could have told me that you love me. That would have been a good reason for me to break up with Nick." Andrew jerked his head back, surprised by the frank words, though, knowing Caleb, he shouldn't have been. "Do you love me, Drew?" Caleb whispered.

"Of course I do. You're my best friend," he answered, his heart pounding furiously.

The corners of Caleb's lips turned up in a tiny smile. He cupped Andrew's cheeks and looked into his eyes. "Are you in love with me, Andrew Thompson?" he asked again.

No matter how scared he felt, how vulnerable and exposed, Andrew wasn't going to hide from this. He wasn't going to hide it from Caleb. And he wasn't going to hide it from himself. Not anymore.

"Yes," he confessed, his voice breaking. "God, yes. I...I love you, Cae."

"Why didn't you tell me?"

"I didn't know. Not until a couple of months ago. Crazy, right? All those years I spent searching for a permanent guy, but I don't think I knew what it'd look like when I found it. Permanence, I mean. I didn't want to follow my parents' model, I knew that much. But I didn't have a good picture of the alternatives." He rubbed his hand on the back of his neck and clicked the ball in his tongue against his teeth. "When I was with Drake, it killed me that I couldn't fool around with you, and then I was so pissed at myself for wanting you when I was with him. It was like a vicious cycle of self-loathing." Andrew closed his eyes and drew in a shaky breath. "Then when he was sick and you came to be with me...even then I wanted you, Cae. I was exhausted and devastated, but I wanted you. My boyfriend was in the hospital dying, and I wanted you."

"Oh, babe," Caleb sighed. He kissed Andrew's temple and caressed his cheek. "I wanted you too. But we never acted on those feelings. You could have. You knew he was with other men. Hell, he probably thought we fucked like bunnies when we were together. But you were faithful to him, Drew, all the way until the end."

"Only because you wouldn't come near me, so I was forced to be faithful physically, but in my mind, Cae, in my heart..."

"We can't blame ourselves for what we felt, only what we did," Caleb said firmly.

"Maybe," Andrew acquiesced. "But I hated myself for it. And then when he died..." Andrew shuddered. "I couldn't let myself touch you. It would have been like giving myself a reward for failing him."

"Failing him?" Caleb asked incredulously. "How did you fail him? You did everything for Drake!"

"I'm a doctor for fuck's sake! What kind of doctor stands by and watches his boyfriend die?"

"The kind of doctor whose boyfriend refuses to take help when it's offered. You were there for him, Drew, and you let him know that. His death isn't your burden to carry. Don't you think it's time you let it go?" Caleb asked. Then he looked pleadingly at Andrew. "I need you to let it go."

"I have. I can. I..." Andrew fumbled with his words. "You know that permanent person? The one I was always trying to find?" he finally asked.

"Yeah."

"I know what permanent looks like now. He's the first person I want to call when I get good news, or bad news, or really any news. He's the person I want to be with when all I want is to veg on the couch, the person I want by my side when I'm at some big crowded party, the person I want with me when I'm stuck at a miserable work function or an awkward family gathering. He's the guy who turns me on even when I've been on call for forty-eight hours and I'm sure the only thing my body is capable of is sleep. It took me years of failed relationships and dozens of self-help books to recognize what was right in front of me all along. But now I know. It's us, you and me, what we have together. That's the permanence I always wanted."

Andrew took a deep breath and gathered his courage before he continued. "You're the one who saved me from a lifetime of loneliness, Cae. Do you want to share that lifetime with me?"

Caleb blinked back tears. "You saved yourself, Drew. I'm just the one who's been lucky enough to come along for the ride. No way am I getting off now. We're just getting to the good part."

THE END

(But wait...there's more—bonus chapter ahead.)

BONUS CHAPTER

When the U.S. Supreme Court released their historic marriage decision, I wanted to celebrate so I wrote a bonus chapter with Andrew and Caleb's reaction to the wonderful news. I hope you enjoy it. –CC

ANDREW THOMPSON and Caleb Lakes walked up to their friends' table at the Swallow's Nest.

"What the fuck are you wearing, Bert?" Noah Forman said as soon as he saw them.

Andrew ran his palms over his chest, flattening his shirt. It was white with a black arrow pointing down. Above the arrow there was block print reading, "Your Head Here."

"It was a birthday present from my father," Andrew said. "And I thought we decided I'm Ernie and Cae's Bert."

Caleb snickered. He set his drink on the table and sat down. Andrew took the seat next to him.

"Your father seriously gave you that shirt?" Noah's partner, Clark, asked incredulously.

"Yup," Andrew said with a nod. "I believe his exact words were '*I know how you like those odd T-shirts, so I picked one up for you*'."

"He was trying to be thoughtful, Drew," Caleb said

gently.

"Right," Andrew said. "This shirt was not in any way a commentary about my wardrobe choices and personal appearance. For the first time in his life, my father was being *thoughtful*." Andrew snorted. He took a sip of Caleb's drink, and then he grinned wickedly. "And just to show my gratitude, I've been wearing it every chance I get and texting him a picture every single time." He waggled his eyebrows. "We're going to New York for Christmas. I can't wait to see what he gets me."

"I thought you guys did Christmas here and Thanksgiving in New York," Clark said.

Caleb rolled his eyes and reached for his glass. "Don't get him started."

"Yeah, don't get me started," Andrew said. "Because then we'd have to talk about how a certain someone"—he nudged Caleb—"agreed to change our trip to Christmas this year so he can go with his mother to some once-in-a-lifetime antique auction the day after." Andrew's tone dripped with sarcasm. "Because what Caleb's parents really need is more furniture and knickknacks in their full-to-the-gills house."

"I told you my mom has been giving away a lot of things because they won't match the new design."

"Right," Andrew said. "I forgot about that extra special trip bonus." He turned his gaze to Clark and Noah. "Cae's parents are in the middle of a huge remodeling project, so when we go to New York, we won't be able stay at their house, which means we have to stay with my parents. A three-hour meal with my father is enough to make me lose my mind; I have no idea how I'm going to survive for three days."

"On the plus side, your dad is into *thoughtful* gifts now. Maybe you'll get lucky and he'll get you that twelve-inch dildo you've been eyeing," Noah said before taking a long pull from the frosty mug. "That should make a fun distraction."

Andrew crumpled his napkin, threw it at Noah, and said, "You know what isn't a fun distraction? That ridiculous Facebook page you made for your dog."

"Hey!" Clark objected. "Spike is adorable."

"Ignore him, angel," Noah said to Clark. "He has no room to talk. You know he posts pictures of every meal." He turned to Andrew. "We all know you don't cook, Bert. If you didn't make the food, why do you feel the need to show it to three hundred and fifty of your closest acquaintances?"

"Because I made it," Caleb said. He threaded his fingers with Andrew's, squeezed his hand, and gazed into his eyes before turning his attention back to their friends. "And he's being sweet and bragging about me."

Andrew mumbled something and took a sip of his drink. Noah grunted and did the same.

Clark smiled. "I always suspected you had a soft side, Dr. Thompson."

IT WAS a fun night, and they stayed out late, so Andrew was surprised when Caleb's phone rang as they were walking in the door.

"Hey," Caleb said. He flipped on the lights and wandered into the kitchen, chatting away. Then there was a long pause followed by squealing and fast talking and a litany of, "Oh my God, oh my God, oh my God."

Andrew walked into the living room, sank into the comfortable couch Caleb had upholstered in some soft fabric that made him want to roll around naked on it, and flipped on the table lamp Caleb had strategically placed at the exact right height for reading. His medical journals were there too, stacked neatly, with the newest one on top. Andrew picked one up and smiled.

They'd bought the house almost seven years ago, and Andrew still discovered little touches Caleb added. The man never said anything; he'd just place the coffee table at the exact distance Andrew needed to stretch out his legs, or put the dental floss in a little ceramic bowl on the bathroom counter after Andrew's dentist said he needed to be better about flossing. Thinking about everything Caleb did inevitably made Andrew feel grateful that he had a person in his life who never failed to put him first.

"Cae!" he called out. "It's the middle of the night. Get off the damn phone and come in here."

"Be right there," Caleb responded from the other room.

Andrew tried not to scowl. He'd started flipping through the journal, not really reading but needing a distraction to keep him from rushing Caleb, when he heard him say, "Thanks for calling. I'll let Drew know, and we can celebrate this weekend." Then Caleb walked into the room.

"Who was that?" Andrew asked.

"It was David," Caleb said, a huge smiling spreading across his adorable face. He flopped down on the couch next to Andrew and tucked his legs underneath his ass. "You'll never guess the news." Caleb was practically vibrating with excitement. The man loved being the one to share breaking gossip.

Andrew tossed the medical journal he wasn't reading onto the coffee table. "David and Jonathan are getting married," he said.

"How did you know?" Caleb frowned. "They *just* got engaged!"

The ounce of guilt Andrew felt about stealing Caleb's thunder was outweighed by the pound of smugness about being right in one guess. "It's killing you to think I might actually have a piece of gossip before you, isn't it?" he asked triumphantly.

Caleb snorted, crossed his arms over his chest, and said, "No. Don't be ridiculous." He paused for a few beats, chewed on his lip, and then said, "So how did you know? Who told you?"

"You are so damn adorable when you're flustered. Do

you know that?"

"Your sweet-talking is not going to distract me, Drew."

"No?" Andrew lowered his voice and twisted until he was facing Caleb. "My sweet-talking is usually met with great success."

"Cut it out," Caleb said, but he was no longer frowning, and Andrew could see the sides of his lips twitching, like he was fighting a smile.

Andrew grasped Caleb's shoulders and eased him backward until he was lying across the couch with Andrew straddling his hips. "You sure you want me to stop, Cae?"

There was a time in Andrew's life when he would have felt sort of ridiculous trying to be seductive. Well, maybe *time* wasn't the right frame of reference, more like relationships. There had been relationships in which he wasn't comfortable talking dirty, or acting silly, or speaking openly. But things were different with Caleb. Andrew was never, ever embarrassed to say or do whatever came naturally in front of the man who always had been and continued to be his best friend.

"Yeah," Caleb whispered huskily as Andrew slid his hand up Caleb's chest. "I, uh, stop."

Andrew bent down and nibbled his way across Caleb's jaw. "Do you even know what you're asking me to stop doing?"

"What?" Caleb mumbled, his voice thick with arousal. Andrew rocked his hips and ground his erection against Caleb's. "Drew!"

THE ONE WHO SAVES ME

"Mmm hmm."

"Quit teasing me."

"I'll quit teasing"—Andrew tugged Caleb's bottom lip between both of his—"when you admit that my sweet-talking worked."

"Andrew Thompson." Caleb's tone held a warning note. "If you don't stop focusing on whatever it is you're trying to prove and start focusing on my dick, I'm going to take care of things on my own."

"I already told you I'd give you what you want," Andrew said smugly. "All you need to do is say I was right."

"Oh, for fuck's sake." Caleb planted his hands on Andrew's chest and pushed him away.

"What're you doing?" Andrew asked, taken off guard.

"I'm getting your skinny self off me."

When he had enough room to move, Caleb shimmied out from under Andrew and propped himself up in the corner of the couch. He stretched one leg across the length of the couch and planted the other on the floor.

"Cae?" Andrew said.

Caleb cupped his own balls through his linen pants and gave himself a squeeze. Then he groaned and quickly unfastened his button and zipper.

"Caleb?" Andrew was surprised by how rough his voice sounded.

"Uh-huh," Caleb answered as he pushed the pouch of his red jock underneath his balls, freeing his hard cock.

Andrew gulped at the sight of Caleb's underwear. No matter how many years passed, seeing what Caleb wore underneath his perfectly tailored clothing always ramped up Andrew's libido. "What're you doing?" he asked weakly.

Caleb dropped his head back and closed his eyes as he fondled his balls with one hand and stroked his dick with the other. "I know it's been a while since you've had to do this on your own, but I'm sure you remember the finer points of jacking off, Drew."

Andrew watched Caleb's gorgeous dick fill and his mouth watered. Before he realized he was moving, he was tracing a vein along the side of the enticing flesh with his finger.

Caleb snapped his eyes open and locked his gaze with Andrew's. "Drew," he sighed.

The longing, arousal, and need in Caleb's voice and eyes snapped what little remained of Andrew's control and pride. He forgot about proving whatever point he'd been trying to make, forgot about winning the battle of wills, forgot about basically everything except tasting the tempting erection in front of him.

He slid to the floor and kneeled in front of Caleb. With one hand on Caleb's thigh and the other holding Caleb's shirt out of the way, Andrew dipped forward and started lapping at Caleb's balls.

"Mmm, Drew."

Hearing the arousal in Caleb's voice encouraged

Andrew further. He moaned and licked his way up the hot shaft to the bulbous head and then took it into his mouth and immediately began sucking on it.

Caleb moaned and combed his fingers through Andrew's hair. "Feels good," he said on a sigh. "Love it when you go down on me."

Andrew didn't respond—he was too busy sucking and licking Caleb's dick. Besides, he knew exactly what Caleb liked in bed. How could he not? He'd spent more than half his life learning this man's body. He rubbed his hand over his own groin, giving himself a little friction while he continued to work Caleb over.

"Oh God," Caleb said after a few minutes. "Gonna, Drew. I..." He bucked his hips, pushed his cock deeper into Andrew's mouth, then stilled and pulsed hot ejaculate down Andrew's throat.

Andrew waited until Caleb was done, and then he stood and pushed his zipper down. With his rigid dick in his hand, he leaned over Caleb's sated body and stroked himself hard and fast. Dark-brown eyes, more familiar than his own, blinked at him. Then Caleb licked his lips and said, "Give it to me, Drew," and Andrew was done. He threw his head back and cried out as he shot his white-hot release onto Caleb.

When he felt like he could breathe again, Andrew opened his eyes. Caleb was sprawled on the couch, his pants still open and his now flaccid dick exposed. He had stripped off his shirt and was using it to wipe Andrew's semen off his chest.

"You missed a spot," Andrew said.

"Where?"

Andrew climbed onto the couch, straddled Caleb's thighs, then dipped his face down and licked Caleb's chin.

"There," he whispered huskily. "I got it."

Caleb sighed happily and traced Andrew's pierced eyebrow with his finger. "So," he said.

Andrew turned his face and kissed Caleb's palm before meeting his gaze. "So," he responded.

"Your sweet-talking is super-hot and distracting, but I still want to know who told you about Jonathan and David."

Andrew laughed. "You couldn't even wait until we zipped up, could you?"

"Nope." Caleb's grin was wicked as he cupped Andrew's exposed package and played with his apadravya piercing.

"Nobody told me," Andrew said. "I just guessed."

Caleb cocked one dark eyebrow. "Seriously?"

"Sure." Andrew scooted off Caleb's lap and settled next to him on the couch. It was a tight fit, but being pressed up against Caleb's warm body was never a hardship. "I mean, David's a pretty traditional guy; they have a kid." He shrugged. "I bet we're going to hear about a lot of people getting hitched now that DOMA's been overturned."

They took each other's hands instinctively; then Caleb kissed Andrew's cheek and rested his head on Andrew's shoulder. "I bet you're right," Caleb said.

They sat together, touching but not speaking.

"You understand, right?" Andrew eventually said, hoping Caleb would know what he meant.

"Yup," Caleb answered.

Feeling like he had to explain, Andrew said, "Marriages end all the time. And even when they don't, they're miserable."

"Don't worry, Drew." Caleb rubbed his thumb over the back of Andrew's hand. "We're on the same page. I'm happy David and Jonathan and everyone else who wants to get married can do it, but that doesn't mean I need to."

Andrew kissed Caleb's temple. "Thanks for always understanding me," he said.

Caleb smiled warmly and caressed Andrew's cheek. "I love you, Drew," he said. "Nothing's going to change that."

"I love you too." Andrew took a deep breath and locked his gaze on Caleb's. "You're my best friend, Cae. *That's* forever."

THE END

ABOUT THE AUTHOR

Cardeno C.—CC to friends—is a hopeless romantic who wants to add a lot of happiness and a few *awwws* into a reader's day. Writing is a nice break from real life as a corporate type and volunteer work with gay rights organizations. Cardeno's stories range from sweet to intense, contemporary to paranormal, long to short, but they always include strong relationships and walks into the happily-ever-after sunset.

Email: cardenoc@gmail.com

Website: www.cardenoc.com

Twitter: https://twitter.com/cardenoc

Facebook: http://www.facebook.com/CardenoC

Pinterest: http://www.pinterest.com/cardenoC

Blog: http://caferisque.blogspot.com

OTHER BOOKS BY CARDENO C.

SIPHON
Johnnie

HOPE
McFarland's Farm
Jesse's Diner

PACK
Blue Mountain
Red River

HOME
He Completes Me
Home Again
Just What the Truth Is
Love at First Sight
The One Who Saves Me
Where He Ends and I Begin
Walk With Me

FAMILY
The Half of Us
Something in the Way He Needs
Strong Enough
More Than Everything

MATES
In Your Eyes
Until Forever Comes
Wake Me Up Inside

FRIENDS
Not a Game

NOVELS
Strange Bedfellows
Perfect Imperfections
Control *(with Mary Calmes)*

NOVELLAS
A Shot at Forgiveness
All of Me
Places in Time
In Another Life & Eight Days
Jumping In

AVAILABLE NOW

He Completes Me
(2nd Edition)

Not even his mother's funeral can convince self-proclaimed party boy Zach Johnson to tone down his snark or think about settling down. He is who he is, and he refuses to change for anyone. When straight-laced, compassionate Aaron Paulson claims he's falling for him, Zach is certain Aaron sees him as another project, one more lost soul for the idealistic Aaron to save. But Zach doesn't need to be fixed and he refuses to be with someone who sees him as broken.

Patience is one of Aaron's many virtues. He has waited years for a man who can share his heart and complete his life and he insists Zach is the one. Pride, fear, and old hurts wither in the wake of Aaron's adoring loyalty, and as Zach reevaluates his perceptions of love and family, he finds himself tempted to believe in the impossible: a happily-ever-after.

Home Again
(2nd Edition)

Imposing, temperamental Noah Forman wakes up in a hospital and can't remember how he got there. He holds it together, taking comfort in the fact that the man he has loved since childhood is on the way. But when his one and only finally arrives, Noah is horrified to discover that he doesn't remember anything from the past three years.

Loyal, serious Clark Lehman built a life around the person who insisted from their first meeting that they were meant to be together. Now, years later, two men whose love has never faltered must relive their most treasured and most painful moments in order to recover lost memories and secure their future.

Just What the Truth Is
(2nd Edition)

People-pleaser Ben Forman has been in the closet so long he has almost convinced himself he is straight, but his denial train gets derailed when hotshot lawyer Micah Trains walks into his life. Micah is brilliant, funny, driven...and he assumes Ben is gay and starts dating him. Finding himself truly happy for the first time, Ben doesn't have the willpower to resist Micah's affection.

When his relationship with Micah heats up, Ben realizes has a problem: his parents won't tolerate a gay son and self-confident Micah isn't the type to hide. If Ben wants to maintain his hold on his happiness, he'll have to decide what's important and own up to the truth of who he is. The trouble is figuring out just what that truth is.

Love at First Sight
(2nd Edition)

The moment naïve, optimistic Jonathan Doyle glimpses a gorgeous blue-eyed stranger from afar, he believes in love at first sight. Unfortunately, he loses sight of the man before they meet and then spends years desperately trying to find him. Just as he is about to give up, Jonathan gets a break and finally encounters David Miller face to face.

Successful, confident David turns Jonathan's previously lonely life into a fairy tale, giving him more than he ever imagined. But the years spent searching were hard on Jonathan, and he's terrified his young son and scandalous past will destroy his blossoming relationship. For David and Jonathan to build a future together, they'll both have to dig deep: David for the courage to share himself in a way he's never considered and Jonathan for the strength to tell the truth.

Where He Ends and I Begin
(2nd Edition)

Aggressive, physical, and brave, Jake Owens is a small town football hero turned big city cop who passes his time with meaningless encounters believing he can't have who he really wants: Nate Richardson, his best friend since before forever. Thoughtful, quiet, and kind, Nate is a brilliant doctor who has always known who he is and has never been able to shake his crush on loyal, courageous, *straight* Jake.

After a passionate night together, Nate realizes Jake isn't as straight as he assumed, but he worries that what they shared was a fluke, a result of too much closeness for too long. For Jake, the question isn't how they ended up in bed together because he has always known that Nate holds his heart, it's how he'll convince Nate that he wants and needs to stay there.

Walk With Me
(2nd Edition)

When Eli Block steps into his parents' living room and sees his childhood crush sitting on the couch, he starts a shameless campaign to seduce the young rabbi. Unfortunately, Seth Cohen barely remembers Eli and he resolutely shuts down all his advances. As a tenuous and then binding friendship forms between the two men, Eli must find a way to move past his unrequited love while still keeping his best friend in his life. Not an easy feat when the same person occupies both roles.

Professional, proper Seth is shocked by Eli's brashness, overt sexuality, and easy defiance of societal norms. But he's also drawn to the happy, funny, light-filled man. As their friendship deepens over the years, Seth watches Eli mature into a man he admires and respects. When Seth finds himself longing for what Eli had so easily offered, he has to decide whether he's willing to veer from his safe life-plan to build a future with Eli.

Made in the USA
Monee, IL
11 September 2020

40622212R00164